AIKEN-BAMBERG-BARNWELL-EDGEFIELD
Regional Library System

Here's what readers are saying about B.J. Hoff's
Mountain Song Legacy.

Book One…

A Distant Music

P9-DZP-159

DISCARD

"B.J. Hoff always delights readers with her warm stories and characters who become part of your 'circle of special friends.'"

—*Janette Oke,* author, *Love Comes Softly*

"For this Kentucky woman, reading *A Distant Music* was like driving through the eastern hills and hollers on a perfect autumn day with the scent of wood smoke in the air and the trees ablaze with color. B.J. Hoff's lyrical prose brings to life this gentle, moving story of a beloved teacher and his students, who learn far more than the three Rs. I brushed away tears at several tender points in the story and held my breath when it seemed all might be lost. Yet even in the darkest moments, hope shines on every page. A lovely novel by one of historical fiction's finest wordsmiths."

—*Liz Curtis Higgs,* author, *Thorn in My Heart*

"I read *The Penny Whistle* years ago and never forgot it. I was delighted to see that it had become a full length novel. *A Distant Music* contains all the elements—compelling characters, fascinating setting, and stellar writing—that I've come to expect from a book with B.J. Hoff's name on the cover."

—*Deborah Raney,* author, *Over the Waters*

"B.J. Hoff is a master storyteller. With impeccable research, vibrant characters, and historical accuracy, Ms. Hoff weaves a story that's impossible to put down."

—*Lori Copeland,* author, *The Plainsman*

"In the lyrical pages of B.J. Hoff's *A Distant Music,* we discover that God is present even in the darkness of despair…and where God is, hope overflows. A warm and satisfying tale of characters who will live in your memory for years to come."

—*Angela Hunt,* author, *The Novelist*

"In some ways, *A Distant Music* is reminiscent of the *Little House* series. Each chapter recalls the details of an event or some character's dilemma. Eventually, though, Hoff connects all the threads into a solid story whose ending will deeply touch readers. *A Distant Music* should find an eager audience. An excellent book to recommend to readers with a penchant for historical novels, particularly those set in late-19th-century America."

—*Aspiring Retail Magazine*

Book Two...

The Wind Harp

"B.J. always does a great job of drawing her readers into the lives of her characters. I'm sure that there will be many who will be eagerly pleading to know 'what happens next.' I will be among them."

—*Janette Oke*, *Love Comes Softly*

"B.J. Hoff continues the story of Maggie and Jonathan, who must endure their share of trials before reaping their reward. Though this novel is historical, B.J. deals with issues that are completely contemporary...and I loved the big dog! Kudos to the author for charming us again!"

—*Angela Hunt*, bestselling author, *The Novelist*

"*The Wind Harp* does not depend on sensationalism to create its moving story. Like a cup of ice-cold water on a hot summer day or sitting under a big old tree by a gently running stream, *The Wind Harp* draws readers in to sit for a spell. They are refreshed and never want to leave. As always, B.J.'s hallmark characterization is supplemented by her skilled depiction of both the light and dark sides of life, presented with a beautiful simplicity that made my heart sing along with the story. If you're after a book that leaves you feeling good about life, or feeling hope about life regardless of circumstances, or just feeling refreshed after reading a wonderful story—don't miss *The Wind Harp*."

—*Sara Mitchell*, author of *Shenandoah Home* and *Virginia Autumn*

"In *The Wind Harp*, this sequel to *A Distant Music*, author B.J. Hoff takes the story of Jonathan Stuart and Maggie MacAuley a step further, delving deeper into their characters and crafting a tale that is truly compelling. These people who come to life in book one take on a new dimension in book two, pulling the reader into their worst fears and deepest dreams. With a different take on an age-old love story, Mrs. Hoff shows us that the old adage is true—good things come to those who wait. I love the way Mrs. Hoff draws me into each character's hopes and dreams, while weaving in enough mystery and drama to keep me turning pages. Not many books keep me thinking about them long after I set the book down, but Mrs. Hoff has such a wonderful way of bringing the characters to life on each page. I feel like I know them—like they have become dear friends."

—*Jill Eileen Smith*, reader

B.J. HOFF

The Song Weaver

HARVEST HOUSE PUBLISHERS
EUGENE, OREGON

Cover by Koechel Peterson & Associates, Inc., Minneapolis, Minnesota

B.J. Hoff: Published in association with the Books & Such Literary Agency, 52 Mission Circle, Suite 122, PMB 170, Santa Rosa, CA 95409-5370, www.booksandsuch.biz.

This is a work of fiction. Names, characters, places, and incidents are products of the author's imagination or are used fictitiously. Any resemblance to actual persons, living or dead, or to events or locales, is entirely coincidental.

Harvest House Publishers has made every effort to trace the ownership of all quotes. In the event of a question arising from the use of a quote, we regret any error made and will be pleased to make the necessary correction in future editions of this book.

THE SONG WEAVER
Copyright © 2007 by B.J. Hoff
Published by Harvest House Publishers
Eugene, Oregon 97402
www.harvesthousepublishers.com

Library of Congress Cataloging-in-Publication Data
Hoff, B. J.
   The song weaver / B.J. Hoff.
     p. cm. — (The mountain song legacy; bk. 3)
   ISBN-13: 978-0-7369-1459-8 (pbk.)
   ISBN-10: 0-7369-1459-5 (pbk.)
   1. Married people—Fiction. 2. Sisters—Death—Fiction. 3. Family—Fiction. 4. Coal mines and mining—Fiction. 5. Kentucky—Fiction. 6. Domestic fiction. I. Title.
PS3558.O34395S66 2007
813'.54—dc22

                                         2007004405

All rights reserved. No part of this publication may be reproduced, stored in a retrieval system, or transmitted in any form or by any means—electronic, mechanical, digital, photocopy, recording, or any other—except for brief quotations in printed reviews, without the prior permission of the publisher.

Printed in the United States of America

   07 08 09 10 11 12 13 14 15 / RDM-SK / 10 9 8 7 6 5 4 3 2 1

for Jim...

Thank you for the music.

Acknowledgments

So many special people have been part of this story. No book is ever completed and published without a major effort on the part of many, including those who love and serve and wait behind the scenes. Let me mention a few:

Nick Harrison, my editor...whose patience is as impressive as his instincts, whose approach to the work produces inspiration rather than frustration, whose expertise is unfailing, and whose sense of humor is unflagging—all of which make him nothing less than a genuine blessing to his authors.

The entire Harvest House family...a remarkable team whose efforts always bring credit to the One they serve with such commitment and faithfulness.

Janet Kobobel Grant...my agent and friend who never asks for more than my best.

Cheryl and Sara...who never stop praying, never stop believing, never stop caring.

Angie...wizard and friend, whose quicksilver mind, bedrock common sense, and relentless sense of humor can't quite mask the sensitive heart of a genuine *song weaver*.

Winnie and Nita and Charlotte...heartfelt thanks for the ideas and the encouragement and the laughs—on a weekly basis—and for making me more friend than client.

My family...*you* are my story and my song.

My readers...God bless you—every one of you!

Beginnings

O God, our help in ages past,
Our hope for years to come,
Be Thou our guide while life shall last,
And our eternal home.

Isaac Watts

~~~~~~~

Skingle Creek, Northeastern Kentucky
December 1904

Maggie Stuart. Maggie *MacAuley* Stuart. Mrs. Jonathan Stuart."

Maggie stood looking out the window at the bright December morning. The snow that had fallen Christmas Eve—her wedding night—still blanketed the ground. Because of the mines being closed over the holiday, the pristine whiteness had not yet turned gray with coal dust.

Even though she was alone at the moment, she felt a little foolish practicing her new name over and over. She turned away from the window to let her gaze play over the bedroom. Everything was new: this room, a new name, a new home.

7

Jonathan's home. How many times had he reminded her that it was now *her* home too? *Their* home.

That being the case, she wondered if she dared act on his suggestion that once they returned from their honeymoon trip, she consider doing some redecorating. She wasn't sure how she felt about that. On the other hand, she wouldn't mind turning the bedroom into *their* room rather than the masculine sanctuary it now represented. With not a feminine touch to be seen, it was almost spartan in its decor: functional pieces of dark, sturdy wood, bare walls, heavy drapes, and shelves groaning with books.

Suddenly the thought of stripping all this away and starting over felt presumptuous, even intimidating…not to mention extravagant. And no matter what Jonathan said, could she really bring herself to start making changes to the home in which he'd lived for so many years? Wouldn't he ultimately resent her for it? Besides, what did she know about redecorating? Miners' families did well to fix their broken furniture and add a coat of fresh paint every few years. Only wealthy people had the means to redecorate.

People like Jonathan's family.

The slam of panic came out of the blue, stealing her breath. There were so many changes, so much that was new. Jonathan would expect her to know how to do things. Things his mother would have done. And his sister.

The thought overwhelmed her. Oh, she knew how to keep house well enough. She'd been brought up to do her share of housework: laundry and ironing, cooking and cleaning. But she knew next to nothing about the *niceties* of maintaining a home. There'd been no money, thus no interest, in that sort of thing in her family.

But she wasn't exactly dimwitted. Didn't Jonathan insist that she'd been the brightest student he'd ever taught? And hadn't she made her way through university as an honor student? Surely she could learn whatever she needed to learn. She'd not disappoint her husband.

My husband! I'm a wife. Jonathan's wife.

That was the newest—the strangest—thing of all. Jonathan wasn't new to her, of course. Across the years he'd moved from teacher to mentor to friend. But now he was her husband. Someone to come to know in new and different ways.

The thought gave Maggie her first cold feeling in her married life.

She sank down on the side of the bed. Beside her, Jonathan's briefcase lay open where he'd left it before going downstairs to fetch the newspaper for reading on the train. At the top of the other odds and ends he'd already packed was Maggie's book—*The Penny Whistle*—that she'd finally given to him yesterday morning… Christmas morning, the day after their wedding.

Naturally she'd told him about the book she'd written. What she hadn't told him was the reason its publication had been delayed. Originally scheduled for late fall, she'd bargained with Mr. Rice at the publishing house to delay the book's release until after Christmas in order to change the dedication appropriately: "*To Jonathan Lawrence Stuart—my mentor, my hero, my husband.*"

The thought of how moved Jonathan had been upon reading the dedication page brought a smile now, albeit a fleeting one. Her thoughts seemed bent on returning to the same treacherous direction as before—her own inadequacies for all that lay before her in her new life.

In a little while they would leave on their honeymoon trip to Lexington. There she would finally meet Jonathan's family: his ailing father and his widowed sister. What would they think of her? Her youth, her inexperience, her lack of refinement…would they be terribly disappointed in his choice of wife? Even the thought of bringing disappointment or embarrassment to Jonathan and his family was intolerable.

The sound of him clearing his throat yanked her out of her thoughts. She looked up and saw him standing in the doorway, his head tilted to one side watching her.

"So—" he said, "are you getting used to it yet?"

"Used to it?"

"Everything." He came and took both her hands in his, tugging her to her feet. "Being married. Having a new name. A new home. A husband who's absolutely wild about you. That's enough for a start, I expect."

He kissed her lightly on the forehead.

At the moment Maggie wasn't eager to talk about *newness.* "I see you're taking my book along," she commented, gesturing to his travel case.

"Of course I'm taking it along! I can't wait to show it to my father and Patricia. A man's entitled to boast a little about his wife's accomplishments after all."

"Don't you dare, Jonathan."

He drew her into his arms. "It's not every day a man has a book dedicated to him, you know."

Maggie framed his face with her hands. "It's really your story, Jonathan. So of course I dedicated it to you."

"Do you have any idea how proud I am of you?" he questioned quietly.

She loved the way he drew her into himself just by searching her eyes. And the way a strand of his flaxen hair fell over one eye when he dipped his head to kiss her. And the way he always breathed her name *after* he kissed her. Oh, she loved everything about him, this man who had been her husband for all of…thirty-eight hours now! She had never known such a feeling as this dizzying whirlwind of love and happiness.

An unexpected chill passed over her, as if to thwart the rush of emotion bubbling up in her. She recognized it for what it was—the old Irish superstition she'd too often heard as she was growing up: Too much joy was likely to invite an equal cup of sorrow.

"Maggie?" Jonathan was watching her, his expression one of concern. He held her slightly away from him. "Are you all right?"

Maggie managed a smile and nodded. "Just trying to think of anything I might have forgotten."

He didn't look convinced. "Are you quite sure you've no regrets about leaving your family so soon after Christmas? We could have waited a day or two more."

They had spent their wedding night at Jonathan's house. *Their* house, he would have reminded her. Yesterday they shared Christmas with Maggie's family, coming back here in the evening to prepare for their trip.

"I've no regrets about anything so long as we're together," she replied, resolved to give truth to her words. Forcing a note of brightness into her tone, she added, "Although I confess that I already miss Figaro a little."

"Ah. So my competition is to be a hound."

"I loved your dog before I married you," she reminded him.

"Yes, I know," he said dryly. "Is it possible that's *why* you married me? So you could move in with my dog?"

"He's an awfully handsome fella. But then so are you."

"And both of us are obviously besotted with you."

He drew her close again as if to act on his besotted state, but Maggie stole a glance at the clock on the bedroom mantel.

"Jonathan—we have to go or we're going to miss the train."

He sighed, still managing a brief kiss before taking a last look around the bedroom.

"Our luggage—"

"Already in the buggy."

"Did Figaro settle in with my folks all right?" she asked as they left the room.

"The big faker. He tried to pull that pitiful-pup routine on me until I was almost out the door. He'll be fine. By now he's probably driving your mother crazy, tagging along on her heels through the house."

They hurried down the steps, making a final check of the first floor before locking the door behind them. Once they were settled into the buggy, Jonathan hesitated before driving away. "Well, Mrs. Stuart," he said, turning to Maggie, "this is our first trip together. How do you feel?"

Maggie thought for a moment and then decided to be honest. "Nervous."

Jonathan's face fell. "Why?"

"Because I'm meeting your family for the first time, and I want them to like me. I want you to be proud of me."

He shook his head. "Maggie, it's not possible for me to be any prouder of you than I already am. And my family is going to *love* you."

"I'm sure I'm not the kind of wife they'd have chosen for you."

"They would never presume to choose a wife for me." He took her hand. "Listen to me, Maggie. You have nothing to worry about where my family is concerned."

"You can't know that."

"Oh, but I can. I know my father and my sister. And I promise you, they're going to love you. They'll love you because you're irresistible and because they'll see how much *I* love you, and because the only thing my family has ever wanted for me is my happiness." He squeezed her hand. "And there is no way whatsoever, my dear, that they'll be able to miss the fact that I am now the happiest man in the world."

Maggie took a deep breath, tempted to scandalize the neighborhood by throwing her arms around her husband this very minute, in broad daylight, never mind who was watching. He was still Jonathan, after all. Her husband, yes. But also her friend. And as he had so many times in the past, he'd dispelled her doubts and fears with his quiet, steady reassurance.

She took one more long look at the man beside her. In that moment she realized that as long as they were together in the shelter of God's love and their love for each other, she had nothing to fear.

Chapter One

Learning to Love

I dreamt not that life
Could hold such happiness.

Wilfred Wilson Gibson

⟨⟨⟨~⟩⟩⟩

Maggie held her breath as she watched Lawrence Stuart slowly rise from his wheelchair. Her concern for Jonathan's father was growing almost as quickly as her fondness for him. The effort it cost him to get up was visible, yet he insisted on walking from the dining room to the front room—which Jonathan and his sister, Maggie noted, referred to as the *parlor.*

On the way from the hotel Jonathan had explained that although his father had to rely heavily on a wheelchair, on "good days" he still forced himself to walk a little, if only from one room to the other.

All through dinner Maggie had tried not to stare, but now, as they sat talking in the *parlor,* she caught herself studying her new father-in-law when he wasn't looking. In his late seventies, despite years

of crippling arthritis, he was a striking man, elegant in appearance
and demeanor. A lawyer by trade, Lawrence Stuart looked honest
and trustworthy.

The longer Maggie was around him, the more she saw her husband reflected in his father. The same refined and gentlemanly
behavior, the same strong and noble features, the same dry, unpre-
dictable sense of humor, and the same deference to others that so
appealed to her in Jonathan were all evident in his father. Even the
stubborn strand of hair that tended to fall over his left eye—silver
rather than Jonathan's flaxen shade—was reminiscent of his son.

Just as Jonathan had said, her earlier apprehension about meeting his family had been unwarranted, although when she'd first
walked into her husband's childhood home, she felt as if she'd
entered a foreign country. The oak doors with their shining brass
knockers were massive and heavy; the entry floor marbled, setting
up an echo with every step; the ceilings high; and the walls lined
with paintings that even to Maggie's unstudied eye looked to be
of excellent quality. But by the time they entered the dining room,
despite the quiet elegance of a table that would have served at least
two dozen people, and china and tableware that reflected the light
like diamonds, she had already relaxed more than she would have
thought possible.

Jonathan's father and sister had greeted her with open arms, and
with open hearts as well. Maggie warmed to Patricia almost immediately. A widow in her early fifties with both her children grown
and away at university, she clearly doted on her father and brother.
If for no other reason, Maggie would have loved her profusely after
seeing her affection for Jonathan.

A tall, slender woman with the same dark eyes as her father and
brother, Jonathan's sister possessed the genteel stateliness Maggie
might have envied in someone else. But Patricia treated her with
such warmth and open friendliness—and took such obvious delight
in her brother's marriage—that even a hint of envy toward her was
out of the question.

To Maggie's considerable relief, if Jonathan's father and sister had been disappointed in his choice of a bride, they kept their feelings well concealed. For the past half hour, Patricia had been regaling her with stories of Jonathan's childhood, stories that Maggie found immensely interesting while Jonathan, seated between the two, clearly would prefer to forget.

"Patty, you're enjoying yourself far too much," he said, shaking his head. "Leave me *some* secrets, won't you?"

His sister ignored him, reaching over to pat Maggie's hand. "Don't worry, Maggie. I'm sure he's over his youthful fascination with frogs and toads by now."

"Father, stop her! *Please.*" Jonathan put a hand to his forehead in mock pain. "This isn't fair."

Lawrence Stuart laughed. "She's just getting warmed up. If you had any thought of impressing Maggie, I'm afraid there will be none of that now."

Jonathan groaned.

"Oh, and wait till I tell you about the frog wedding," Patricia said, leaning across Jonathan toward Maggie.

"The frog *wedding?*" Maggie repeated, looking at Jonathan.

"You don't want to know," Jonathan said as he scowled at his sister. "Patty, if you can bring yourself to stop disgracing me long enough, why don't you take Maggie upstairs and show her your paintings?"

"Oh, that's right!" Maggie said. "Jonathan told me you're an artist."

"Hardly. But since he so obviously wants to spoil my fun, come along, Maggie. We'll humor him."

"She *is* an artist," Jonathan said, standing. "She has quite a reputation in Lexington."

"All over the state now," his father put in. "Patty's had some very successful showings over the past few years."

"Let's leave them alone," Patricia said, getting to her feet and reaching a hand out to Maggie. "This way they'll talk man talk instead of embarrassing me."

Maggie met Jonathan's smile with one of her own, then got up and let his sister lead her from the room.

◆▸·◂◆

Jonathan watched his sister and Maggie start upstairs. He punched up the fire before taking a chair close to the fireplace and across from his father.

"She's absolutely lovely," his father said, smiling. "I liked her immediately, and you can see for yourself that your sister has taken to her too. And you look to be in fine form. Fit and happy. I'm glad, son."

"Thank you, sir. I *am* happy."

"And you're staying well?"

Even though it had been years since Jonathan had been plagued with heart trouble, one of the first questions from his father any time he came home had to do with his health.

He nodded and his father looked satisfied.

"I'm eager to read Maggie's book. What an accomplishment for one so young."

Jonathan shifted in the chair. "Are you bothered by Maggie's age, Father? That there are so many years between us?"

His father lifted an eyebrow. "It seems to me that would be none of my business. But since you asked—no, I'm not in the least concerned. I trust your judgment. Besides, seeing the two of you together, it seems to me that God has blessed each of you with the ideal mate."

Pleased, Jonathan realized he'd been waiting for this. He'd written about Maggie and their marriage, of course, and his father had immediately replied with his congratulations, along with a note from Patricia that said simply, "About time!" Unfortunately, his father's health wouldn't let them make the trip to Skingle Creek for the ceremony.

Even though he'd recently turned forty, Jonathan still considered his father to be the wisest, most discerning man he'd ever known and, as always, coveted his approval.

"Jonathan, your last letter said there was something you wanted to talk to me about. Some kind of bad business with Maggie's sister and her husband."

Although Jonathan had written only the briefest account of Eva Grace's abusive marriage to Richard Barlow, he'd been eager to get his father's legal advice about the situation. "Eva Grace—Maggie's sister—was also my student a few years ago," he said, leaning forward. "A wonderful girl. She and Maggie are very close, so you can understand how all this ugliness with her sister is affecting her."

He went on to tell his father the whole story about the brutal beatings Eva Grace had suffered at her husband's hands, how she'd left Barlow some months back and gone home to her family in Skingle Creek, and Barlow's subsequent attempt to force her to return to Lexington with him.

"I think I mentioned in my letter that Eva Grace is carrying Barlow's child," he said.

Frowning, his father nodded.

"When Barlow came to Skingle Creek—and in two letters afterward—he threatened to take the baby away from Eva Grace once it's born. She's due to deliver anytime now, and Maggie is worried sick that Barlow will come after the child. Can he do that?"

Still frowning, his father steepled his hands at his chin, not replying right away.

"Just so you know," Jonathan added, "Maggie has seen the marks of Barlow's savagery for herself. And come to think of it, I suppose Eva Grace's physician would have seen them too."

His father looked up. "I'm not sure that would help, but would he testify if necessary?"

"I feel certain *she* would."

Lawrence's frown darkened. "The doctor is a woman? I'm afraid she'd not be as credible in court."

Jonathan gripped the arms of the chair. "That's absolutely absurd. As I understand it, Dr. Gordon is a fine doctor with impeccable credentials."

His father made a palms-up gesture. "You know how things are, Jonathan. We may not like it, but we're not going to change the system in a few weeks. The day is coming, I believe, when women won't be treated like chattel, but it's not going to happen soon enough

to help Maggie's sister." He paused. "You might as well know that
even with witnesses, we'd almost certainly lose in court. If we even
made it to court."

Jonathan pulled a long breath and got to his feet. "I hate to tell
Maggie this."

"Well, *don't* tell her, not just yet. Give me some time to think
about things and discuss the situation with Jeff. It's always possible
he might come up with something I haven't thought of."

Jeff Prescott was a senior partner in the law firm and a close
friend of the family. It was no secret that Lawrence Stuart trusted
him as much as if he were family.

"This Barlow—you say he's fairly well-regarded here in
Lexington?"

Jonathan nodded. "According to Eva Grace, yes. Apparently he
rose quickly in business and ever since has been active in community affairs. And in church."

His father's mouth pulled down. "While he beats his wife behind
closed doors." He made a move as if to stand, then seemed to think
better of it.

"I know Maggie would greatly appreciate any advice you might
have to offer, Father. And so would I."

"Well, Maggie's part of our family now, so of course we'll try to
help her—and her sister—any way we can." He glanced toward the
entryway and the staircase. "Before the ladies return, I want to tell
you again how happy I am for you, son. I've prayed for years that
you'd make a good marriage, and it seems you've done just that. My
deepest wish is that you and your lovely Maggie will be as happy
as your mother and I were."

Jonathan didn't miss the trembling of his father's hands. Lawrence
Stuart had never been an openly emotional man, not with his wife
nor his children. He almost always expressed his affection more
with deeds than words, but none of them had ever had occasion
to doubt his love.

On impulse, Jonathan went to him. Earlier he had noted how
thin his father had grown, thinner than he had ever seen him. But

only when he clasped the other's shoulder did he sense that the father who had once seemed so strong and indestructible had become a frail old man.

Jonathan had all he could do to control his own emotions as he tightened his grip on his father's shoulder. "If I can be half as good a husband to Maggie as you were to Mother, I know we *will* be happy, sir. I have every intention of following the example you set for me."

His father reached up and covered the hand on his shoulder with his own. "You were always a good boy, Jonathan. You made your mother and me very proud. I have no doubt in my mind that you'll do well by your Maggie."

Jonathan's eyes burned. He didn't trust himself to say anything more. Because it was so unlike his father to be this vocal, he felt as if he'd been given an uncommon gift.

⋙⋘

On the way back to the hotel it started to snow again, a heavy, wind-driven snow that quickly veiled the darkened streets and buildings in relentless white.

"I'm beginning to think we should have hired a sleigh instead of a cab," Jonathan remarked. "I suppose you're enjoying this."

"You know I am! It's so beautiful…and so romantic."

He rolled his eyes but tugged her a little closer to him in the darkness of the hack.

"So how do you feel about my family now?"

"I think they're wonderful! I see so much of you in your father. How could I help but love him? And Patricia—she couldn't *be* any nicer, could she? I feel as if I've known her forever. And they were both so kind to me, Jonathan."

"Why wouldn't they be?" he said, squeezing her hand. "You invite kindness, Maggie."

He stopped her protest, insisting, "It's true. People *want* to be nice to you."

He touched her face, brushing the back of his hand along her chin.

"Jonathan—"

"The driver can't see us, nor can anyone else," he assured her, tilting her face up to his and tracing her cheek with his lips.

"You're sure?"

"Quite. We are totally, *romantically* alone."

He bent his head and kissed her, and Maggie took a deep breath.

She was secretly pleased that they were staying at the hotel instead of with his family. She hadn't known before tonight just how quickly she'd be comfortable with his father and sister. In spite of the fact that she no longer felt intimidated by them, she was happy she'd have Jonathan to herself for most of the week.

They'd had so precious little privacy in their time together. With her living at home—and with Da being as strict as he was—there had been no real opportunity for them to "court." Days were spent at the school surrounded by their students, and the few evenings they could manage together were usually spent with Maggie's family. They couldn't even take a quiet walk together without coming upon friends and neighbors, many of whom were eager to talk to the principal and teachers of their children.

To suddenly find themselves facing entire days...and nights... alone together was a rare experience indeed, and one that Maggie was still trying to get used to. She wanted to learn as much about Jonathan as she possibly could. As recently as a few weeks ago she would have said she knew him well. But knowing him as her former teacher, later as her supervisor and friend, wasn't remotely the same as knowing him as her husband.

Years had passed since they'd first met. This was no longer a little girl's hero worship for an exceptional teacher or a schoolgirl's crush.

She had known Jonathan Stuart to be a quiet man, self-contained, and often contemplative. Strong but self-deprecating. Sharply intelligent but practical. A devout and highly principled man, but never didactic.

Now she was discovering formerly unknown facets of his personality that surprised and often delighted her. An unexpected lightness and an almost boyish playfulness that watched for ways to make her smile or laugh. A way of loving her with infinite tenderness and dizzying passion, bringing her to tears with his gentleness, taking her breath away with his touch. An abandonment, a total relinquishment of himself to his God that at one moment was almost childlike—the next, holy. And a genuine, selfless love, a concern for others that was as much sacrificial as generous.

She loved this man to the point of drowning in him. She had been his wife for only two days, but she knew the time had already come when she could no longer feel at home anywhere but in his presence.

So much was known, so much was still unanswered.

Chapter Two

A Gathering Storm

Love thyself last.

Ella Wheeler Wilcox

~⁓⁓

The next morning Jonathan was enlisted to help Maggie put up her hair. While she pinned up one length, he held another section in place and passed her the occasional hairpin as needed. He supposed he wouldn't have much liked for it to be common knowledge that he'd been a part of this kind of thing, but in truth the whole ritual fascinated him.

Maggie's hair had always intrigued him. Even when she was still a child, he'd sometimes wondered how such a small head could hold such a mass of heavy hair without toppling. But at some point over the years, the incorrigible mane of wiry curls had been transformed into a fiery spill of copper and gold that made his heart skip a beat.

Standing behind her, watching her in the mirror as she worked her way through this unexpectedly intimate undertaking, he was surprised to realize that it seemed as much a mystery to her as it did to him.

"Eva Grace has me incredibly spoiled," she muttered as she attacked yet another swatch of hair. "She usually helps me with this. I've never been any good at dressing my own hair. Not at all."

"Is there anything more I can do?" Jonathan ventured. "I don't seem to be contributing very much."

She met his eyes in the mirror. "You can stop smiling, for one thing. You seem to find this entirely too amusing. Here—I need another pin."

He handed it to her, still grinning like a simpleton.

She tilted her head a little, stabbing the hairpin into place.

"Why must you go through all this anyway? Why don't you just wear it down or tie it back with a ribbon as you do at school? That's the way I like it best," he volunteered.

She shot him a look of reproach. "I can't do that anymore, Jonathan. I'm a married woman now."

"Indeed." He thought about that for a moment. Apparently there was a connection between being a married woman and putting her hair up. She must know something he didn't.

"Well, you wouldn't want your wife to go around with her hair flying in the wind like some floozy, would you?"

"I...wouldn't. No, of course not," he said with more emphasis. "Absolutely not."

She nodded and reached for another hairpin. "Mum says a woman shouldn't take her hair down except for her husband," she said, lowering her gaze.

Jonathan studied the crown of her head and then the plush knot she'd somehow anchored in place at the nape of her neck, the tendrils of copper already escaping their confines at her temples.

He swallowed against the dryness in his throat. "I couldn't agree more with your mother," he said, handing her another hairpin.

❧❧

Still in her dressing gown, Maggie stood back a little to admire the new suit she'd just laid out on the bed. Unbeknown to her, Jonathan had connived with Cora Dillon, who had fashioned her wedding gown, to also fashion two new suits from material he himself had selected: the lovely, deep-forest green she planned to wear today and the caramel-colored "traveling outfit" she'd worn yesterday for their trip to Lexington. Both were of the softest wool imaginable and perfect fits.

Her initial protests at his extravagance had lasted only until she saw the warm look of approval in his eyes yesterday, the first time she'd worn the travel suit. She hoped he'd be just as pleased with her appearance today.

She glanced across the room to see that he was still standing at the window, watching the snow. Maggie had been surprised to realize that the weather held a fascination for him that went beyond mere interest. He seemed particularly taken with thunderstorms and snowstorms.

Storm aptly described what was going on outside today. She allowed herself one more admiring look at her new suit and then went to stand next to him. "How long do you suppose it's been snowing?"

"It must have started up again well before daybreak. And there doesn't seem to be much sign of it stopping soon."

Outside the window, the snow came in blowing waves. Uneasiness tugged at Maggie in spite of her attempts to simply enjoy the scene. Last night's snowfall had been playful, a capricious dance that rose and fell on the wind. This seemed more a heavy invasion.

"Do you think we'll be able to get around the city today?" she asked, taking hold of Jonathan's arm.

Even though he claimed to have no desire to live in the city, Maggie knew he still felt genuine affection for the place where he'd grown up and had been looking forward to showing her some of his favorite haunts. She hated to see him disappointed.

Jonathan turned to look at her. "I thought you liked the snow."

"Oh, I do. When we were all still at home, Nell Frances and I could scarcely wait for the first snow of the season so we could build a snowman." She smiled at the memory. "Not Eva Grace, of course. She thought both of us were as mad as a bag of squirrels. She stayed inside and watched out the window. No, I was just thinking how disappointed you'd be if we were to end up snowbound."

"Oh, I don't know," he said, touching her hair. "I can think of far worse things than being snowbound with you. But you needn't worry. It takes more than a snowstorm to bring Lexington to a halt. We'll manage just fine. But dress warm."

"I'm going to wear my new suit," Maggie said, pointing to the bed. "I can't wait any longer."

"Why don't I have a fresh pot of coffee sent up since I suspect we might be here for a while?"

Maggie rolled her eyes at him, scooped up her suit off the bed, and headed for the dressing room, happiness humming through her.

⤜⟡⤛

Jonathan had arranged for a cab to pick them up in front of the hotel at ten-thirty. By ten o'clock Maggie still hadn't emerged from the dressing room, so he returned to the window and again stood looking outside. He saw that the snow had intensified and felt a tug of concern. He hadn't wanted to spoil Maggie's excitement by admitting the possibility that they might actually end up stuck at the hotel. And as yet it shouldn't be a problem. In truth, getting stuck *away* from the hotel would be much more of a problem. Was he being foolish, taking her out in such a storm?

The door to the dressing room opened just then, and he turned to see her step out with a flourish and do a little whirl for his inspection. His intuition had been right on the money about the new suit. Its deep, rich green emphasized the fiery copper of her hair, the faint blush of her complexion, and the design nipped and tucked in all the right places to show off her adorable figure.

The minx! That impish glint in her eye plainly said she knew she had him tongue-tied, and not for the first time.

"I love it, Jonathan!"

He continued to stare. "I love it more."

Had he ever, even in his youth, imagined that he would one day be so happy? There were times, like now, seeing his love for her reflected in her eyes, when he thought he might strangle with the joy she brought to him. All he wanted for the rest of his life was to return that joy to her.

He started toward her, bent on showing what he was feeling since words had clearly failed him, but he stopped when someone rapped on the door.

He glanced at Maggie. "Probably someone letting us know the cab is here," he said. He opened the door to reveal a youth in the hotel's black-and-gold bellboy uniform.

"Mr. Stuart?"

Jonathan nodded.

"Western Union, sir."

Jonathan frowned, hesitating a moment before taking the paper the boy held out to him. When the youth made no overture to leave, Jonathan fished in his pocket for a coin and handed it to him, then stepped back into the room and closed the door.

"Jonathan?"

He glanced at Maggie and then at the telegram.

His father had a telephone in the house. He would have called. No one local would send them a telegram. They would simply call the hotel.

He felt Maggie watching him, hard, as he opened it.

Even before he could begin to read, she was at his side, clutching his arm.

> Eva Grace taken bad. She's asking for you. Come home right
> away. Your da—Matthew MacAuley.

Maggie's grip on his arm tightened like a vise. Bringing his hand around to cover hers, he found it cold.

She made a sound like a sob and leaned into him, trembling. "Jonathan—"

He gently pressed her head against his chest and held her securely against him. "Yes, I know. We'll go at once." He cast an uneasy glance across the room as another blast of wind-driven snow rattled the window.

❖·❖

They had been sitting in the train station well over two hours when Jonathan got up and walked over to the window again, just as he had no more than fifteen minutes ago. And fifteen minutes before that. He'd made at least a dozen trips back and forth since they'd first sat down on the bench. Maggie knew that his next move would be to approach the middle-aged man with the tired eyes behind the ticket window and ask for any news.

She glanced around. They weren't the only ones waiting for a train. An elderly woman on a nearby bench sat staring worriedly out the window while the white-haired man beside her dozed. Across from them stood a woman with two small children. Every so often she would cross to the window, peer out, and then return to her station near the bench, both fussy children in tow. Near the entrance a young man fidgeted, shifting from one foot to the other, adjusting his carrying case, his gaze darting from one corner of the building to another.

Jonathan was on his way back to her now. Maggie could tell from his tightly drawn features that there was no news.

"They're clearing the tracks ahead," he said, sitting down beside her again. "It's only a matter of time now."

Maggie made no reply for a moment, but she couldn't ignore the growing sense of urgency pressing at her. "If it keeps snowing like this, the tracks can't possibly stay clear. And we need to leave *now*. We have to get home."

"Look," he said, pointing to the window. "It's not so dark now as it was earlier. I think it's going to clear up soon." He took her hand. "It's going to be all right, Maggie. It is."

She studied his face and saw the effort it was costing him to bolster her spirits. But in this instance, even Jonathan couldn't help her. Even so, she wished they weren't in a public place. She wished she could just go into his arms and let him hold her, impart his strength to her.

"I know you're trying to reassure me, Jonathan," she said, keeping her voice low. "And I appreciate it. But we both know that sometimes things *aren't* all right—and might never be all right."

Dear Lord...please don't let this be one of those times.

He pulled a long breath, squeezed her hand, but said nothing.

How could everything have changed so quickly and without warning? In the midst of a happiness so overwhelming there was no thought that anything could ever dim it, and now, all in a moment, a fear as real and grave as she'd ever known cast its shadow. In only seconds—as long as it took to read a telegram—life had gone from incredible joy to crushing dread.

Maggie's head ached as fear hammered at her. Da never would have called them home from their honeymoon had the situation been anything less than dire. He hadn't even said whether the baby had been born. Just that Eva Grace had been taken bad and they should come home now.

Her stomach roiled again, and she swallowed hard. Poor Jonathan. She was nothing but a burden to him just now. He didn't know what to say, what to do, how to help her, yet he was trying so hard to put on a bright face for her sake.

Oh, Evie. How did it come to this for you? You—always so lively and bright...you used to shine...

All through her teenage years, Eva Grace had been the most comely girl in school. Probably it was fair to say that for years she'd been the prettiest girl in Skingle Creek. Her place had always been at the center of things, as the focus of attention. For the boys, a prize to be won; for the girls, someone to admire and emulate.

But Evie had made no secret of the fact that she hated Skingle Creek, that somehow, some way, she would escape it.

Was that why she married Richard? To get away from the town

of their childhood and the hard existence that fell to a miner's wife and family?

No. Almost certainly her sister had loved the man she married— or at least thought she did. Eva Grace was too honest, too fine a person to latch on to a man just to escape a bitter life. She would have gone to Richard Barlow as a young bride with stars in her eyes and love in her heart only to be horribly beaten and mistreated.

For her unborn baby's sake, she had fled his cruelty and returned home. Betrayed, broken, wounded in body and spirit, she'd nevertheless found the courage to escape, to leave everything behind but her resolve to protect her child.

Maggie shuddered, more from the cold in her soul than the drafty train station. How could this be happening to her sister? What would they find when they reached Skingle Creek? And how long would it be before they could get there?

Jonathan patted her hand, gripped it, and then released it. He again got up from the bench, but before he could reach the ticket window, their train was called.

Maggie almost went limp with relief. She stood, only to find that her legs were shaking as badly as her hands. She swayed a little, but Jonathan saw and rushed to catch her arm, steadying her.

As they stepped outside, she discovered that the skies indeed had brightened somewhat. But it was still snowing.

Chapter Three

Going Home

Sometimes, I think, the things we see
Are shadows of the things to be.

Phoebe Cary

Snow veiled most of the slow train ride back to Skingle Creek. Twice they had to stop and wait while the tracks ahead were cleared. An hour the first time, nearly two hours the second. Jonathan must have looked at his pocket watch no less than every fifteen minutes during each delay.

Maggie didn't ask about the time. She didn't care what time it was. Her only concern was to start moving again, to get home. With each delay her thoughts traveled further away from Jonathan than they'd been since she'd come back from Chicago and started teaching at the school.

She'd been scarcely aware of the world outside the train window since they left Lexington, only vaguely taking notice as they raced by the snow-covered trees, the creeks and ponds that had become glazed mirrors, the roofs of farm houses that sagged with the white weight blown upon them, and the dark lines of track that curved into each turn along the way.

At some point, she had already gone home in her memory. It was still winter in her thoughts as she walked to school with her two sisters. Nell Frances lagged behind to delay the start of the school day, and Eva Grace charged ahead to get out of the cold. Mondays they were all three quiet and often grumpy, depending on how they'd spent the weekend. Fridays were better. They dawdled, even in the morning, sometimes stopping for a brief snowball fight. Hurrying on the way home in the afternoon, they would tease Eva Grace about her latest beau or argue among themselves as to whose turn it was to help with supper or do the dishes, not really minding the chores ahead because the weekend usually held some fun along with work.

Especially when it snowed. Snowmen and snow forts, snow angels and sledding, Christmas and ice skating. Snow always brought good times.

But not today. This day the snow brought dread like a falling rock landing on her chest, smothering her and weighing her down. Fear came upon her, a howling wind unleashed inside, battering her without mercy. She couldn't stop thinking of Eva Grace, of the doctor's warnings about the toxemia, and every thought was a physical blow.

Her mind lost all sense of order. Her thoughts darted back and forth from the past to the more recent days when Evie had come home after leaving Richard. One moment she was gripped by the memory of her sister helping her with homework by the light of an oil lamp at the kitchen table, only to remember next how, in weeks past, Evie had encouraged her love for Jonathan, even confronted her with the stern announcement that she and Jonathan needed to face the reality of their love for each other.

So many memories...

So lost was she in remembrance that it came almost as a surprise when she realized the darkness of the winter afternoon had gathered in on them, and they were finally home.

A blast from the train whistle. Smoke and ash falling by the window. Jonathan's hand on her arm. His voice gentle, but edged with the same apprehension that clutched at Maggie's heart ever since the telegram came.

"We're here, Maggie," he said, increasing the pressure on her arm. He helped her up. "We're home."

❖❖

"I can't tell you how much I appreciate this, Ben. You should have brought my buggy, though, instead of risking yours."

"Mine's a bit heavier, I think. It's always done pretty well in the snow."

Jonathan had wired ahead, asking Ben Wallace, their pastor and Jonathan's closest friend, to meet them at the depot. On an ordinary day they could have walked to the MacAuleys from the train station—it wasn't all that far. But this was no ordinary day. It was still snowing, and the wind was even more raw than it had been earlier.

Besides, they needed to get to the MacAuleys as quickly as possible. Maggie looked tight enough to snap if they had to wait much longer.

After getting her settled into the buggy under a heavy lap robe, Jonathan and Ben went to retrieve the luggage from the platform.

"Eva Grace—have you seen her?" Jonathan asked.

His friend nodded. "I went as soon as I got your telegram. I was going anyway. I'd already heard she was in trouble."

"And?"

Ben shook his head. "Not good."

Jonathan's heart sank. "The baby?" he asked, his mouth dry.

"She was still in labor when I stopped by. That was about half past two. Dr. Gordon was with her." The pastor's usually pleasant features were taut, his eyes shadowed.

"Tell me, Ben. If it's that bad I want to know before Maggie does."

"It's that bad, Jonathan," said the older man. "I'm afraid it's very bad indeed."

❧•❧

Dr. Sally Gordon's buggy was parked in front of the house. Clearly she'd been there for quite some time. The horse's blanket was covered with snow, the wheels only partly visible above a drift. This kind of snowstorm wasn't typical for the area. Jonathan fervently wished it hadn't surprised them today.

He helped Maggie out, taking both her hands in his for a moment as he searched her eyes. "All right?" he asked.

Her features were pinched with apprehension, and her hands trembled in his. But she took a deep breath and nodded.

Ben came up just then and put a hand to Jonathan's shoulder. "I'd best go on home. Regina's nervous about being alone with the children in the storm. But promise you'll send word if you need me."

Jonathan nodded, immeasurably grateful for this loyal friend who was always there when needed. He heard Figaro barking in back of the house, but he would have to wait. Later he would go to him, but not now.

Maggie's father met them on the porch, sweeping Maggie into his arms and then shaking Jonathan's hand. Inside, he pulled Maggie close again, his eyes meeting Jonathan's over the top of her head. The devastation on the older man's craggy face wrenched Jonathan's heart and set off a warning bell.

Maggie's brother, Ray, was standing in front of the window, his eyes red, his youthful expression one of pain and bewilderment.

Jonathan nodded to him, and the boy, clearly awkward with this newly changed relationship with his schoolteacher mumbled something too low to catch.

"'Tis good you've come," Matthew said, his voice hoarse.

"Eva Grace—how is she?" Maggie asked. "Has she had the baby yet?"

Her father turned ashen. He made a sound like he was about to choke but no words came.

Just then Maggie's mother appeared in the doorway, holding a small bundle swaddled in blankets.

A soft "oh" escaped Maggie, and she went to her mother.

Jonathan had never seen Kate MacAuley in such a state. She looked positively…destroyed. Haggard. Her eyes were dark caverns, her face ashen, the skin so tight over her features it might crack. Her fair hair, usually neatly secured at the nape of her neck, had come loose and fell in limp strands.

Tears slowly tracked down her face as she stood watching them.

"Mum?"

Jonathan heard the tremor in Maggie's voice and quickly went to stand behind her. He put a hand on her shoulder, felt her trembling, and strengthened his grip.

"Eva Grace has a baby girl," announced Kate MacAuley in a voice that sounded as if she couldn't quite get her breath. "Such a tiny thing…but the doctor says she's healthy."

She smoothed the blanket away from the baby's face for Maggie to see.

Maggie touched the baby's face with one finger. "Oh, she's so small!"

Kate held the sleeping infant up for Jonathan to see.

"But so pretty. And Evie? How is she?" Maggie asked.

Her mother brought the baby back to her chest, wrapping it as close as she could against her heart, burying her face in the small bundle.

Behind him Jonathan heard Matthew groan.

"Maggie…your sister is gone," he said.

Stunned, Jonathan turned to look at him.

"Just a few minutes after the baby was delivered," Matthew added, his words thick and slurred. "Eva Grace…she's gone."

Jonathan stared at him and then whipped around to catch Maggie as she cried out and swayed against him.

✦· ·✦

The next few hours were a nightmare unlike anything Maggie had ever imagined. The room wheeled as she stood beside her sister's lifeless form on the bed where she'd given birth. The same bed she'd slept in as a child.

Guilt thundered in on Maggie. A suffocating guilt, that she hadn't been here when her sister died. Guilt that she had worried about the baby more than she had Eva Grace. Fear that the blows Evie had suffered at the punishing hands of Richard Barlow might have damaged her unborn child had dogged her all throughout her sister's pregnancy. But she had focused most of her concern on the baby rather than Evie, in spite of Dr. Gordon's concern about toxemia.

Maggie stood very still, yet the room seemed to rock beneath her. She reached for something to hold on to and felt Jonathan's arm go around her waist, holding her steady. She was aware of her mother's ragged keening on the other side of the bed, her hands covering her face...her father's struggle to maintain his self-control as his features crumbled with the effort...her younger brother's absence from the room...her own thoughts, the memories that had drifted in and out of her mind throughout the train ride home.

How could it be that the still, waxen form on the bed was her sister? Only days before, at the wedding, Evie had teased her, laughed with her, squeezed her hands, and wished her happiness.

Eva Grace was only twenty-seven years old. Three years older than Maggie. It hadn't been that long ago that Evie had been the belle of Skingle Creek, the loveliest girl in town, the brightest light of the family, the darling of most everyone who knew her. Vivacious and pretty and clever with an uncompromising sense of fairness and a precocious sense of humor. Eva Grace MacAuley had *sparkled*. She had been impossible to resist. Everyone loved her.

This couldn't be her sister. This swollen body with the bruised eyes that would never again meet her gaze with the glint of a shared secret or a private joke. Those still hands that had held her baby daughter for only a few moments and never would again.

Maggie shook as she stared down at the bed where death had stolen a daughter, a sister, and a young mother…where one life had ended and another had begun…where dreams had died and hope had departed. There was nothing left here except cold emptiness and terrible grief that mocked the echoes of a young girl's laughter and the memory of her bright dreams.

"She's with God now, Maggie."

She looked at Jonathan. "But I don't want her with God. She should be here…with us…with her baby."

She saw that her words caused him pain, but she could do nothing but shake her head and hug her arms to herself.

Across the room the baby whimpered.

Maggie looked to see Dr. Gordon standing at the window, cradling the infant in her arms, touching a small, nippled bottle to the baby's mouth in an effort to feed her.

She watched them for a moment and then eased away from Jonathan to bend and kiss her sister's forehead.

She was cold.

Evie hated being cold.

She straightened then, went into her husband's arms, and allowed herself to weep against him, but only for a moment. Finally she turned, her gaze at first resting on her mother, hunched and still weeping at Evie's bedside. She looked at her father, his hand on his wife's shoulder, his usually strong features slack with bewilderment and grief.

She turned back to Jonathan, gripped his forearms for a moment, met his eyes, and nodded to assure him she wouldn't fly apart.

"Go to Ray," she murmured. "He doesn't know how to be…what to do."

She saw the hesitation in his eyes, his reluctance to leave her. "Please, Jonathan," she said. "I'll be all right."

As soon as he turned to go, Maggie went to her parents, gathered them into her embrace, and held them while they wept.

She didn't allow herself to look at her lifeless sister again. Not even once.

Chapter Four

The Long Goodbye

The pains of death are past,
Labour and sorrow cease,
And Life's long warfare closed at last,
Thy soul is found in peace.

James Montgomery

The evening of the wake for Eva Grace the wind was still up, driving the snow in wild gusts. It was a bitter, raw night, but the weather didn't stop the people of Skingle Creek from showing up at the MacAuleys to pay their respects. Until well after midnight a steady stream of the town's residents moved in and out.

There was no pretense at Irish merriment at this wake, only lighted candles and the prayers and shared tears of those who visited. Jonathan stood with the family for the duration, and he felt certain that almost everyone in town had stopped in at one time or

another. Even the few newcomers who might not have known Eva
Grace had come out of respect for Matthew and Kate.

Finally the house was quiet, the visitors gone, the family abed
for a few brief hours. In the deeply shadowed living room, lit now
by a few flickering candles, Jonathan stood with Maggie beside the
coffin. He had not seen her weep even once throughout the evening,
although he knew that only the slenderest of threads was holding
her together.

Maggie's other sister, Nell Frances, was unable to make the trip
from Indiana because of the impending birth of *her* baby, due any
day now. Earlier Maggie had admitted to him how keenly she felt
the absence of her other sister. She had confided something else
to him as well: that not having the chance to say goodbye to Eva
Grace before she passed on was a regret she feared she would always
live with.

She leaned against his shoulder, and he felt her tremble as she
repeated what she'd told him earlier. "Oh, Jonathan, if only I could
have been here at the end," she murmured in the darkness. "I'll
always wish I'd been with her."

She broke down then, and in a way Jonathan was relieved. Even
as a child Maggie had been able to steel herself in the worst of situ-
ations, had managed to keep her emotions under control in order
to be strong for everyone else. But her self-control hadn't always
worked for her good. More than once he'd feared she might eventually shatter, so taut was she drawn against the weight of her own
sorrow.

She needed to grieve. No one was meant to suppress this level of
pain indefinitely. So when she tried to pull away and recover herself,
he steered her back to him. "No, sweetheart," he said softly. "You
don't have to be strong. Not now. Not with me."

Later, as she bent to touch her lips to her sister's forehead for one
final goodbye, he stood behind her, grasping her shoulders, for she
was trembling again, harder this time. When had she last had anything to eat? *Had* she eaten? He'd been so preoccupied for hours that
he hadn't eaten and hadn't paid attention to whether Maggie had.

She turned back to him and sighed. "Oh Jonathan...she's so cold...and you know how Evie hated being cold."

Jonathan felt powerless. From the first, once he realized that he loved Maggie, he'd been seized with a fierce desire to take care of her, to make her happy, to keep her isolated from hurt. And now to see her like this, to see the pain wounding her heart and searing her spirit and know there was nothing he could do to ease her agony was almost unbearable.

But at least he could see to her physical needs. With great effort he coaxed her into the kitchen where he fixed her a plate with some of the food brought in earlier.

"I can't eat," she said dully.

"You *must* eat, sweetheart. We both will. We must."

With him sitting across from her, watching, she managed a few bites, as did he. They ate without speaking until Maggie broke the silence. "Da wants you to say a few words tomorrow at the cemetery."

Jonathan nodded. "I know. He asked me tonight."

"I'd like that too, Jonathan. Evie always held you in such high regard. And she was...so happy for us when I told her you'd asked me to marry you."

In truth, according to Maggie, Jonathan was actually indebted to her sister for convincing Maggie to face her feelings for him rather than deny them. He wished now he had thanked Eva Grace for the part she'd played in bringing them together.

"If you'd rather not do that, Jonathan, I'd understand—"

He reached across the table and took her hand. "It's all right, Maggie. Of course I'll do it."

They were clearing the table when they heard the baby cry out. A stricken look froze Maggie's features, and she stopped, her gaze darting to the direction of her parents' bedroom. A moment later the baby quieted, and they heard the sound of Kate's voice as she crooned softly.

"Poor wee thing. Everyone's been too preoccupied, too sad, to give her the attention she needs. This is so hard for Mum. It's too much for her," Maggie said.

"Your mother is stronger than you think, sweetheart. She'll get through this."

She looked at him.

"She will, Maggie. And so will we. Now why don't you go see if Kate needs any help? She might need a bottle warmed."

A few moments later Maggie came back carrying the baby. The infant was still wailing. "I told Mum to go back to bed, that we'd feed—"

She broke off, her eyes brimming with dismay. "Oh, Jonathan! The poor wee babe doesn't even have a name!"

He went to her. "She *will* have a name. And soon, I'm sure. You know Eva Grace's child will never be neglected." Awkwardly he reached to take the baby. This was strange territory for him. From time to time he'd held an infant sibling of one of his students during home visits, but even that had been awhile ago.

"I'll hold her while you warm a bottle," he said, studying the warm, squirming bundle in his arms. To his relief the baby's cries quieted to soft sobbing. Her eyes were open, her little fists suspended in the air.

"Isn't she a pretty thing though?" Maggie observed, a sad smile touching her lips.

"She is indeed," he said, carefully taking a chair at the table. "And you know, I believe I can already see Eva Grace in her. The blue eyes. All that blond hair. And, look, Maggie! She has a dimple beside her mouth just like Eva Grace."

Maggie bent to look. "Why so she does! Oh, I'm so glad Evie got to see her. And Mum said—" She stopped to wipe the wetness from her eyes before going on. "Mum said she *was* able to hold her for a few minutes."

Jonathan balanced the baby in the crook of his arm and touched his free hand to Maggie's cheek. "Maggie, you have to believe that Eva Grace died in peace. She saw that her child was whole and healthy. She knew she'd be well taken care of by her family. And as for Eva Grace herself, she's known the Lord from the time she was a child. Try to find comfort in that…and in the baby. That's what Eva Grace would want."

Maggie nodded and straightened. "I know," she said, her voice unsteady. "Perhaps after tomorrow…" She turned away and went to the stove to get a warming pan.

Jonathan tucked the baby a little closer. He understood what Maggie meant by "after tomorrow." Before they could even begin to think about the days ahead, they must say that last goodbye. He glanced down at the infant in his arms and had all he could do not to weep for the motherless, nameless child he was holding. *How she would have loved you if she'd only had the chance…*

But Eva Grace *had* had the chance to love her baby. She had loved her enough to flee the violence of an abusive husband for the sake of her child, loved her enough to risk her own life carrying her, enough to sacrifice her life so her tiny daughter could live. She had known the incredible love that only a mother could begin to understand even if only for a brief few months. And at the last, when she'd heard her baby's first cries, surely that love had overcome any fear she might have experienced, any pain she might have suffered.

Please, God, let it be so.

❖•❖

By the morning of the funeral it was no longer snowing. A silent, severe cold settled over the mountains, turning deep ridges of snow and piles of slush into ice.

Kate MacAuley sat in her bedroom alone, the first time she'd really been alone since Eva Grace's death. Everyone else was busy readying the house for the service, putting up the food that continued to be carried in, one dish after another. Tidying the kitchen. Sweeping out the cinders and debris tracked in the day before. All the things needing to be done before the service. She had been firmly ordered in here by Matthew and Maggie and told to *rest*.

Merciful Lord, how could she rest? Indeed, would she ever truly rest again? To rest meant being able to draw a breath without pain seizing her heart, being able to pray without falling to pieces in a spasm of weeping, being able to sleep without seeing her daughter nearly out of her head with pain, giving a tortured birth to a baby daughter she had held only minutes before giving up her own life.

Perhaps her only true rest would be found, eventually, in her own draped wooden casket like the one now on view in the front room.

She was shaking again. Kate was cold all the time now. In truth, she couldn't think of Eva Grace at all without being gripped with this bone-numbing cold. She reached into the pocket of her best dress and pulled out the letter Eva Grace had left for Maggie, the letter she'd written days before, even before Maggie's wedding. Kate knew what was in it. Evie had told her at the beginning of her labor pains, told her what she'd written to her sister and begging Kate to understand why.

"Just in case," she'd said, sending an icy coil of fear twisting through Kate.

Looking back, she was convinced her daughter *had* known or at least had suspected what was ahead for her. Didn't that account for her resolve to set her thoughts down on paper and her insistence that Kate promise to give the letter to Maggie?

If nothing else, she had feared the worst. And Kate realized now that she had shared that fear. A pall had hung over her own anticipation of the baby almost from the day Dr. Gordon told them about the toxemia. The dreaded blood poisoning wasn't unknown to Kate. Too many women right here in Skingle Creek, small town though it was, had died of the same vicious illness.

Rubbing the letter between her fingers, Kate was struck by guilt. She should have given it to Maggie by now—*before* now. But she had thought to wait for the best time. She was still waiting. Such a hard thing Eva Grace had asked her to do. Kate knew she was acting against her daughter's wishes by withholding the letter, but as yet she couldn't bring herself to pass it on. It was so…final. But her conscience increasingly tormented her, and she knew she could no longer delay the inevitable. Today, after the burial, she would give Maggie the letter.

Please, God, give me...and Maggie...the strength to do the right thing.

Chapter Five

A Message from Eva Grace

At length the harp is broken;
And the spirit in its strings,
As the last decree is spoken,
To its source exulting springs.

Richard D'Alton Williams

The Protestant cemetery lay at the other end of town from the company houses and halfway up Medders Hill, a difficult, tiring trek even in the best of weather. The snow and ice made it even more arduous and unsafe, but it was obvious that most of the town's families were accompanying the MacAuleys to the grave site.

By now the family was exhausted and in poor condition to face the harsh wind and bitter cold, but there was no relief for the suffering of this day. As much as propriety would allow, Ben Wallace kept the graveside service brief. Jonathan and Maggie stood with Maggie's parents between them, Jonathan at Matthew's side, Maggie beside her mother. Ray, his hands shoved deep into his pockets, his cap riding low on his head, looked on from his place at the other side of Jonathan. With typical kindness, Ben's wife, Regina, had volunteered to keep the baby at home with her.

Near the end of the service, at Ben's nod, Jonathan stepped forward. He'd fretted throughout the morning as to whether he could manage to keep his composure long enough to somehow comfort the family—Maggie's family...and his.

Eva Grace's death had affected him deeply, not only because she was Maggie's sister, but also because he had known her from her childhood and had cared about her throughout all the years she'd been his student. He'd also developed a great fondness for the MacAuley family long before he and Maggie had grown close.

He glanced at Maggie before he began and saw that she was clearly holding herself together with only the most rigorous self-control. Her features were tight, her eyes darkly shadowed from lack of sleep and the throbbing headache she'd confessed to him earlier that morning. Yet she met his gaze straight on and even gave him a small nod as if to reassure him.

He cleared his throat once and then again. Even to his ear his voice sounded thin and unsteady. "Eva Grace...was my student for many years. I knew her as a child, as a young girl, and finally as a splendid young woman. I can never say enough about the qualities that made her a pleasure to teach. She was an inspiration to the younger children, a cheerful, willing helper, a joy to her family, and the best possible influence on all who knew her."

He swallowed, searching for just the right words. What could he possibly say in the face of such a tragedy, with one so young being taken from her loved ones all too soon?

He believed in the mercy and wisdom of God, but at this moment he was finding it nearly impossible to articulate that mercy and wisdom without sounding trite or vacuous. The best he could manage was to express what he believed. Even so, it didn't come without great effort.

"There is no minimizing the empty place she leaves behind and the loss her loved ones have suffered. This is one of those times when life brings us questions without answers, when our prayers seem to go unheard. It's all we can do to believe that God is still here, working in the shadows, loving us in the silence. There are things we will never understand this side of heaven. But we do know this: Eva Grace left an incomparable legacy to us in the memory of a beautiful life well-lived and a precious baby daughter who will be loved with as much devotion and affection as her mother could desire for her."

Jonathan's throat tightened, swollen with his own sadness. By God's grace he had made it this far without faltering. But now his voice broke, and he trembled as he raised his head slightly to look out on the crowd of mourners.

"I can't help but remember Eva Grace as she was on her graduation day—so filled with the hopes and dreams and promises for the new life she was about to enter." He hesitated, and then added, "My dear family and friends, with all my heart I believe that *now* is Eva Grace's *true* graduation. Her faith in God was strong, and I'm convinced that her hopes and dreams and promise for a new life, a *better* life, have all been fulfilled in the most glorious of ways."

He bowed his head then, not so much to hide the tears in his eyes, for some of those gathered around the graveside had seen him weep before today, but more to offer a silent prayer for the loved ones of Eva Grace on this, her ultimate graduation day.

❧⋅❧

Later that evening Jonathan, Maggie, and Kate sat around the coal stove in the living room. Matthew had insisted that Jonathan stay by the fire while he and Ray went to fill the coal buckets and lay in more wood.

Jonathan wasn't fooled. Matthew was no doubt feeling the need to get away from the house, away from the trappings of the funeral, the wake, the walls that echoed with the murmurings of death. And

Ray—well, the boy was enough like his father that Matthew's need was most likely his own.

The baby was sleeping quietly in the bedroom. Neighbors and friends had gone back to their homes and their own lives. This was a hard time, in some ways the most wrenching time of all, when the house was finally silent and the family was left alone with their thoughts, their memories, their sorrow.

Seated beside Maggie on the sofa, her hand in his, Jonathan was glad for the fire, which was brisk and hot and comforting. His attention went to Kate, sitting across from them on a chair beside the window. His chest felt heavy at the sight of her. How was it possible that she had faded so quickly?

Maggie's mother had always had such a light about her. Over the years he had known the MacAuleys, Jonathan had come to realize that even more than the rugged Matthew, Kate was the one who bolstered the family in difficult times, who encouraged and supported her husband and children as well as eased the tensions and kept the peace. She faithfully kept what the other immigrants in Skingle Creek referred to as an "Irish hearth," making certain the fire never went out and the door was always open to anyone who would enter.

She was the very heart of her family, but now her own heart was broken, her light flickering. How would she and Matthew get through this time, this season of grief that had come upon them like an avalanche? Even Matthew, that great, rough-hewn oak of a man, had aged years in three days.

Three days. It was almost impossible to realize how happy he and Maggie had been only three days ago. Newly married, deeply in love with each other and with life, off to begin their honeymoon and their new life together. Tragedy had been the furthest thing from their minds.

Maggie's pressure on his hand as she said his name yanked him out of his thoughts. He looked at her and then followed the direction of her gaze to her mother.

"I was saying that the two of you must go home soon now, Jonathan." Kate MacAuley's voice was low but steady. "Other than to take your dog home, feed him, and fetch clean clothes, you've not been home since you came back from Lexington."

Maggie turned her gaze on him again, and Jonathan knew what she was asking.

He gave a small nod, saying, "We'll stay over yet tonight, Kate. It's too late—and too cold—to leave. Sometime tomorrow we'll go."

Kate looked from him to Maggie, and in that instant Jonathan knew they weren't fooling her. She knew neither the weather nor the time had anything to do with their staying longer.

Her shoulders were hunched, her hands knotted on her lap. A ragged sigh escaped her. "All right then," she said, not meeting his eyes. "That being the case, there's something I need to give you."

She slipped her hand inside the pocket of her skirt and withdrew a piece of paper. "Here, Maggie," she said. "This is for you. And for Jonathan as well. It's a letter from Eva Grace—"

She looked as if she were about to break into fresh tears. Maggie leaped to her feet and went to her, but Kate quickly rallied. "She wrote this a few days before she died. 'Just in case,' she said. 'Make sure to give this to Maggie.'"

Standing, she handed the folded paper to Maggie. "Don't read it just now, *alannah*. I'll be going on to bed. Your da and Ray will be in soon. Wait until later, when you and Jonathan are by yourselves. You should read it together."

Maggie watched her mother as she held the paper, her expression questioning and troubled. "All right, Mum," she said, kissing Kate gently on the cheek. "You go to bed. Maybe you can rest tonight. You'll try, won't you?"

Kate smiled at her. "Don't fret yourself about me, Maggie. And don't be letting the fire in the kitchen stove go out now. The cold will be fierce by morning."

Jonathan went to her then. He put his hand on her shoulder, finding it too thin, too frail by far. He bent his head so that he too could kiss her goodnight, but she surprised him by grasping him by his forearms and searching his eyes.

"I can't think," she said, her voice trembling, "what any of us would do without you, Jonathan. What a gift you have been to this family." She turned then and hurried to the door as if to escape before she broke down in front of them.

Jonathan's eyes misted. When he turned to Maggie, he saw that she too was on the verge of weeping.

"Mum's right, you know," Maggie asserted. "I don't know how I would have gone through this without you. You're my rock, Jonathan—and theirs too."

He put a hand to her hair, taking in her pallid complexion, her eyes weary and hollow. "You're exhausted, Maggie. I wish you'd go to bed."

She flinched. "I can't," she said, her voice hoarse. "I told you. I can't bear the thought of sleeping in that room…"

Her words drifted off, but he understood. They had bundled together on the couch or on chairs the few hours they'd slept while staying here. Maggie couldn't bring herself to spend the night in the same room she'd shared with Eva Grace. The same room in which her sister had died.

She glanced down at the paper in her hand. "Mum said we should read this together. But not yet. I don't think I can. Not yet."

Putting an arm around her shoulder, Jonathan pulled her to him. "Let's go to the kitchen. There's been enough food brought in to feed most of the town, and I dare say you've not touched a bite of it today. I'll fix you something, and then you're going to rest."

She started to protest, but he stopped her. "I mean it, Maggie. How are you going to be strong for your family if you can't stay on your feet?"

After a moment she nodded, leaned into him, and let him move her toward the kitchen.

Long after her father and Ray had gone to bed, Maggie sat with Jonathan at the kitchen table, half of their cold supper still in front of them, with the oil lamp on the table the only light in the room.

Jonathan went to punch up the fire in the stove and then came back and carried their plates to the sink.

"I think we should read this now," Maggie said, taking the folded paper from her pocket.

Jonathan refilled both their glasses with milk before sitting down across from her again. "Are you sure you don't want to wait?"

She pulled in a long breath. "Whatever is in this must have been important to Evie. She wasn't a great one for writing. I can count on one hand the number of letters she sent me while I was away at school and in Chicago. Besides, I think Mum meant for us to read it tonight."

She pulled the lamp a bit closer and unfolded the paper. Her eyes were so tired and swollen she had to wait for them to focus before she could see the words clearly enough to make them out. Abruptly she changed her mind and handed the letter to Jonathan. "Would you read it? Please, Jonathan?"

He looked at her and then turned his attention to the letter. For a moment he scanned down the page, and Maggie saw him pale.

"Jonathan?"

Finally he began to read.

> Dear Maggie,
>
> If you're reading this, then I won't be there to explain any of it, so I'll try to make myself as clear as possible.

A sob tore from Maggie's chest, and Jonathan reached out to clasp her hand. She nodded that he should go on reading.

> I realize that what I'm asking of you isn't fair. Indeed, it's a hard thing altogether, but I think once you read this letter you'll understand why I feel the need to ask it.
>
> Maggie, I'm asking you to raise my child—you and Jonathan.

Maggie gasped. Jonathan increased the pressure on her hand but went on reading.

> *The folks know about this letter, Maggie. They've read it, and we've talked about it. They understand why I feel that I have to write it. As you can imagine, Ma was quick to assure me they would raise my baby if anything should happen to me. But she also understands why I believe it should be you and Jonathan who undertake that responsibility. I can only pray that you will understand.*
>
> *You and Jonathan are young, and no doubt you'll have children of your own before long. I want my baby to grow up in a home like we had, Maggie, with other children and parents young enough to enjoy their family and make a happy, lively home for them. It's no secret to you that Da isn't well anymore, and though our mother has always seemed younger than she is, in truth she doesn't need the burden of raising another child at her age. Moreover, Ray will be leaving home before much longer to live his own life, and then there will be no one but Ma and Da to see to a little one.*
>
> *I don't believe that would be the best thing for them or for the baby. And I want the very best thing for her. (Yes, I think of the baby as a girl, perhaps because, as I told you, I can't bear the thought of a boy who might grow up to be even remotely like his father.) But boy or girl, I want my child to grow up as I did, in the midst of a happy family, a loud Irish family who loves their children more than everything and have the energy to keep up with them. And I want her to grow up with brothers and sisters.*
>
> *I also want her to be raised by parents with a strong faith, as we were, parents who will teach God's love in the way they love their children. Ma and Da did that for us, and I know you and Jonathan will do the same for your own family.*
>
> *I'll be the first to admit that it isn't fair of me to ask such an enormous burden of you and Jonathan, with the two of you being newly married and all. And I hope it won't come to that. I sincerely do. But if it does, and if you're willing, I want you both to know that whatever happens to me, I'll have peace and I'll be comforted*

*knowing my child will have the best possible home ever and will
grow up loved as much as if she were your own.*

*And that's what I want, Maggie. I don't want you to raise my
baby as "aunt" and "uncle." I want you and Jonathan to be her parents, to be mother and father to her so she can grow up with real
parents and be as special to you as your own children will be. You
can tell her about me—I hope you will—but don't let her grow up
being sad about the mother she doesn't have. Be her mother, Maggie,
and Jonathan her father.*

*There's one more thing, and then I won't ask anything else of
you. You know what I went through with Richard, Maggie. And you
know the real reason I found the courage to leave him was out of
fear that he might hurt the baby. Please, please, Maggie, no matter what it takes, no matter what you have to do, please don't let
Richard take my baby. Keep my baby away from him!*

*I hope you and Jonathan will forgive me for asking you to take
on such a huge responsibility. But with all that Dr. Gordon has told
me about this problem I have—this toxemia—with that and the
way I've been feeling of late, I just had to write down the deepest
wish of my heart. My baby means everything to me, Maggie, and,
oh, how I hope I'm here to watch her grow up and raise her myself.
But just in case I'm not, I wrote this letter.*

*What a wonderful and rare blessing it is to have a sister and a
brother-in-law I can trust in all assurance with the most precious
thing God has ever given me.*

*Thank you for being such a wonderful sister, Maggie, and for
being my dearest friend when I needed you most.*

Love,

Evie

It was as if Evie had stepped into the room herself to plead with
them for her child. Maggie heard her sister's voice behind every
word, but more than that, she heard her heart. She thought of what
it must have taken for Evie to write that letter, how difficult it must
have been to confront the fear and the wrenching anguish that she

might not live to raise her own child and yet find the strength to look to the future for the sake of her wee one.

She thought of all the nights her sister had lain weeping for the evil that had been done to her and the fear she harbored for the baby. And she thought of all the ways she would miss Evie, all the firsts that would come round day after day, week after week, month after month to remind her of a loss that would always leave a corner of her heart empty.

When she was finally able to lift her head, she saw tears tracking down Jonathan's face even as he tried to comfort her.

"Jonathan—"

He put a finger to her lips and then touched *his* lips to the wetness on each side of her face. "I know, sweetheart. I know."

"What can do we do? I can't ask you to—"

He clasped her shoulders and held her away from him just enough to meet her gaze. "You don't have to ask, Maggie. Surely you know that. Your decision is *my* decision."

There *was* no decision. There hadn't been from the first words of her sister's plea.

"It's not fair to you…"

Determination flared in his eyes. "Don't *ever* say that to me again, Maggie. Don't even *think* it."

Maggie searched his face and saw the kindness, the goodness she had never failed to see looking back at her.

"You're quite sure…"

"I've wanted a family more years than I can count, Maggie. For so long I *prayed* for a family, to be a husband and a father. I'd almost given up all hope. And then there you were. I don't have to think about this, Maggie. Can you understand that? It's a gift. Eva Grace… and God…have given us a precious gift. When someone gives you a gift, you don't have to think about whether or not you'll accept it. You reach out for it and be thankful."

"But how will we ever manage? You need me at the school—"

"Maggie…sweetheart." He framed her face with his hands and

held her gaze. "We'll make it work. One step at a time, we'll work it out. I promise."

Again Maggie began to weep, but this time instead of feeling the weight of an unbearable sorrow darken the empty chamber in her heart, she felt the grateful smile of her older sister come to rest upon her spirit.

Chapter Six

Taking Gracie Home

What e'er in life shall be their share
Of quickening joy or burdening care,
In power to do and grace to bear,
May they in Thee be one.

William Vaughan Jenkins

~~~

They named her Grace Katherine. *Gracie.*

On Saturday, Jonathan and Ray loaded the cradle Maggie had used as an infant, along with the baby bed and high chair—all made by Matthew—aboard the MacAuley's wagon for delivery to Jonathan and Maggie's house. Packed in among the other things was the layette Kate had sewn during Eva Grace's waiting time.

After packing his and Maggie's things in the buggy, Jonathan left Maggie with her mother and started home, with Matthew and Ray following in the wagon. They spent the next few hours unloading the wagon, heating the house, and giving the recently neglected

Figaro some much-needed attention. Jonathan also did what he could to turn one of the spare bedrooms into a hastily-ordered nursery.

Returning to the MacAuley's, they found Kate and Maggie putting the final touches on an early afternoon dinner, comprised in part by some of the food brought in by friends and neighbors, but supplemented by Kate's incomparable homemade bread and applesauce cake.

For the first time in days, Jonathan actually felt hungry as he surveyed the spread in front of him. It also pleased him to note that Maggie's mother had brightened somewhat during the hectic morning, though he didn't doubt for a moment that the parting to come would be excrutiatingly difficult for her—and for them all. For now, though, they were gathered around the table as a family—and it was good.

Maggie had placed Gracie in her cradle and scooted her up between herself and him. Jonathan noticed that she glanced down at the baby every two or three minutes, as if to reassure herself that she was still there. She also kept one foot on the cradle and every now and then gently set it to rocking. For the time being, Gracie seemed thoroughly content to lie there and take in her surroundings.

Maggie and Jonathan had told the family of their decision first thing the day before. Jonathan couldn't be sure, but he thought Matthew was relieved, though he plied them with numerous questions about how they would manage. Kate agreed that it was the right thing to do, but she'd wept a little all the same.

Jonathan glanced across the table to see Kate pushing her cake around on her plate with her fork. He sensed a question in the making.

"How are you going to take care of a baby and teach at the school as well, Maggie?" Kate finally asked. "Have you thought about that?"

Maggie looked at Jonathan, and he cleared his throat. "We wanted to talk with you about that very thing, Kate," he said, choosing his words carefully. "Maggie's not too keen on giving up her teaching position altogether. She apparently thinks I'm incapable of running the school without her."

He glanced at Maggie, receiving a look that clearly told him to go on.

"In truth, I don't fancy the idea of her leaving her position either. At least not entirely. I really do need her at the school. So we were wondering, Kate, if you would consider looking after the baby— after Gracie—for part of the day? Maggie thinks we can work out a schedule that will allow her to keep her class while still not working quite as many hours as before."

"If you don't feel up to it, Mum, it's all right," Maggie hurried to add. "It's not that I *have* to continue teaching. We just thought—"

Did Jonathan imagine Kate's eyes brightening and the slump leaving her shoulders as she looked up?

"Of course I'm up to it," she declared. "I think you *should* go on teaching. That's the reason you went to college, after all, and Jonathan clearly wants you to continue. Besides, you never were the type to be housebound for too long a time."

"Are you sure, Mum? I mean, a baby is a lot of work—"

Kate actually managed a rueful smile. "I expect I know more about how much work a baby is than you do, though you're about to find out. You and Jonathan just figure out a schedule, and I'll help however I can."

Jonathan tried not to show his relief. Even though the decision to take Eva Grace's baby as their own was the right thing to do, he had no idea how he'd manage at school without Maggie. Finding and hiring a replacement for her in the middle of winter would certainly be difficult. Besides, he didn't *want* a replacement. He wanted Maggie.

Just then he saw something in his mother-in-law's expression that made him wonder if he *shouldn't* show his relief. He suspected Kate *wanted* to do this, but maybe she ought to know they definitely *needed* her to do it.

"*Thank you, Kate!*" he said. "I'll admit I was hoping you'd agree. Matthew? Is it all right with you?"

Matthew was watching his wife with a speculative expression. After a moment, his gaze shifted to Jonathan. "Aye. It seems the right thing to do, if it's what Kate wants."

"It is, Matthew," Kate said quietly. "I believe it's what Eva Grace would want as well. I'd like…to be a part of Gracie's life."

Maggie rose and went to put her arms around her mother. "Oh, Mum! There was never a thought that you *wouldn't* be an important part of Gracie's life! You and Da both. And you too, Ray. Remember how Evie helped take care of you when you were just a wee thing? Now you can help take care of *her* little one."

Ray turned red, but he nodded and smiled. "I'll help out," he said in a voice that cracked, marking his change from boy to man.

Kate wiped at her eyes with her apron and then declared the matter settled.

Jonathan glanced down at the blond-haired infant in the cradle beside him to find her studying him with a curious expression.

He leaned over to touch her cheek—so soft! She squirmed and flailed her arms until she caught hold of his finger. Something stirred in the deepest part of him, something new and stronger than he'd ever felt before, even with the youngest and most helpless of the students whose lives had touched his over the years.

She was so very tiny and so defenseless. In that instant Jonathan wanted nothing so much as to lift her out of the cradle and hold her against his heart. And so he did. He felt as clumsy as a bear reaching for a butterfly as he scooped her up. Holding her snugly but carefully against him, he felt overwhelmed by the warmth and sweetness cradled in his arms.

He glanced at Maggie to find her watching him, her eyes alight with an emotion he couldn't have begun to name. He knew the others were watching him too, and there was a time when he might have been embarrassed to have such attention focused on him. But at the moment he seemed strangely immune to any feeling of awkwardness. After all, Gracie was the one everyone was watching. A baby was always the center of attention, not her father.

Her father...

Shaken by the thought that had come to his mind so unexpectedly, yet so easily, Jonathan could almost taste the word on his lips. *Her father.* He was to be—no, he *was* a father. Gracie's father.

Without warning, the word turned to show a different side, becoming for just a split second something ugly, even menacing.

He *wasn't* Gracie's father. Not her *real* father. Eventually it would have to be discussed, this subject that never quite left him, that wrung him tight with anxiety each time he thought of it. They would *all* have to discuss Gracie's biological father. Not just he and Maggie, but the entire family. There were precautions to be observed, steps that had to be taken.

But this wasn't the time. Not today.

The subject of Richard Barlow and the threat he represented to the infant Jonathan held against his heart would wait. By Eva Grace's request and with her blessing, *he* was Gracie's father.

And he had every intention of remaining so.

❧•❦

When they finally came to their own bedroom that night, the baby had been fed and now lay sleeping in the small room directly across the hall. Figaro, already Gracie's self-appointed guardian, stood in the hallway, looking from the baby's room to Jonathan and Maggie, obviously hard-pressed to make a decision. At last, with a long sigh that might have been resignation or frustration, the big hound gave Jonathan a soulful look as if to make sure his master understood the circumstances and then plopped down just inside the door of the baby's room, resting his head on his paws.

Jonathan made a fire in the bedroom fireplace and moved the big overstuffed rocking chair from its place by the window to face the fire. Both he and Maggie sat in it, watching the flames lap the logs and set the sparks to dancing. Maggie, wrapped in a soft blue robe, snuggled as close to Jonathan as possible. He buried his face in her hair, still slightly damp from her bath, breathing in the faint fragrance of vanilla that always seemed to follow her. Tonight there was also a hint of the baby powder she'd patted over Gracie before putting her to bed.

They didn't talk right away, but simply sat resting by the fire. Maggie was quiet for so long he finally looked to see if she'd fallen asleep. But she was staring into the fire and looked entirely awake.

"What are you thinking about?" he asked.

Still not moving, she sighed a little. "Evie. And us. And Gracie. And how life can change when we least expect it."

She turned toward him. "Do you realize we've been married less than a week and we're already a *family?* For a moment just now, as we were sitting here, it seemed as though none of this had happened recently. That instead of tonight, it was months or even years in the future—a future we'd planned and were prepared for."

Jonathan studied her, looking for a hint of what she was feeling. "Are you having doubts about what we've done? About raising Gracie?"

She shook her head. "Of course not."

"It's understandable if you are, you know," Jonathan assured her. "We've made a decision that's going to have an enormous impact on our lives, a decision we had to make quickly with no preparation."

Again she shook her head. "I don't doubt our decision, Jonathan. It's just...I think I'm still trying to get used to everything. Things have been so hectic I haven't had time to take in the enormity of what's happened. Everything is coming at me all at once. And you and I have had so little time to be alone together, to talk things through. Jonathan, we've hardly had time to *think!* And in a few more days school will take up again, and we'll be even busier!"

Not only was she exhausted, but she was agitated and obviously worried.

"For now just right now, tonight, Maggie—what's bothering you most?"

She twisted around still more to face him. "I suppose trying to imagine how we're going to manage everything with my teaching and Gracie. The additional responsibilities. I mean, we're *newly-weds,* Jonathan. I had this picture—didn't you?—of spending almost all our time together—getting to know each other, coming home together after school, having a nice, leisurely supper, and then perhaps taking a walk or reading by the fire. Just being together." She broke off and then blurted out, "Goodness, Jonathan, we haven't even shared a bed since—"

Immediately her face flamed and she slapped her hand over her mouth. "I didn't mean—"

"That's a situation I'm fully aware of and hope to remedy very soon," he said, trying not to smile at her embarrassment.

"Maggie—"

She resisted only a moment when he tried to gather her close.

"Everything will work out. I told you before, we'll *make* it work. Your family will help, and we'll come up with a schedule at school that will allow you some extra hours. I've already started working on it."

"You have?"

He nodded. "In my head, at least. Tomorrow we'll talk about it. Now, tell me what's *really* troubling you."

She shuddered and looked away. "I think I'm afraid."

"Afraid? Of what?"

When she turned back to him, her expression was crestfallen. "Oh, Jonathan, I know I'm just being selfish, but—but most women have time to *prepare* for motherhood. I haven't even had time to get used to being *married.* What if I turn out not to be a good wife *or* mother? What if I fail Gracie? And *you?* What if I can't do this, Jonathan?"

For a moment—only a moment—Jonathan was overwhelmed. He was physically and emotionally drained, trying to deal with the same concerns that were troubling her. In truth, he was suffering from the worst feelings of inadequacy he could remember. How could he possibly give her the reassurance, the confidence, she was so clearly looking for?

He didn't know, but this didn't seem the time to admit his *own* fears.

He took a deep breath and, brooking no resistance, pulled her into his arms, holding her gently but firmly. "Maggie, you have never failed at anything in your life. You've done everything you ever set out to do and then some."

She started to say something, but he silenced her, touching a finger to her lips. "Besides," he went on, "you're not going to do this alone. We're going to do it together. I'm going to learn to be a father at the same time you're learning to be a mother. And we *will* learn the way everyone else learns: by experience. I'm not expecting that we'll be perfect parents, but we'll do our best to be *good* ones. It's true we're going into this with no preparation, but I wonder if one is ever really prepared to raise a child."

He tucked a wayward curl behind her ear. "We won't fail, sweetheart. I promise you. We won't fail Gracie. And we won't fail each other. You've always trusted me before, trust me now."

She searched his eyes and apparently found what she needed. She gave a small nod, slipped her arms around his neck, and kissed him.

He kissed her back. They sat in silence for a time, Jonathan deeply content to savor the warmth of the fire, Maggie's slender form cuddled next to him, the silence of the house, the simple pleasure and comfort of being home again. He would grow old never taking the gift of this *oneness* for granted, never wanting more than he had at this moment. In all the dreams he'd had when he was a younger man, dreams about what it would be like to have one special someone to love and share his life with, nothing had ever come close to this experience of loving Maggie.

He bent to look at her and found her asleep, her features more peaceful than he'd seen for days. He thought about lifting her from the chair and carrying her to bed, but decided they were fine just as they were.

He touched his lips to the top of her head, tucked the blanket more snugly around them both, and again wrapped her in his arms. His last thought before he drifted off to sleep was a silent prayer of thanks.

Chapter Seven

At Home on a Winter's Night

And bless the door that opens wide
To stranger, as to kin;
And bless each crystal windowpane
That lets the starlight in.

Arthur Guiterman

The next unexpected snowfall wasn't quite so unwelcome as its predecessor. The storm delayed school's reopening by an additional five days, allowing Maggie and Jonathan more time at home with Gracie.

She was a good baby, seldom crying unless she was hungry, except at a certain time in the early evening, when the shadows of night began to draw in from the mountain. At that time each day she would take to crying a bit—not a fierce, demanding cry, but more a soft wailing. Maggie couldn't help but wonder if this was when she was missing her mother. Who knew what kind of connection existed between a child and her mother, even between earth and heaven? Was it possible that loneliness could set in from time to time, when even an infant felt the loss of the one who had carried her and given her life?

Maggie made sure she was always nearby at this time of day to pick wee Gracie up and cuddle her close. She would rock her and sing softly to her until the crying ceased. Then she handed her over to Jonathan, who would continue rocking and talking to her in a quiet, soothing voice while Maggie warmed the bedtime bottle.

Tonight was no different. It wasn't quite dark as Maggie sat by the window in the room they now called the nursery, rocking Gracie as the wind moaned around the eaves and blew snow against the windowpanes. It had snowed all day, stopping only for an hour or so before gaining strength and starting up again.

Humming as much to herself as to Gracie, Maggie had been rocking long enough that she'd lost track of time. Jonathan and Figaro were going back and forth, inside and out, bringing in more wood. Fortunately they'd had more coal delivered at the end of last week during a lull between the two storms.

No doubt some would think it strange that she found a fundamental comfort in being trapped inside. But their house was cozy in spite of the wildness swirling outside. Their pantry was stocked, they'd had a hot meal, and the lamplight cast a warm glow over the room. Rather than rebelling at these long days of being confined, she relished the time alone with her new husband and her new daughter. She wished Jonathan didn't have to brave the storm, but he insisted that it made him appreciate the snugness of their home even more.

When she realized that Gracie had grown completely still, she was surprised. Her evening bouts of crying usually lasted longer. She glanced down to find the baby wide awake, watching her with a small frown, as if she were puzzling over something.

Maggie smiled at the intent expression on those tiny features. She touched the miniature nose with the tip of her index finger—and Gracie smiled! A rosebud smile that rounded her cheeks and banished the frown. And when Maggie lowered her head to kiss her gently on the forehead, the baby caught a lock of hair and clutched it tightly, locking Maggie's face within inches of hers.

Warmth blanketed Maggie's heart. "Oh, Gracie, you are my own sweet girl," she murmured. "I couldn't love you more if I had carried you beneath my heart."

"And she's going to grow up knowing that."

At Jonathan's quiet words and his hand on her shoulder, Maggie carefully dislodged her hair from the baby's hand and lifted her face for her husband's kiss.

"Has she already had her bottle?" he asked.

"No. She just suddenly stopped crying."

"Let me warm my hands a little and I'll take her," he said, going to stand in front of the fire.

Figaro came and plopped down beside the fire, looking hopeful that he wouldn't need to move again. When Maggie got up to hand Gracie over to Jonathan, the big hound actually closed his eyes and feigned sleep.

"After Gracie goes to bed," Maggie said, "perhaps you can have a second piece of pie. I saw the way you were eyeing it after supper."

"I was merely remembering how good the *first* piece was," he said as he and Gracie settled into the rocking chair.

"Just be grateful my mother made it," said Maggie. "Pies are not my specialty."

"Indeed? Other than making me happy, what *is* your specialty?"

She thought about it. "Warming baby bottles is the only thing that comes to mind at the moment."

"Well, that's certainly important," he said expansively.

❖⬦❖

Gracie hadn't been down for more than a few minutes when someone stamped his feet out front and pounded on the door.

Figaro bounded down the steps and stood waiting, tail wag ging.

"Who in the world would be out in this weather?" Maggie said, coming into the hallway.

Jonathan opened the door on Maggie's brother, who stood pounding the snow off his high boots as he shook it off his cap.

"Ray!" Maggie tugged him inside. "This is a nice surprise." Just as quickly she sobered. "Is something wrong at home?"

He shook his head, handed over the sack he carried, and then bent to pet Figaro, who was whining with anticipation, his tail whipping about in a circle.

"Ma sent me round to see how you're faring. She's been fussing about the baby and all."

"Oh, of course she would be," Maggie agreed, taking his coat. "Come on into the kitchen. You can have a piece of Mum's mincemeat pie. I just cut Jonathan a slice. And Figaro—*you* go back upstairs and stay with Gracie."

The big hound gave his equivalent of a frown, but after one last pat from Ray turned and galloped back up the steps.

"Well, I had some cake at home," Ray said. "In fact, that's what's in the sack. Ma sent you and Jonathan a couple of pieces. And a loaf of nut bread."

"You can still have pie," Maggie said, leading the way to the kitchen.

"Yeah, I reckon." He hesitated. "So is Gracie asleep or what?"

Maggie realized he wanted to see his baby niece.

"She is. But you can look in on her if you want."

"I don't want to wake her up—"

"You won't. She's a sound sleeper. Jonathan, why don't you go up with him?"

While they were upstairs, Maggie started a fresh pot of coffee and set out what was left of her mother's mince pie, the apple cake slices, and the nut bread.

Jonathan showed his appreciation when they returned by kissing her on the cheek. Ray eyed the table with a gleam in his eye.

"She's grown some already," he said as he pulled out a chair and sat down. "She looks a lot like Evie, wouldn't you say?"

"Even more so when she's awake," Maggie agreed, bringing the coffeepot to the table and pouring a cup for each of them.

"I wouldn't want her to take after Barlow, that's for sure," Ray said. "What are you going to do if he tries to take Gracie back to Lexington?"

Maggie's hand trembled as she set the pot on the table. "We won't let him, of course."

"How can you stop him? He's her dad—" He stopped without finishing, shooting a look at Jonathan as if he feared he'd offended him. "I didn't mean—"

Jonathan turned his hand in a dismissing gesture. "I know what you meant, Ray. And you're right. Barlow may very well try to gain custody of Gracie. It's up to us to make sure he doesn't get it. My father and one of the attorneys in his firm intend to prove he's unfit to raise her. Don't worry. They'll know how to deal with Barlow."

Ray's features cleared, and Maggie tried to put the thought of Richard Barlow out of her mind. No doubt Jonathan sensed the need to ease the tension because he quickly changed the subject.

"This is nice, Maggie," he said, motioning for her to sit down beside him. "Makes me forget what it's like outside."

"I wish it'd let up," Ray said. "I haven't been able to get out to the farm for days now. 'Course, even if I could make it out there, there wouldn't be much I could do. I hope Cousin Jeff won't decide he doesn't need me anymore."

Jonathan pushed the last piece of mince pie toward him. "I've already had a piece. You take this one, and I'll tackle the cake. You like working for your cousin, don't you?"

Ray hesitated only a moment before digging into the pie. Maggie couldn't help but marvel at how *large* her baby brother was these days. He was nearly as big as Da!

"I like working at the farm," Ray said. "Working for Cousin Jeff—" he shrugged. "Well, he's a grouch."

"Ray." Maggie's objection was perfunctory. Their cousin *was* a grouch.

Her brother shrugged again. "He's talking about selling the farm, you know."

"No! Why?"

"Says he's tired of all the work. He's talking about moving to Indiana, out close to where Nell Frances is."

"That'll upset Da. They're the only family we have around here."

Ray nodded. "It'll upset me too. I'll miss the farm." He paused. "And the money. Reckon I'll go into the mines once the farm is gone."

"You will *not!*" Maggie burst out.

Her brother gave her a sour look. "That's not for you to say, Mags. Besides, there won't be much choice. Da's going to have to quit before long, and there's no work of any kind around here for me except mining."

Maggie shot a look at Jonathan.

"I'd hate to see you leave school too soon, Ray," he said. "Surely we can help you find something other than the mine, should the need arise."

"Don't know what it'd be," Ray said, returning to his pie.

"Why did you say Da will have to quit soon?" asked Maggie.

Her brother looked up. "You've seen how he is. I don't think there's ever a time his back's not hurting him. He's like an old man when he gets home from work."

"Oh, I wish he weren't so stubborn about going to see Dr. Gordon. I know she could help him. She almost said as much to me once."

Her brother made a snorting sound. "Fat chance of Da going to a woman doctor."

Jonathan nodded. "I tried to talk to him about it once. He put me in my place in short order."

Maggie frowned. "You never told me about that. What did he say?"

"It was a long time ago. Before we were married." Jonathan gave a rueful smile. "He basically told me to mind my own business."

Maggie sighed.

Finished with his pie, Ray scooted away from the table and stood. "I'd better get back. Ma will wait up till I get home."

"You're welcome to stay over, Ray," Jonathan offered, also getting up. "No sense in going back out in that weather."

"I don't mind. Besides, like I said, the folks aren't going to rest until I get home and give them a report."

"Mum's probably afraid we'll break the baby," Maggie said dryly, getting to her feet. "I'm still surprised she let me out of the house with Gracie."

At the front door, as Ray shrugged into his coat and put on his cap, he turned to Jonathan. "I don't quite know what to call you now, sir."

Maggie hadn't thought about that. It *would* be awkward for Ray, his schoolteacher also being his brother-in-law.

"Why not 'Jonathan' with the family and 'Mr. Stuart' at school? And for goodness' sake, don't call me 'sir' here at home."

Ray grinned. "That sounds okay to me." They shook hands, and he went on his way.

Back in the kitchen, as they put away the leftover food and tidied up, Maggie said, "Ray likes you, Jonathan. I mean, he's always liked you, but he likes you as a brother-in-law too."

"He's a good boy."

"He's almost a man," Maggie said. "It hardly seems possible. I still remember feeding him in his high chair. Next thing you know I'll be feeding Gracie in that same chair."

She went to him, took the dishcloth out of his hands, and put her arms around his neck. "It all goes so quickly, doesn't it? It seems like yesterday that I was still in school and you were my teacher. And now we're married. And Ray—just look at him. And before we know it, Gracie will be walking."

He laughed at her. "Not anytime in the next few days, I hope." He kissed her on the forehead. "But you're right. Life *does* go fast." His gaze went over her face. "Which is why we need to make the most of every single moment."

He pulled her more snugly into his arms and kissed her again, this time not on the forehead. "That being the case," he whispered against her temple, "I think we should go upstairs...while we're still young."

Chapter Eight

A Disappointment

We look before and after,
And pine for what is not;
Our sincerest laughter
With some pain is fraught;
Our sweetest songs are those that tell
Of saddest thought.
Yet if we could scorn
Hate and pride and fear;
If we were things born
Not to shed a tear,
I know not how thy joy we ever
Should come near.

Percy Bysshe Shelley

On the Friday before school was to resume, Pastor Wallace paid a visit to Jonathan and Maggie. Usually a visit from Jonathan's closest friend was an event to be enjoyed. Today, however, Ben seemed uncommonly formal.

Once they were settled in the living room, Ben held Gracie for a moment. "Isn't she lovely?" he commented, admiring her one more time before returning her to Maggie.

They proceeded to make small talk for a few minutes more. Then Jonathan, sensing his friend was unusually ill at ease, moved to diffuse the tension.

"This is a treat, Ben. It's officially your first visit since Maggie and I were married. Welcome to our home."

The pastor glanced away. "Actually, I'm not here in a…social capacity, but more as president of the school board."

"Oh yes. Well, we've already got the word that school will take up again on Monday. In fact, we plan to spend the weekend getting things caught up here at home so we'll be ready first thing next week to start our delayed winter term."

"Yes, well, that's why I'm here." The pastor paused, casting a look from Jonathan to Maggie. "There's something we need to talk about. And it's rather awkward, I'm afraid."

Something stirred in Jonathan, something he'd almost forgotten. "What's wrong, Ben?"

The pastor let out a long breath. "Apparently, with all that's happened over the past few weeks—your marriage, Eva Grace's passing, Gracie's birth, the bad weather—it seems we slipped up."

Jonathan moved away from Maggie's chair to sit down at the other end of the sofa from Ben. "Slipped up?"

Ben gripped his knees with his hands and nodded. "You do remember when we talked about the restriction against married women teaching?"

Jonathan swallowed. Not a word had been said about this issue since a few weeks before the wedding. For a time he'd assumed that Ben had taken care of it. Then, later, what with the turmoil of events, he'd forgotten about it. Until now.

He looked across the room. Maggie was sitting stiffly with Grace propped against her shoulder.

He realized now what was coming and knew it was his fault. He'd led Maggie to believe there would be no problem in her resuming her position at the school. He and Ben had foolishly taken it for granted that there *wouldn't* be a problem. He'd owed it to Maggie to make certain, but he hadn't followed through.

"Surely the board doesn't mean to hold us to that ridiculous prohibition," he said.

Ben nodded. "I'm afraid they do. They insist that with Maggie being married now, she can no longer teach at the school."

"Ben, that's absolutely absurd!" Jonathan shot to his feet. "There has to be a way around this. You're the president of the board. Surely you can do something?"

"I'm afraid I've done all I can. And it really isn't the board's fault. They're just following the state laws." He got to his feet. "Jonathan... Maggie...I sincerely apologize for this. I let it go far too long because I thought we could work something out. And now I've created a problem for both of you."

Jonathan raked a hand through his hair. He didn't know who to be upset with, himself or the legal system. And yet even though he didn't necessarily agree with this particular restriction, at least not in all cases, he understood the rationale behind it.

"This isn't your fault, Ben. I don't know why I was so obtuse as to assume this wouldn't apply to us."

Maggie looked to be locked in place. She had stopped rocking the baby and sat staring at him and Ben.

"Don't worry, Maggie," he told her. "We'll take care of this somehow."

"Jonathan."

She spoke his name quietly but firmly. "I think Pastor Ben is right. I don't believe there's anything we can do. And we should have realized that from the beginning. Like you, given everything else that was going on, I hadn't even thought about it until now. There's been so much to do, so much else to think about."

She stopped and glanced down at Gracie, who had fallen asleep. "But it's all right," she said, raising her head. "Really, it is. Perhaps it's even for the best. I can be with Gracie all the time, and Mum won't have to help."

Jonathan knew her well enough to know this brave face was for Ben's benefit. Without answering her, he turned back to his friend. "Ben, I need Maggie at the school. You know what a good teacher she is. The children have come to depend on her. We had this all worked out with her mother. Kate agreed to take care of Gracie while Maggie and I are at the school, and we were going to work out a schedule that would allow Maggie to teach fewer hours so she wouldn't be away from the baby too long at a time."

He paused. "Ben, those children *need* Maggie, that's the thing. And *I* need her. I'm long past the point of being able to run the school alone. There are too many students for that."

"Jonathan, we don't expect you to run the school alone. We'll begin a search for a new teacher immediately, as soon as the weather breaks."

Out of the corner of his eye, Jonathan saw Maggie flinch.

"Meanwhile, I'm to go back to school Monday without a teacher to help? That's impossible, Ben. They at least have to let Maggie stay on until you find someone." A thought struck him. "And that brings up something else. They let Carolyn Ross teach on a temporary basis before we hired Maggie. Carolyn was a married woman. Why was that allowed?"

"That was different, Jonathan. Mrs. Ross is a *widow* woman and without children. And she merely volunteered to help out until we hired a full-time teacher. We're not just going to hang you out to dry, Jonathan. I'm sure the board will be willing to let Maggie continue until we can hire another teacher. And, again, I can't tell you how sorry I am that I didn't get this settled long before now."

Jonathan shook his head. "You don't owe us an apology. It's as much my fault as yours for not seeing it through when we first talked about it."

Ben headed for the door. "I'll let myself out. You and Maggie will want to talk."

Jonathan followed him anyway. After helping him with his coat, he searched his friend's eyes. "If there's anything you can do, Ben, I know you will. I understand if you think I'm biased because Maggie's my wife, but the truth is that she makes a real difference with those children, especially the little ones. She's *good* for them. And a town like Skingle Creek won't attract a teacher of her caliber all that easily."

Ben sighed. "Believe me, Jonathan, I don't like this either. But the law is for the good of women and their families, you know."

"When we first talked about this a couple of months ago, you said there ought to be extenuating circumstances," Jonathan reminded him. "Do you really believe Maggie and I would ever neglect our child? Do you think Gracie will be any less loved or cared for during those few hours a week she's with her grandmother instead of with us?"

Ben shook his head. "Of course not. But unless we can think of something else, I can only encourage you to accept things as they are. But I *will* go to bat for Maggie staying on until we can find another teacher, I promise you that."

Distracted, Jonathan gave a short nod. "I'm sorry if I was sharp. I'm hugely disappointed. And I know Maggie is, in spite of that stiff upper lip she's showing. Ben, you know I want what's best for Gracie, but I want what's best for my students too. And Maggie is definitely part of that."

His friend nodded. "Let's pray about it then. Right here, right now."

The two men stood shoulder to shoulder as they brought the situation before their God, asking for wisdom they didn't have, a solution they couldn't find, and in it all, His best will for Maggie, for Gracie, and for the children of Skingle Creek.

As they prayed, Jonathan was vaguely aware of Maggie slipping quietly around the corner of the hallway and starting up the stairs.

◆》•◆《

Later he found her in the bedroom, looking out the window.

"Gracie's down for her nap?"

She nodded but said nothing.

He came behind her and put his arms around her. "I hate this," he said, pressing his cheek against hers. "I should never have let it happen."

She turned in his arms. "You can't fix everything, Jonathan, although I confess I'm always quick to assume you can. There's nothing you could have done about this. And I meant what I said. It may be for the best. I won't mind being at home with Gracie all the time. Goodness, I already have my hands full learning to be a mother."

He searched her face. "You are a *wonderful* mother, Maggie. You slipped into the role as if you were born to it. But I don't want to lose you as a teacher, either. I don't want the *children* to lose you."

"You heard Pastor Ben. They'll start looking for a new teacher right away. And I'm sure they won't object to my staying on until they hire someone. So you need to let it go now. Just…let it go."

She was being so strong, so practical. That was Maggie. She'd always been able to put a brave face on things. But he'd seen the tightening around her eyes. She was hurt. She was disappointed. And he hated it.

He pulled her into his arms and pressed her head against his chest. He didn't know what to say to her, didn't know how to comfort her. And he was angry. Mostly with himself. How could he have been so irresponsible as to think this would all take care of itself?

"Maggie, there may still be something we can do. I just need a little time to think—"

She eased back from him. "Jonathan, listen to me. Please. I don't need anything else besides what I have. I have you, Gracie, a wonderful family, a home. It would be the worst kind of sin to want more."

She held his gaze with those incredible deep-set eyes of hers, as if she could convince him just by the strength of her own intensity. And it almost worked.

"In truth, Jonathan," she said quietly, "there's something else I'm much more concerned about than losing my teaching position."

"What?"

"Richard. Richard Barlow. You haven't forgotten that he threatened to take Evie's baby, have you?"

The reminder brought a stab of pain to the base of Jonathan's skull. "No, I haven't forgotten."

"Have you contacted your father about Evie? Does he know that we have Gracie?"

He nodded. "Yes. And don't forget, before we ever left Lexington he assured me he'd have Barlow investigated."

"That's good. But it's not enough. We have to take some precautions, Jonathan. Because I know what I saw in Richard's eyes that day when he tried to take Evie back to Lexington. He *will* come after Gracie. He'll try to take her."

"Our lines are probably down now because of the storms. But tomorrow I'll go to the company store and place a call to my father. He'll know what to do. We'll want to start the adoption process as soon as possible."

"How can we do that with Richard still in the picture?"

"We have to get him *out* of the picture. If we can prove that he beat Evie—and by doing so endangered the baby—we should be able to put a stop to any interference on his part."

Maggie gripped his forearms. "We can't let him near Gracie, Jonathan. *We can't!*"

"And we won't," he assured her, catching both her hands in his. "He's not going to take Gracie away from us, Maggie. I give you my word. Whatever it takes, we'll keep her safe with us."

She let out a long breath and slumped against him. "I get so frightened when I think about that man. There's no telling what he might try."

"Maggie, there's always a chance he won't try *anything*."

She looked up at him. "What do you mean? Jonathan, you didn't hear him! You didn't see his eyes."

Jonathan nodded. "I know. And I understand why you're frightened. But it's just possible, now that some time has passed, he may have moved on. Barlow is intrinsically selfish, we know that. He may have decided he doesn't want a child complicating his life. There might even be a new woman in the picture."

She studied him. "Do you really believe that's possible?"

Do I? Or am I just trying to convince myself along with Maggie?

"I have to believe that anything is possible with a man like

Barlow. For the present, at least, I don't think we need to worry too much."

"But he does know about Eva Grace and the baby by now. You said your father's partner was going to notify him."

"Yes, and I didn't mean we won't take precautions. For now, though, try not to let worry interfere with your enjoyment of Gracie."

After a moment, she gave a reluctant nod. "You're right. I'm afraid that's what I've been doing." She stopped, putting a hand to his face. "Jonathan—about the teaching. I really do accept things as they are. I'll be content to stay home. However things work out, I'm fine. God knows where He wants me, and I'm fine with that. It's just as I told you. I couldn't possibly want anything more than what I already have. As long as I have you and Gracie, I don't need anything else."

Warmed by this expression of love for him, Jonathan brought her closer. "Oh, Maggie, what a gift you are to me. You and Gracie, a family of my own, our home. No man could be more blessed."

"You're going to be a blessedly *hungry* man if I don't get downstairs and start supper," she said, giving him a little push to extricate herself from his embrace.

He tugged her back. "It's still early," he murmured. "And Gracie's sound asleep. We can always eat later."

She narrowed her eyes and slipped out of his arms. "Not *that* much later, you outrageous man."

From his place in the hallway Figaro gave a chuff of agreement.

Chapter Nine

Two Are Better Than One

Best and worst, whate'er they be,
We shall share together.

Winthrop Mackworth Praed

~~~

The next three weeks passed in a flurry of activity, but somehow life settled into a fairly normal routine. The snow melted. Gracie thrived. And Maggie gained a two-month exemption for her position at the school. Until the weather eased, there could be no serious search for her replacement, so the school board agreed to keep her employed through the end of March.

Although their mornings and most evenings were hectic, Maggie and Jonathan had established a workable pattern on weekdays. They dropped off Gracie on their way to school in the morning and picked her up on the way home. Housework was kept to a minimum until the weekend. They planned and marketed for meals in advance, and they learned to share responsibilities at school and at home.

Figaro accompanied Gracie to the MacAuleys every day, though Maggie knew the children missed having him at the schoolhouse. They had grown used to his being part of their day, either napping in Jonathan's office when classes were in session or running free in the schoolyard during lunch time and recess.

No doubt the great hound missed the students as well. But Maggie was fairly certain he would miss Gracie more. By now he had appointed himself the baby's guardian angel, personal watchdog, and best friend, and there was no telling what it would take to pry him away from the object of his devotion.

Fortunately, Maggie's mother seemed unperturbed by his being underfoot. What went unsaid among them all was the fact that having the big, protective hound on the premises created a sense of security they wouldn't have enjoyed otherwise.

In the busy but fulfilling evenings, Jonathan would tend to the baby while Maggie fixed supper and tidied whatever clutter they'd left behind that morning. They took turns with Gracie's bath and feeding schedule, and when she was finally down for the night, they graded papers, worked on the next day's lessons, and managed a quiet hour or so for themselves. They reflected on their day or simply relaxed in front of the fire, content with the quiet of their home and being together.

Most days Maggie's mother tried to coax them into staying for supper when they came for Gracie. And they did so often enough that Jonathan insisted on taking groceries over at least once a week. Maggie hated to admit it, but not only was her mother spoiling Gracie, she was getting a bit spoiled herself—having a warm meal waiting at the end of the school day.

Gathering was a good thing for them all as a family. Da got home not long after she and Jonathan arrived, and Ray came in an hour or so later after sweeping up and doing odd jobs at the company store, the exact parttime job Maggie had held as a girl.

Having all of them there seemed to ease her mother's sadness.

With her family around the supper table, Kate MacAuley seemed content, if not actually happy. No doubt evenings were lonely for her, with Da asleep by the fire soon after supper and Ray off somewhere with his friend Tim Duggan until bedtime. With Maggie and Eva Grace no longer there to talk with when the others were gone, the hours must have loomed long and empty.

Mum's spirits had often seemed to sag low on winter evenings, when darkness gathered early and a hush fell over the house. Even as a child, Maggie had sensed the heaviness that hovered near her mother when there was little or no family activity taking place around her. It was as if the absence of her loved ones drained her energy. With the selfishness and self-centeredness of youth, Maggie and her sisters hadn't let concern for a parent divert them from their own pursuits. But every once in a while the distant, wistful expression in her mother's eyes would stay with her after leaving the house and intrude on whatever she was doing, wherever she happened to be.

Tonight—Friday night—as they left her parents' home after a particularly convivial evening with her family, she was finding it impossible to shake the image of her mother's drawn features as she stood at the door waving goodbye. Ray had already taken off with Tim to join up with some of the other teenage boys at the square. And Da, with still one more workday to go before Sunday, had looked bone-weary and gripped with pain during supper. His only smile this evening had been for Gracie.

Her mother was alone again.

❖·❖

"I'd offer you a penny for your thoughts, but I have a feeling I'd need several dollars to cover the cost." From the easy chair by the fireplace, Jonathan was watching her over the top of his newspaper. Figaro lay dozing at his feet, occasionally opening one eye just enough to make sure his charges were still in the room. Lately the big hound divided his evening hours between watching over Gracie upstairs and spending time with Jonathan and Maggie downstairs.

Maggie, sitting at the table by the window, realized she'd been wool-gathering instead of grading the papers she'd brought home. Her intention had been to get the schoolwork out of the way early so she would have the rest of the weekend to devote to Jonathan and Gracie and—a less pleasant thought—housework. She'd been staring out the window, the night's darkness relieved only by the thin wedge of moonlight filtering through the pine trees out front.

She put her pencil down with a sigh. "I'm worried about Mum."

"Worried?"

She nodded. "She's so sad, Jonathan."

"I thought she seemed unusually cheerful tonight."

"She was good because we were all there. But did you see the look on her face when we got ready to leave? You could almost tell she was steeling herself for the rest of the evening. She's missing Eva Grace terribly."

"You have to give her time, Maggie. Probably a *long* time." He paused. "That's true for you too."

"Oh, believe me, I *do* know. In fact, I think being a mother to Gracie not only makes me more aware of how awful this is for Mum, but it's also made it more painful for me as well. Every time I look at Eva Grace's baby girl, my heart feels as if it's going to break all over again. She'll never know her real mother, and Eva Grace will never know *her.*" She paused. "And I miss her. I miss my sister," she added quietly.

Jonathan studied her for a long moment, folded his newspaper, and patted the space beside him in the chair. "Come here."

Maggie didn't hesitate. She crossed the room and curled up next to him in the oversized chair, soaking up his warmth and that of the fire. This had become almost an every-evening ritual for them, sharing the big chair and enjoying the fire together. Sometimes they talked; sometimes they sat in silence. It brought Maggie a peace that nothing else could match.

Jonathan wrapped his arms around her. "I know you miss Eva Grace. Of course you do. But you *are* Gracie's 'real' mother, Maggie. You're the only mother she's ever going to know."

Maggie started to interrupt, but he went on. "Naturally we'll tell her about Eva Grace. But it's *you* she's going to call 'Mother,' sweetheart, and it's you she's going to *love* as her mother. We'll keep Eva Grace's memory alive. And the memories won't always be sad. The time will come when you'll be able to celebrate her memory and rejoice in the kind of person she was: strong and good and resolved to give her daughter life and a chance for happiness. Her every thought was of Gracie, right up to the end, when she asked us to raise her."

He pushed a strand of hair behind her ear. "For now, be grateful that you had a sister like Eva Grace. But at the same time, give yourself the freedom to be Gracie's mother. Her *real* mother."

Maggie studied him. Her mind grasped his words and filed them away. A time might come in the future when she would need them again to remind herself that although she hadn't given birth to Gracie, she was her mother. By Eve Grace's request and consent—and by her love for the tiny girl that increased daily, she was Gracie's *mother*.

She buried her face against Jonathan's chest, feeling his heart beat the rhythm, not only of his own life, but hers as well. He *was* her life, after all. He and Gracie. Her family. She had never thought of it quite that way, but the ones she loved—they were her very life, her very world.

She wept a little then, and as if he knew she needed the release of her tears, Jonathan remained silent and simply held her.

❧·❦

Kate returned from the bedroom with her mending to find Matthew in his rocking chair staring out the window. "I thought you'd dozed off," she said, sitting down on the end of the sofa across from him.

He shook his head but said nothing.

Setting a button in place on Ray's shirt, Kate pulled a thread through and began to sew. "Is your back hurting, Matthew?"

"No more than usual. No, I was thinking about our Maggie. How she is with Jonathan and how he is with her. And how both of them are with wee Gracie."

"They're grand with her."

He nodded. "They are. But don't you find it hard to keep from laughing at the way they handle her? As if she's a baby doll that might break if they put too tight a grip on her?"

He grinned. "That Jonathan. He all but carries her about on a silk pillow. And have you seen—he can't look at anything else but the babe or Maggie. And he always has a bit of a dazed expression about him at that. Those two will have him falling over his own feet most of the time, I'll wager."

Kate's hands stilled, and now she also smiled. "He's a wonderful daddy."

Matthew gave another nod. "He is that. The babe will lack for nothing, including attention."

He was quiet for a time, and Kate went back to her mending.

"He's a good man, Jonathan is," he said after a few moments more.

Surprised but greatly pleased at this rare show of talkativeness in her husband, Kate again paused in her mending. "Maggie couldn't have found herself a better man, and that's the truth. He treats her like fine china, and doesn't he nearly melt every time she steps into the room?"

Silence again.

"Do I treat you well enough, Kate?" Matthew's gaze was needle sharp.

Kate stared at her husband. He might just as well have asked her the question in another tongue, so bewildering were his words.

"Matthew, have I ever complained?"

"No, but you wouldn't. Though the good Lord knows there have been times when I've given you cause."

Her confusion growing, Kate stared down at the sewing in her lap. "Matthew, is something wrong?"

"Wrong?"

She could hardly say what she was thinking, now could she? That he was acting like a total stranger and not the man she'd been living with for nearly three decades. "You just don't seem quite... yourself," she said, looking up.

"Because I'm awake, you mean, instead of passed out on pain pills like I usually am every night?"

"No, Matthew! I didn't mean that—"

He waved off her protest. "It's true enough, I know. I'm little more than a cabbage-head these days by the time supper's over. Those infernal pills—"

He hauled himself to the window and stood looking out. "I can hardly think straight when I'm on them, but the pain grinds me to pieces if I don't take them. I hate to think what they might be doing to my brain...what's left of it."

Kate's heart turned over. "Why won't you at least consider going to see Dr. Gordon? You've never trusted Dr. Woodbridge, after all. Why not see another doctor?"

He turned around to her, a humorless smile slashing his face. "Better the devil I know than the one I don't."

"Oh, Matthew, really!"

"Now, Kate, we've had this out already. 'Tis a dead horse."

"'Tis your insufferable pride, that's what it is! You'd live in misery from one day to the next rather than disavow your stubbornness. Dr. Gordon is a good doctor—everybody says so. And she just might be able to help you."

A scowl turned his features to a thunderhead. "She wasn't a good enough doctor to save Eva Grace, now was she?"

Caught off guard by this unexpected indictment, Kate stood to face him. "That's unfair entirely, Matthew. Dr. Gordon did everything that could have possibly been done for Eva Grace, and you know it. You were here. You saw what happened. Are you saying Lebreen Woodbridge could have done more?"

His scowl darkened still more as he hunched his shoulders and thrust his hands into his pockets. "There's no way to be knowing that, is there?" he grumbled.

"You *do* know it, just as well as I do. There was nothing anyone could have done."

His eyes were damp, his mouth slack. The misery in his expression wrenched Kate's heart and squelched her annoyance. She went to him. "Oh, Matthew. Let's not quarrel. Not about this. Not about our girl."

"I'm sorry, Kate," he said, his voice rough-edged. He clasped her shoulders and pulled her to him. "I suppose you're right. I suppose there was nothing anyone could do. But sometimes I get to thinking about her, and I can't help but wonder if there wasn't *something…anything…*"

His words fell away, and for a moment he slumped against her.

"We can't think that way, Matthew. It will drive us both mad." Kate took him by the hand and led him to the sofa where they sat for a long time in silence, holding each other while she quietly wept and Matthew, obviously, tried not to.

The pain was still raw, like a hacksaw filing away at her heart. Perhaps it was even harder for Matthew, she realized. Most of the time he thought he needed to keep his feelings to himself, showing nothing even to her. Yet grief contained was heavier than sorrow shared.

"We will get through this," she said quietly. "We must. For our other children—and for wee Gracie. And for ourselves. God will carry us through until we're able to walk on our own again. He will."

He nodded, saying nothing, his bearded cheek pressed close to hers.

Kate continued to hold him, this man she had lived with so long she scarcely remembered life without him. His need for her comfort, as always, drew him into her heart.

She wiped her eyes and took a deep breath. She had to be strong for him. She *had* to. When she faltered, Matthew grew uncertain, even frightened. She had seen it so many times over the years. Her weakness weakened *him.* Her strength seemed to bolster him, restore him. But ever since Eva Grace's death, weakness had dogged her like an unrelenting buzzard. Physical weakness, yes, but emotional and spiritual weakness as well. Most days she felt as if it were all she could do to make it through to nightfall. Her body seemed lifeless, her mind numb.

Caring for the baby helped. Lately she had begun to feel a faint hint of strength returning. Her days had purpose again. Gracie needed her and depended on her. And Maggie and Jonathan needed her help so they could get on with building their life together. Every time she was tempted to give in to the weakness, to give up and stop trying to come out of the cave of sadness her grief had dug for her, something would tug at her, reminding her that she couldn't quit. There were still those who depended on her.

Especially Matthew. It had taken her years to realize that he wasn't as strong as he let on to be. Oh, physically, he'd been an oak tree for most of his life. And even though he claimed his faith couldn't hold a candle to her own, Kate had seen that faith at work and knew it surpassed his own perception of it. In most ways he was a mountain of a man. But emotionally—and unknowingly, she thought—he looked to her for his own resilience. If he found it in her, he could call his up. If she wavered, so did he.

She wondered sometimes if that wasn't the way it was meant to be. If a man and wife were to be as one, if they truly made each other complete, then didn't it only make sense that what one lacked, the other would supply? That they would find what they needed in each other?

And if once in a while she grew weary of letting him think she was strong, when in truth, at that moment she was anything *but*, wasn't that merely a gift she could give him without complaint? A kind of grace God allowed her to offer the man who was indeed a gift to *her*?

Such thoughts were deep. Too deep. The best she could do at this moment was to hold on to her husband, give him whatever warmth and consolation she knew how to give. Let him draw from what strength she had left in her.

She could only hope it was enough.

Chapter Ten

Jonathan's New Idea

Christ,
Grant us this boon,
To look with Thine eyes of pity and love
On all men's need:
To feel from within, with Thee,
The bite of pain, of hunger, of wrong:
To live wholly beyond ourselves,
In deep and active desire
Of help for the needy and weak.

John S. Hoyland

Jonathan looked up from his desk to scan his classroom. It was a good opportunity to study his students, as they were all deep in concentration, working through the test papers he'd handed out twenty minutes before. The sight of all those young, intense faces never failed to move him. Some brought an ache to his heart, others a smile. But each evoked a feeling of almost paternal interest and affection. Most days he saw more of these children than their parents did. Certainly he cared deeply about their welfare.

One thing about children: No matter how hard things might be with family financial struggles, inclement weather, even learning challenges, they somehow kept an innocent cheerfulness that never failed to lift his own spirit. Conditions were particularly difficult at present for mine families, but for the most part, the children retained their carefree liveliness.

He also enjoyed the diversity in his classroom and appreciated the differences among the students. His gaze came to rest on Selma Lazlo, and he couldn't stop a smile at her shining head bent over her test paper. Here was a child who, along with her younger brother, Huey, had once wrenched his heart with her guarded, solemn features, her shabby appearance, and her difficulty in relating to other children—and adults as well.

The products of a violent, abusive home, both Selma and her brother were now living with Ben Wallace and his wife, Regina. Although Selma apparently had not been physically mistreated, little Huey had been badly beaten over an extended period of time. The mother who beat him was now deceased, having been shot by their father. In fact, Burian Lazlo was presently confined to the county jail, awaiting sentence for the murder.

In the brief time since the Wallaces had taken Selma and her brother into their home, the children had undergone remarkable changes, and not merely in terms of their physical appearance. The sober, furtive mannerisms that once characterized the two of them had gradually given way to a more childlike lightheartedness and cheerful demeanor. Even their schoolwork had greatly improved, and they were beginning to make friends among their classmates.

His attention shifted for a moment to the other side of the room, where the older students were finishing up a history quiz. For a change, thirteen-year-old Annabeth O'Toole wasn't flirting with Mike Zinco at the desk behind her but was actually frowning in concentration.

Annabeth worried him. Her widowed father had his hands full holding down a job in the mines and raising two sons and a daughter. Annabeth, the oldest of three, was a precociously pretty blond who looked a good two or three years older than she was. She managed to ensnare just about every boy within range with her dimples and long eyelashes.

Jonathan didn't envy Colm O'Toole the onerous responsibility on his shoulders. His daughter, even at her young age, was turning out to be one of the most comely girls in school. Growing up without a mother to counsel her had to make her adolescent years more difficult for Annabeth—and for Colm as well—than they might have been otherwise. He wished he could think of something that would turn Annabeth's attention from boys to a less hazardous sort of diversion. So far he hadn't come up with anything, but he was still mulling it over.

Just then a movement by Maggie's brother, Ray, caught his eye. The boy was leaning back, one hand raking his sandy red hair as he frowned at the test paper in front of him. Obviously confounded, he repeatedly tapped the desk with his pencil and twisted his mouth to one side.

Jonathan expelled a long breath. Ray was no student. He was bright enough, no doubt about that, but he disliked the books and the classroom. He'd much prefer being outside planting a crop or feeding animals. Maggie and her family were intent on the boy getting a good education, and Jonathan was hardly one to minimize the importance of his doing just that. But, realistically, he had little hope of keeping his young brother-in-law in the classroom more than another year or so.

He looked back to his own desk, to the paper he'd been making notes on earlier. A number of ideas, mostly for the school and his students, though not entirely, had been buzzing around in his mind over the past few weeks only to be pushed to the back of his thoughts during the time of his marriage, Eva Grace's death, and taking over the care of Gracie. For several days now they'd renewed their struggle for his attention.

At the moment he needed to bring the period to an end and prepare for dismissal. He folded his notes and tucked them into his pocket to review later.

"Time," he said and started down the aisle to collect the test papers.

❧·❧

After supper that night, while Maggie was giving Gracie her bedtime bottle, Jonathan put a recording of Mendelssohn's "Spring Song" on the phonograph. As they sat together on the sofa, listening to the piece that had quickly become one of Maggie's favorites, Jonathan smiled to himself. He'd once wondered if Maggie would enjoy the phonograph as much as he did or if, lively as she was by nature, she might find the simple act of sitting and listening to music somewhat boring.

Clearly his concern had been needless. Most evenings, if he was later than usual in turning on the phonograph, she kept after him until he did. Yet when he would have showed her how to start it herself, she refused. "I'll not risk breaking something so valuable and so special to you." No amount of coaxing could change her mind.

She was still rapt in the music when she lifted Gracie onto her shoulder to burp her. "It seems to me," she said, "that what makes music so special is that you don't need to understand it to enjoy it."

Jonathan looked at her. She had a way of tossing out these little statements and then stopping for a moment, as if she were looking for some sign of agreement from him before going on.

He nodded, waiting.

"You, for example, most likely *do* understand what we're listening to, but I can't think you enjoy it a bit more than I do, even though I haven't a thought as to what it's all about or how it comes into being."

Jonathan didn't always get her point, but this time he did. "You're exactly right. That's because even though I know something about music, I listen with my heart, the same as you do."

At that instant Gracie let go a satisfied burp, and Maggie smiled.

Jonathan reached to touch Maggie's hair and then the baby's head.

"Speaking of music—I have an idea. Something I've been considering for some time now. I'd like to know what you think."

She tucked the baby close, got up, and went to the rocking chair. "Tell me while I rock Gracie."

After seeing her settled in the rocker, Jonathan asked, "Do you remember the night of my birthday party at the schoolhouse, the night you gave me the penny whistle from you and Summer?"

Her eyes misted. "Oh, yes," she said softly. "Of course I remember."

"Then you remember the music the students and their parents performed as a kind of birthday gift."

She nodded. "I'll never forget that night. How could I? I even wrote about it in my book."

"Yes," he said, "you did. Just as you wrote how the music changed the people in the room–and the town—afterward. How things got better after that, at least for a time."

"That's how I remember it. Something happened that night. I'll never understand it, and you said *you* didn't understand it either. But for a long time after that night, things were different in Skingle Creek. The town came together. For the first time in a long time, people grew closer, almost like a big family. And they looked forward, instead of giving up."

He nodded. "Things are bad in town right now, Maggie. The men's wages have been cut again, and the weather has shortened their hours. The mine bosses are fighting all mention of a union, even though they know it's going to happen sooner or later. That's caused a lot of anger and frustration among the miners. To make matters worse, we had so many men injured last year in the cave-in—including Matthew—that some are no longer able to work. The town needs something to lift their spirits, to keep them going."

He paused. "There's no arguing that they need actual physical and material sustenance more than the kind of thing I'm thinking of. Still—"

"What *are* you thinking of?"

He hesitated. "I don't actually have it worked out very well in my mind yet. It's just an idea—"

"Tell me."

⋙·⋘

Maggie studied him as she rocked the baby. He looked genuinely excited. This was a facet of Jonathan's makeup that still surprised her. She had to admit that up until their engagement, when she grew to know him better, she had seen him as a decidedly serious, dignified, and studious man. And in truth, he was all that at times. But she had come to realize that he also possessed a distinctly light-hearted side, a relentless sense of humor, and a boyish enthusiasm for ideas and new ventures—his own as well as those of others.

How had she missed these facets of his personality over the years?

Well, he'd been her *teacher*, after all. From first grade through graduation. Although she'd always been keenly aware of his kindness and his gentleness, she'd known him primarily as the most prominent authority figure in her life other than her parents. That role itself demanded respect from his students, imbuing him with an aura of gravity, whether real or imagined.

At the moment, however, he seemed hard-pressed to contain the enthusiasm that appeared primed to spill over at any second.

"You're familiar with the way the miners sing on their way home from work?" he asked now.

"Sing? Oh, yes. They've done that for as long as I can remember. I've always liked hearing them."

"But have you ever noticed just how *good* they are? How well they sing? And how much they seem to enjoy it?"

Maggie glanced down to find Gracie already asleep. She touched her cheek with her index finger and brushed a kiss over the soft, warm spot she'd touched. "Let me put Gracie to bed," she whispered, getting up from the rocker. "I'll just be a moment, and then you can tell me all about your idea."

"I'll go up with you."

Halfway up the steps Gracie opened her eyes and, seeing Jonathan following behind, let out a wail for him, which Maggie knew pleased him no end.

It was another half hour before they finally got her settled and back to sleep—and before Jonathan could relate his idea in detail.

Afterward, sitting together on the sofa, Maggie said carefully, "It's a grand idea, Jonathan. But perhaps somewhat...ambitious, don't you think? Do you really believe you can persuade enough men to take part?"

"Yes," he said firmly, his expression not dimming a bit. "Oh, not at first. We both know the miners have their own way of doing things. But I've thought a lot about this, Maggie. And I've prayed about it even more. I believe I can make it happen, and I'm convinced it will be a good thing. For the miners and for the town."

Maggie was *trying* to share his enthusiasm, she really was, but it seemed like such a fanciful idea. The people of Skingle Creek needed so much. The churches tried, but they couldn't begin to keep up with the need for such essentials as food and clothing. It had already been a hard winter for many, and it wasn't over yet.

As if he recognized her skepticism, Jonathan took her hand, saying, "What? I can tell you have some reservations."

She searched his face, her heart warmed by the light in his eyes and the earnestness of his expression.

"I think that no one but you could make it work. But I believe you *will* do it."

He smiled. "I confess that I do covet your faith in me. But do you mean that? Or are you saying it just to salve my feelings?"

"I wouldn't do that."

"Oh, I believe you might. But I'll not press the issue. So you'll help me then?"

"Help you? I can't think what *I* could do."

"You can work on your father, to begin with."

Maggie lifted an eyebrow. "Da?"

"The miners look to Matthew as a leader. If I can get him involved, most of the others will come around. Matthew will see to it."

Actually, he had a point. For years Da had been recognized as the one to go to when a miner had problems of any kind. He'd been a foreman before the cave-in a little over a year ago, but by his own choice had gone back to being a fire boss after his injury. No matter what position he might hold, however, Matthew MacAuley was one of the most experienced, diligent, and reliable miners among them, and to a man they treated him as their leader.

"If you want my opinion," she said, "you'd do better to talk to Da yourself. There's no one he respects more than you. I'm still his knock-kneed daughter. He seems to find it hard to refuse you anything."

"You were never knock-kneed."

"How would you know? You never saw my knees until we were married."

"You had a knack for skinning them, as I recall, tomboy that you were. I remember handing you the iodine more than once. But back to Matthew. You really believe he'll listen to me?"

"You convinced him to let you marry me, now didn't you?" she said, giving him a nudge.

"A good point," he said.

Maggie knew from the look in his eye that Jonathan's idea would soon bear fruit.

Chapter Eleven

Visitors

We are stronger, and are better
Under manhood's sterner reign:
Still we feel that something sweet
Followed youth, with flying feet,
And will never come again.

Richard Henry Stoddard

Jonathan had known since noon he was going to be working late, but he hadn't realized it would be *this* late. Fortunately, Carolyn Ross offered Maggie a ride to her parents' house, and he insisted that she go on without him. He'd also told her that the family shouldn't wait supper for him, and it was a good thing. By four-thirty he still hadn't finished preparing his monthly report to the school board when he glanced out his office window and saw Ben Wallace coming up the walk.

"I was hoping you'd still be here," said Ben as he walked into Jonathan's office.

"Report time," Jonathan said, pointing to the papers in front of him.

"I know how much you enjoy that."

"Indeed."

"Well, I have some news I thought you'd want to hear."

Jonathan motioned him to the chair across from his desk. "Good news, I hope."

"Not for Burian Lazlo, it isn't," Ben said as he sat down across from Jonathan.

"What's happened?"

"He was sentenced today. Tom Mason called the deputy's office as soon as he heard."

Jonathan tensed. "And?"

"They're transferring him to the state penitentiary tomorrow. Apparently the jury didn't go for his self-defense story. He'll be behind bars for a long time. At least twenty years."

Jonathan gave a low whistle. "So long?"

"Well, he did kill his wife, Jonathan."

"I know. But twenty years in prison. I can't imagine."

His mind played over the events that had led Lazlo to this dire place. The father of Huey and Selma Lazlo had shot his wife when he caught her setting fire to their house, not long after it was discovered that she'd been beating little Huey for an undetermined length of time. Apparently Lazlo had never been abusive to the children, but he had known about his son's beatings and done nothing, distancing himself from his children physically and emotionally.

In checking the family's background, Ben had learned that the Lazlo woman suffered from some sort of mental illness and had a history of setting fires. As for her husband, he was known to be a belligerent sort who drank heavily. Those two poor children had been raised by a man who apparently didn't care enough about them to offer them any sort of protection from a mother whose mind wasn't right and who was a danger to herself and her entire family.

"You do realize that this raises the subject of adoption again for Regina and me."

Ben's words brought Jonathan out of his thoughts. "You still plan to adopt the children, then?"

"Oh yes. We've talked of little else for weeks now."

Huey and Selma Lazlo weren't the first children the Wallaces had taken in for a time over the years. But this was the first situation that lent itself to the possibility of adoption. A childless couple, Ben and Regina had hoped and prayed for children for years. Jonathan fervently hoped the Lazlo youngsters would prove to be the answer to their prayers.

"Have you any idea where we ought to start, Jonathan?"

"Assuming the children will be as pleased with the idea as I am, I'll be happy to contact my father. He's an attorney, you know. I'll get some information for you. I can't think you'll have any problem whatsoever, Ben. Especially with Lazlo's extended sentence."

"We're going to approach the children with the idea in a few days," said Ben, getting to his feet. "As soon as they've had a chance to get used to the idea that their father won't be around for a long, long time."

Jonathan nodded, stood, and eased his shoulders. "I'll write to my father tonight or tomorrow."

"I appreciate that, Jonathan. Maggie and the baby are well, are they?"

"Oh yes. Gracie's growing like mad."

"I expect she keeps you busy."

"Definitely busy. But happy as well. She's such a good baby. We're still stumbling our way through this parent thing, but so far we don't seem to have done any major damage."

They shook hands. "I hope Regina and I will be joining you in the 'parent thing' soon."

"Oh, you already have. We just have to make it official now."

Jonathan saw him to the door, drawing a long breath before returning to the paperwork on his desk. Reports were his least favorite part of his job as principal. He much preferred the classroom.

Over the next half hour he had all he could do to keep his mind on his work. Ben's excitement about the prospect of becoming a father had served as a reminder not to take his own role as a parent for granted. Who would have imagined that at the age of forty, after all those years of bachelorhood, he'd be a husband and a father?

There was no denying that his life had undergone some radical changes. Although he hadn't had time to grow into the role of being a husband before becoming a father, he hoped he hadn't been a *total* failure as either. Heaven knew he hadn't quite stopped reeling yet. In truth, Gracie's arrival in their lives might have overwhelmed him altogether had he not longed for a family for so many years before she came along.

So deep in thought was he that he actually jumped when he heard the entrance door slam shut. Again he was reminded of the need for new hinges.

Something else he never seemed to find time to do.

He glanced at the clock on the wall. Nearly half past five. It was already growing dark. Maggie would be getting worried if he didn't show up soon.

The young man who appeared in his doorway was familiar, but Jonathan struggled for a moment to place him. Slender with a neatly trimmed beard, he wore an overcoat flung open and a wide smile.

Jonathan pushed himself up out of the chair.

"Hello, Mr. Stuart. You don't recognize me, do you?"

It was the intensity of his expression and the way he leveled his eyeglasses on the bridge of his nose with his index finger that triggered recognition.

"Kenny! Kenny Tallman!" Jonathan hurried around his desk to grasp the younger man's hand. "I thought you were somewhere in South America."

The other laughed. "India, more recently. But I decided it was time to come home."

His hair had deepened to the color of dark sand, and he wore it longer than he had as a boy. Jonathan noted the lean features, the slightly faint pallor of his face. Kenny had always been slight, but now there seemed to be a look of unwellness about him.

"Well, come in, son. Sit down. Here, let me take your coat."

"Oh, I can't stay, sir. I was on my way home—to my father's house—and I saw the light, so I thought I'd just stop for a moment and say hello. I wasn't surprised to see that you still work late."

Jonathan leaned against his desk. "So you're staying with your father?"

"For now."

Jonathan studied him, again remembering him as a child. Kenny hadn't had an easy time of it as a boy. In fact, he'd seemed an unhappy youth most of the time. His father, Judson Tallman, had been a hard, uncompromising man, both as mine superintendent and as a father. As for Kenny's mother, Charlotte Tallman had abandoned her husband and son before Jonathan arrived in Skingle Creek. She had never returned.

While Tallman had apparently never mistreated his son physically, he'd spent years absenting himself from the boy, showing little interest in any area of Kenny's life—up until the night the boy had been instrumental in saving Maggie from the attack of Billy Macken and Orrin Gaffney, the school's worst bullies. From that time on, Tallman had softened somewhat, involving himself a bit more in his son's school activities and at the same time beginning to show a certain measure of pride in the boy. A pride that was, in Jonathan's estimation, well-deserved.

A thought struck Jonathan. What would Kenny's return mean to Maggie? She and Kenny had been best friends throughout most of their adolescent years. They had been viewed later as a couple by their classmates. As they grew older, many—including himself—thought they would eventually marry. Had Kenny come back because of Maggie? Hoping to renew their relationship? And if he had, what would Maggie's reaction be?

"So you're the principal now too, I hear."

Kenny's voice dragged him back to his surroundings. "Yes, yes, I am. But I still teach too."

"That's good. I can't imagine you *not* teaching, Mr. Stuart."

Jonathan fumbled to regain his composure. "What brings you back to Skingle Creek, Kenny? Are you on furlough?"

Kenny shook his head. "No, I'm probably back in the States to stay. At least for some time. I picked up a touch of malaria that I can't seem to shake, so the Mission Board brought me home."

"Malaria? That's serious, isn't it?"

"Well, the climate in South India isn't exactly conducive to recovery from it. But I'll be all right eventually, I expect, now that I'm home."

"Tell me about your work," Jonathan said. "I remember Maggie mentioning that you wanted to build ships. I doubt you're doing much of that on the mission field."

The other's eyes lighted and he smiled. "Maggie? Where is she now?"

Jonathan hesitated and answered carefully. "Why, she's here."

"Here in Skingle Creek?"

"That's right. In fact, she teaches here at the school."

"*Really?* I can't wait to see her! How is she?"

"She's—" Jonathan stopped to clear his throat. "She's fine."

"*Maggie!*" Kenny said, still smiling. "We lost touch over the years, but I've never forgotten her."

Heart pounding, Jonathan again had to clear his throat. "Did you know—" He stopped and then tried again. "Did you know that Maggie and I are...married?"

He felt a wave of heat stain his face as he waited for the other's reaction.

Kenny's mouth dropped open. He stared at Jonathan. "You and Maggie?"

Jonathan nodded. "I expect that seems somewhat strange to you."

Something flared in the younger man's eyes and then ebbed. He studied Jonathan with an unnerving steadiness. "Not *strange*, no. No, I'm just...surprised. But that's swell, Mr. Stuart, it really is. I'm happy for you—for both of you."

Jonathan glanced away to escape that intent, searching stare.

Silence hung between them for a long, heavy moment before Kenny finally spoke again. "You and Maggie," he said quietly. "I think that's wonderful."

Jonathan looked back to find him smiling. "Do you?"

"Of course. You were both always so special. I expect you're just right—perfect—for each other." He extended his hand to Jonathan. "Congratulations. How long have you been married?"

Jonathan managed a small laugh. "Not very long at all. Sit down, Kenny—please. I won't keep you long, but let me fill you in a little."

As the other shrugged out of his overcoat and took a chair, Jonathan settled himself on the corner of his desk. He told him then about his and Maggie's marriage, about Eva Grace's death, and finally about Gracie and the fact that they were raising her.

Kenny shook his head. "Eva Grace. I can't imagine her gone. She was always so protective of us younger students, always the one to step in to break up any trouble. What a terrible thing for Maggie and her family." He looked up. "So you and Maggie are going to adopt the baby, I take it?"

Jonathan nodded. "We hope so, yes."

"This couldn't have been easy for the two of you."

"Not easy, no. But we wouldn't have it any other way. We love Gracie as if she were our own."

"Mr. and Mrs. MacAuley—are they doing all right?"

"Losing Eva Grace has taken its toll on them, but they're strong people, as you probably remember."

"I remember I sometimes envied Maggie her parents. They always seemed to love their children so much. They were good parents."

"The best," Jonathan agreed. He hesitated. "How's your father, Kenny?"

Kenny shrugged, not meeting Jonathan's gaze. "He's well. You know Dad. He's always well. He doesn't change much."

With that Kenny stood and slipped into his coat. "I need to get going. But I'm really glad I got to see you, Mr. Stuart. You'll tell Maggie I asked after her?"

"I will, indeed. She'll be eager to see you, I'm sure."

"Maybe we can get together soon," Kenny said. "I'd like both of you to meet my wife."

Jonathan blinked. "Your...wife?"

Kenny grinned. "Yes. Anna. We met on the mission field and got married about a year ago. I'd have brought her along, but she's in the family way and still exhausted from our trip home."

Relief washed over Jonathan like a waterfall. "You're married too. That's wonderful, Kenny! I'm so happy for you."

It *was* wonderful. And he *was* happy for him. Happier than Kenny would ever know. Indeed, Jonathan was downright ecstatic to learn that Kenny was married.

"We'll have you and your wife for supper very soon," he said with genuine enthusiasm. "I'm sure Maggie won't let me rest until I deliver the two of you to our front door."

Kenny reached to shake his hand again. "That would be great, sir. I want Anna and Maggie to meet. I know they'll like each other."

"Of course they will. You can count on my being in touch soon."

Jonathan watched him leave, eager now to get on his way so he could tell Maggie about Kenny's return. As he grabbed his overcoat and extinguished the lamp, it occurred to him that only a few minutes ago he was almost sick with apprehension about telling Maggie that Kenny was back. Now he could scarcely wait to break the news to her.

Kenny Tallman married. What fine news!

Chapter Twelve

Meeting with Matthew

Scatter stars in our darkness, Lord God,
And turn our lament to a song.

Anonymous

Within a week Jonathan had his idea firmly in mind. Once he'd drafted out some rough plans on how he might best organize a choir and make it accessible to the miners, he began his recruitment campaign. As planned, his first objective was to enlist Matthew MacAuley. He had it on Maggie's word that her father might be a likely candidate. He hoped she was right. Matthew, he knew, could make all the difference in the responses from the other miners.

He caught his father-in-law on a Sunday afternoon after they'd all had dinner together at the MacAuleys. It was an unusually warm day for early February, and Maggie and her mother had taken Gracie for a walk. Ray was out at their cousin's farm, putting in a weekend of work, so Jonathan and Matthew were alone in the house.

They'd spent the last half hour after the meal reading the newspapers in the living room. Finally Jonathan put his aside. "There's something I'd like to talk to you about, Matthew."

The other threw him an impatient glance over the top of his paper.

Jonathan ignored the lifted eyebrow. "Hear me out, won't you? This may sound a little far-fetched to you at first, but I've not lost my wits, I promise you."

"Well, now, this sounds interesting." Matthew slowly folded the newspaper and removed his eyeglasses, watching Jonathan closely.

"Well, I hope you *will* find it interesting," Jonathan said, proceeding to explain.

The longer he spoke, the more the other's eyes widened. Twice Matthew tried to interrupt, but Jonathan pressed on before he could.

By the time he finished his spiel, he was almost out of breath. "I'm convinced it will be a good thing, Matthew. For the town and for the men as well. I've come to you first because Maggie and I think that if you'll give it a try, the other miners will too."

"You want us to *sing?*"

Jonathan nodded.

"In a group."

"That's right.

"A bunch of coal miners singing in some kind of a—what, a *choir?*"

"Well, we probably won't call it that, but yes, you've got the idea."

"What *would* you call it?"

"What indeed? I haven't gotten that far yet."

"Well, now, that's a surprise. I thought from the sound of things you had this all tied up, neat and tidy," Matthew commented, his tone dry.

"Maggie says you have a fine voice."

"Did she now?"

Jonathan nodded. "So…would you be interested?"

The older man ran a hand down the side of his beard. "You're serious?"

"Entirely."

"How in the world did you ever dream up such a thing, man?"

The obvious incredulity of Matthew's question very nearly made Jonathan falter. But if he couldn't convince this man, it was highly unlikely he'd convince any of the others.

"It's just an idea. I've been thinking a lot about the town and the hard times that have plagued the people over the past year. I hoped to come up with something that might lift their spirits a little."

"There have always been hard times in Skingle Creek, Jonathan. Most likely there always will be. We're a mining town."

"I understand that, Matthew, but doesn't that make it all the more imperative to give the people something besides problems every now and then? Something cheerful? There's nothing like music to brighten things up, you know, and—"

"You want to brighten things up for the people in Skingle Creek?" Matthew sat up straighter in his chair, thrusting his bad leg out in front of him a little more. "Start by finding a way to put three square meals on the table and warm coats on the backs of their children. Jonathan, I know you mean well, and I understand you've a great love for music and all, but music won't feed our families or pay the doctor bills."

Jonathan groped for the words that might convince Matthew his idea had merit, though discouragement had begun to creep in. "You're right. But surely you know that if I could think of a way to help the families in Skingle Creek in a more practical way, I'd do it. But this is what I *can* do, and while it might seem altogether worthless to you, I think there's something to be said for giving folks a means to—well, if not *forget* their troubles, at least set them aside for a time."

Matthew put a hand to his chin, keeping his silence so long that Jonathan worried he was going to dismiss the idea out of hand.

"I expect you prayed about this."

Jonathan brightened. Perhaps he needn't give up just yet. "Why yes, at length."

"What kind of songs would we be singing?"

The question was unexpected, but it didn't catch Jonathan entirely off guard. "Old songs mostly. I'm thinking about folk songs from the British Isles—Ireland, Wales, England. Some hymns, of course. Perhaps some spirituals as well."

"Songs from Ireland, you say?"

"Certainly."

He was interested.

"We'll do only the kind of songs the men would take to. Many they'd already know, I'm sure."

Matthew was studying him with an unnerving expression. "Why would you do this?"

"I'm sorry?"

"Well, I hardly think you need any more work to do. It's always been my impression that you have more than enough to do as it is. So why would you undertake yet another project?"

"Matthew, it's just as I said. I honestly believe it would be good for the men and, eventually, for the town. It's been a difficult year, what with the cave-in, the bad weather's toll on the work at the mine, and the sickness that's set in among some of the families. I've *seen* the benefits of music in my own life and in the lives of others. There's nothing quite like it to lift the heart. In some cases it's actually a tool of healing."

The older man stroked his chin. "So how would this work, then? We'd have to sing in public, would we?"

"Well, eventually I hope the men would agree to that, yes. But not until we've had plenty of rehearsal time together."

"This would be only for the miners?"

Jonathan shook his head. "No, it would be open to any man who has a mind to sing. But most of the men in town *are* miners, so that's why I'd concentrate on music that's agreeable to them." He paused. "So what do you think? Will they give it a try? Will *you?*"

His father-in-law fixed a measuring stare on him. "I have to tell you, Jonathan, you're right about the idea being a bit far-fetched."

Jonathan's hopes took another tumble. If Matthew wouldn't participate, he wasn't likely to get the other miners involved. "Yes, I suppose that's a fair judgment, but—"

Matthew lifted a hand to wave off the interruption. "But even I can see that the men—the miners in particular—could use something to break the monotony of their days. And as it happens, they're a singing bunch."

"I know! I've heard them on their way to and from work, and, frankly, I've heard some very good, strong voices."

A thoughtful look settled over the older man. "Not all of them will do it, mind."

"But you think some will?"

Matthew shrugged. "Perhaps. One thing, they're drawn to music. You've seen them at the square on Friday nights when some of the lads are playing their fiddles." He stopped. "But when would we manage to get the lot of us together? The men are bone-tired after a day's work, Jonathan. And those on the night shift have to sleep during the day."

Jonathan had forgotten about the extra shift. That complicated things. But it didn't necessarily make an impossible situation.

"Do you think they'd be willing to take an extra hour on a late Sunday afternoon or early evening?"

Matthew's answer was slow in coming. "Possibly," he finally said.

"Will you help me with this, Matthew?"

"You want me to talk to some of the men, I expect."

"I think your influence is the only way I'll ever get them interested. They respect you. If they find out you're going to take part, they'll be far more likely to sign on."

The other narrowed his eyes. "And if it turns out to be a colossal failure, I'll never be hearing the end of it." He eased his shoulders a bit and added, "We wouldn't have to wear any funny suits or anything, would we?"

"Funny—oh, no! No, absolutely no."

Matthew stifled a yawn and then dropped his hand away. "Did Maggie put you up to this?"

Jonathan shook his head. "No, the blame's all mine. She's not completely convinced it will work." When Matthew again arched an eyebrow, he hurried to add, "But she thinks it has a credible chance if you take part."

They heard the sound of Maggie and her mother coming up on the porch. "Well, then," Matthew said, "I'll get back to you after I talk with some of the men. We'll see what happens."

Jonathan thanked him, already impatient to get started. He had great faith in Matthew's influence over his fellow miners.

Chapter Thirteen

Old Friends and New

Did you know you were brave,
Did you know you were strong?
Did you know there was one leaning hard?
Did you know that I waited and listened and prayed,
And was cheered by your simplest word?
Did you know that I longed for that smile on your face,
For the sound of your voice ringing true?
Did you know I grew stronger and better
Because I had merely touched shoulders with you?

Author unknown

Maggie tried to ignore the covert glances Jonathan kept shooting her way in the kitchen where he was helping her put the finishing touches on supper. If she weren't so impatient with him, she might have been amused. He could hardly be more obvious. Clearly he was wondering how seeing Kenny this evening was going to affect her.

A sigh escaped before she could stop it.

Jonathan turned from the counter to look at her. "Something wrong?"

She almost told him what was wrong and at the same time was tempted to tell him that as happy as she would be to see her old childhood friend again, she was even happier to hear that he had a wife. As far as she was concerned, Kenny deserved nothing but the best, and she hoped his marriage was as perfect as she considered her own to be.

Instead, she kept her silence. If she didn't know him better, she would have thought Jonathan was feeling insecure. But that was entirely absurd. He was the most self-contained, steady, purposeful man she had ever known. What did he have to feel insecure about? Certainly not her feelings for him! As if there were a man anywhere who could hold a candle to him. As if an old pal from the past, even a childhood friend and high school beau, could earn so much as a second thought from her now that she was a married woman— and married to the man she'd loved practically all her life. As if she could take her mind off Jonathan Stuart long enough to even notice another man, whoever he happened to be.

He was watching her closely now, no doubt waiting for an answer to his question.

All right then. She'd *give* him an answer, albeit an evasive one. "No, nothing's wrong. I just want everything to be perfect for supper. And I'm not the best cook in the world, as you already know."

"Everything will be fine," he said. "And there's absolutely nothing whatsoever wrong with your cooking."

A bark from Figaro outside the back door sounded as if the big hound was adding his own approval.

Jonathan had a spot of flour on his cheek, and Maggie reached to dab it off. Then she brushed a quick kiss on the same place.

His eyes lighted. "What was that for?"

Maggie went back to stirring the gravy. "I don't expect I need a reason to kiss my husband."

"You're not getting off that easily." He tossed his towel on the counter and circled her waist from behind.

Maggie deliberated another moment before turning to face him. She allowed him a kiss before stepping back to look at him. "Jonathan, would you please tell me what's going on?"

He frowned. "What do you mean?"

Maggie reached for his hand. "Whether you realize it or not, ever since we invited Kenny and his wife to supper tonight, you've been watching me like a rooster patrolling a henhouse. Would you like to tell me what exactly is bothering you?"

"What...I don't know what you're talking about."

Maggie noticed he wouldn't quite meet her gaze.

"I am *talking* about the way you keep watching me. And the way you've been bringing up Kenny's name for days now to see what sort of response you get."

Well, at least he had the grace to flush.

"That's not so at all," he said.

"Oh, but it *is* so. Are you sorry we invited Kenny and his wife to supper tonight? It was *your* idea, you know."

"No, I'm not sorry. I'm looking forward to it." He paused. "Aren't you?"

Maggie put the whisk on the counter and faced him. "I expect I *would* be if you weren't acting so peculiar."

"That's ridiculous. I'm not—"

"Yes, you are, Jonathan. And I'd like to know why."

He surprised her. Rather than offer yet another denial, he gave a decidedly lame shrug and an even lamer smile. "I didn't realize I'd been so obvious," he said quietly. His expression remained that of a small boy trapped by his own mischief. "I'm not sure, actually. I suppose I feel somewhat strange. Since you and Kenny used to be...close. It seems awkward somehow."

Maggie stared at him. "Close? Back when we were *children,* perhaps. Jonathan, I haven't seen Kenny for years."

He winced. "I know. And I know I'm being foolish—what with his being married and—"

"*His* being married? What about *us? We're* married too, aren't we? Jonathan, why should you care one way or the other that Kenny's back in Skingle Creek?"

She studied him. "No...you're not...you can't *possibly* think anything would change the way I feel about you?"

There. That was it. Something flickered in his eyes, and Maggie knew she'd hit a nerve. Instinctively she moved closer to him. "Jonathan, do you really trust my love for you so little?"

He squeezed his eyes shut but quickly opened them again. "No. No, of course not. It's not that—"

Maggie searched his gaze. "That's how it seems," she said gently. "Jonathan, don't you understand, even now, what you mean to me? You're *everything* to me. No one will ever change that. No one *could.*" She paused. "You can't treat our love like fine china, as if it might break as easily as a porcelain cup. It's not so fragile that anything can ever shatter it. Not *ever.*"

He let out a long breath and lifted his hands, palms up, seeking forgiveness. "I'm sorry, Maggie. Don't be upset with me. I *do* trust you, of course. I suppose I'm still not quite used to the idea that you're actually my *wife,* that we're finally together."

Maggie reached to draw his face to hers and kissed him. "I suggest you *get* used to it, you foolish man," she said, feigning a sternness she didn't feel as she settled herself into his arms.

He kissed her, long enough that she had to push him away. "I'm going to burn the gravy if you don't keep your distance. Now go look out the front and see if there's any sign of them. I don't want Figaro bolting around the house and jumping on Kenny's wife, what with her expecting a baby."

With obvious reluctance, he released her and started for the door.

"And Jonathan—"

He turned back.

"I love you more than everything. Remember that. "

He smiled and gave a small nod. "Thanks be," he said, using one of Maggie's expressions.

"Yes," she said softy, watching him leave the kitchen. "Thanks be indeed."

❧ ❧

Maggie's only awkward moment came when Kenny and his wife, Anna, first stepped inside. She had gone upstairs to fetch the waking Gracie and somehow ended up behind Jonathan, peering around him like a shy child as their guests entered.

"Kenny, Anna, welcome to our home," Jonathan announced, glancing back over his shoulder in search of Maggie.

He and Kenny shook hands, leaving Maggie to wonder what sort of a greeting was appropriate from her to such a close friend—but one she hadn't seen for some years—and the wife she'd never met.

She needn't have worried. Kenny made it easier than she would have thought possible. Seeing her, the old familiar grin broke over his face, and he opened his arms to her. Maggie stole a quick look at Jonathan before reciprocating, but he smiled broadly, reaching for the baby so Maggie could accept a hug from her old friend.

"Ah, you're a sight, Maggie!" exclaimed Kenny, nodding as if he found her just as he'd expected. He then drew his wife to him. "I want you both to meet Anna, my wife. Anna, here are the famous Maggie and Mr. Stuart you've heard so much about."

Maggie turned to the woman at Kenny's side and was met by a sweet, if somewhat shy, smile and a warm, dark-eyed gaze. Kenny's wife was an inch or so taller than Maggie and almost as slender except for the fact that, as Jonathan had indicated, she was clearly with child.

"I'm so glad to finally meet you, Maggie," she said, her voice quiet, her Irish accent distinct. "I feel as if I've known you for an age. And Mr. Stuart—I expected you to be nine feet tall from the way Ken goes on about you."

"It's 'Jonathan,' Anna, please. To you as well, Kenny. I'm not your teacher anymore. Anna, Maggie and I couldn't be happier that you've brought Kenny back to us. He's been missed."

Maggie couldn't have hoped for the rest of the evening to go even half as well as it did. In between reminiscing about school days, Jonathan plied Kenny with questions about India and his work on the mission field. As for Anna, Maggie liked her immediately. Indeed, she liked her a *lot,* and she thought Anna enjoyed herself, her initial shyness fading as the evening wore on. She was clearly taken with Gracie, giving her a bottle while Maggie saw to their meal and then insisting on going upstairs to help put her to bed.

"I want to learn everything I can from you," she said. "In two more months I'll be doing all this myself."

As they left the baby's room, she put a hand to Maggie's arm, saying, "I can't thank you enough for having us tonight, Maggie. I've been a bit worried, you see, about coming here. Ken, of course, knows most everybody in town, with myself not knowing a soul until now."

"Oh, you'll like it here, Anna, I promise you. The coal dust takes a bit of getting used to, but it's a friendly town. You'll feel at home in no time." She paused. "You *will* be staying, won't you?"

"I'm not quite sure as yet just what we'll be doing. Ken needs to get his strength back before we make any decisions. Eventually, of course, he'll need to find a job."

"So you're not going back to the mission field?"

Anna shook her head. "At least not soon. We've both prayed a great deal about things, and we're convinced the Lord has led us back here for a reason."

"Well, I'm glad He did," Maggie said, starting down the steps. "I've been hoping for a friend for a long time. It seems that all my school chums have moved away. Tell me about yourself while I get supper on the table. Did Kenny tell you that my family is from Ireland too? We already have a lot in common."

They went on talking until they reached the kitchen. A few minutes later they found Jonathan and Kenny out back with Figaro, the big hound showing off in the worst way for company.

"You need to come inside and wash up now," Maggie told them. "We're putting supper on the table. And leave Figaro out here. He can come in later."

"Jonathan spoils that dog as if he were a child," she told Anna as she dished up the roast and potatoes. "Though, in truth, I expect I'm almost as guilty."

"Oh, he's such a handsome animal. Ken wants a dog. He says he was never allowed one as a boy."

Maggie looked at her. "How do you find Mr. Tallman?"

Anna lifted her eyebrows, and for a moment her expression turned almost impish. "He fancies himself quite the potentate, now doesn't he?"

"Don't let him intimidate you," Maggie cautioned. "He can be a hard man, but I'm sure he's glad to have Kenny and you home."

Anna sighed. "Those two—they're something of oil and water, aren't they? Ken doesn't seem to understand that his father is simply afraid to show him any softness." She smiled again. "He's not that way at all with me. He's almost courtly. Ken just shakes his head. He doesn't know what to make of his da when I'm around."

"So you and Mr. Tallman get along? That's wonderful! And so good for Kenny. He needs to see a softer side of his father."

Anna watched as Maggie removed the centerpiece she'd fashioned from candles and ivy to make room for the last of the dishes. "Has there—" She stopped and then went on. "Has there never been any word about Ken's mother in all these years?"

Maggie looked up. "Not that I've heard, no."

"It was hard for Ken, wasn't it?" Anna said softly. "Growing up without a mother. I can't think what that must have been like for him. It still bothers him, you know, when he speaks of her abandonment."

Maggie nodded, remembering the sadness that had always clung to Kenny when they were growing up. "It *was* hard. Kenny didn't have an easy time of it back then."

"He credits you and Mr. Stuart with the best part of his life during those years, you know. He's *that* fond of both of you. He told me once that even during the worst times of his childhood, you and Mr. Stuart were his anchors. How absolutely *right* it is that the two of you married each other."

Maggie's heart turned over at Anna's words. "Kenny's friendship meant a great deal to me too. He was forever rescuing me from one thing or another." She smiled. "Well, the bad times are clearly over now, thanks to you. It's so good to see him as happy as he is."

Anna remained quiet for another moment. "I'm older than Ken, you know," she said, her words quiet and without inflection. She watched Maggie as if gauging her reaction.

Actually, Maggie had already guessed there might be an age difference.

"There are six years between us," Anna went on. "It bothered me at first. But Ken won me over. I'm afraid I didn't resist for very long."

"Well, as Kenny probably told you, there are a lot more years than that between Jonathan and me," said Maggie with a laugh. "And it's certainly worked out just fine for us."

Anna relaxed. "The important thing is to love each other, isn't it? To want the same things and share the same faith? That's really what matters, it seems to me. Being together is…everything."

On impulse, Maggie reached to squeeze her hand. "Oh, Anna, I'm so glad you're here! Before my sister died—"

Maggie had to stop for a moment, caught off guard by the pain that even the thought of Evie's death still inflicted.

"Ken told me about your sister, Maggie. I'm so terribly sorry. I know I can never take her place, but you and I are going to be good friends, don't you think? Perhaps that will help at least a little."

Maggie warmed to the goodness in that kind, sincere face. "It will help a *lot*, Anna."

Their men came bustling into the dining room just then, laughing and talking in a way that squeezed Maggie's heart. It occurred to her in that moment that this was the way a house *ought* to sound: filled with the laughter of family and close friends.

She met Jonathan's eyes across the room, and not for the first time, she caught the sense that he knew her thoughts and shared them.

Chapter Fourteen

An Unwelcome Letter

Look to the road of unmarked place
And not the one well-known,
Leave fear behind, step out in faith—
You do not walk alone.

Anonymous

⁓

The euphoria of the weekend turned out to be short-lived.

On Monday, Jonathan dropped Maggie off at her parents' house before going on to the company store to pick up the mail and a few groceries. When he returned, he was frowning.

Maggie took one look at his face and knew something was wrong. Uneasiness clenched her stomach, but when she would have questioned him, the small shake of his head told her that whatever it was would have to wait until they were alone.

Having just had Sunday dinner all together the day before, they hadn't planned on staying at Maggie's parents for supper today, so a few minutes after Jonathan's return from the store they prepared to leave for home.

First, though, they waited for Maggie's mother to read the letter from Nell Frances that Jonathan had brought along with their mail. Maggie's sister had had her baby, a third little girl, only two weeks after Gracie was born. Today's letter indicated that the baby was doing well, and they hoped to make a visit home when the winter weather broke.

Maggie knew a visit from her funny, outgoing sister would do their mother a world of good. Indeed, Nell Frances's company would be good for the entire family, herself included. But right now she couldn't concentrate on anything but the ominous expression on Jonathan's face.

The moment they pulled away from the house, she quizzed him.

"Let's wait until we get home," he suggested, keeping his eyes on the road.

Gracie stirred in her arms, and Maggie tucked the outer blanket more snugly about her, covering her face to protect her from the wind.

"You're obviously upset, Jonathan. I want to know why."

Even then he didn't reply until she prompted him again. "Jonathan?"

"There's a letter from an attorney in Lexington." He paused. "Richard Barlow's attorney."

The name of Eva Grace's brutal husband set off an alarm bell in Maggie. "Richard's attorney? What does he want?"

She watched Jonathan's throat work as he swallowed. "Barlow is making plans to come for Gracie. The attorney didn't say exactly when, just that Barlow intends to claim his daughter."

"No!" A wave of anger surged in Maggie. She put a hand to his arm. "He can't do that! He can't take Gracie, can he? After everything Richard did to Evie?"

In reply, he merely shook his head.

"Jonathan, there wasn't a word from him after Evie died. Nothing! And he was notified. Your father saw to it, remember? He said that legally Richard had to be told about Eva's death and Gracie's birth. Yet he never contacted us, not once."

"Still, we knew this could happen."

"No! I thought when we didn't hear from him...I thought we *wouldn't* hear. Oh, I can't believe I was that naive."

"I should have prepared you better. I'm sorry, Maggie."

"It's not *your* fault," Maggie said. "I should have known he wouldn't just walk away."

"Gracie *is* his daughter, Maggie."

"And Evie was his wife," Maggie shot back. "But that didn't stop him from beating her half to death. Jonathan, what are we going to do? We can't let him take Gracie! You know what he did to Evie. There's no telling what he'd do to a defenseless baby."

"Maggie, listen to me—"

But Maggie was beyond listening. In truth, Jonathan's calm was beginning to irritate her. This was no time to be calm, no time to be reasonable. Somehow they had to stop Richard Barlow. They *had* to!

"As soon as we get Gracie home," Jonathan said, "I'll go back to the company store and call my father. We have to make certain this is handled in exactly the right way—legally. He'll know what to do, Maggie. Try not to worry. He'll take care of it."

"But your father—he's not well, Jonathan."

"Don't forget that I talked to him when we were in Lexington. He promised that his senior partner, Jeff Prescott, would investigate Barlow. We'll be in good hands with Jeff. Don't worry."

How could she *not* worry? "We can't let Richard near Gracie. I wouldn't put it past him to take her from us for sheer spite. You can't imagine what he's like. He's an awful man!"

He turned to her again. "Maggie, no one is going to take Gracie away from us. *No one!* I trust my father, and if he trusts Jeff Prescott, so do I. Besides, there's nothing you and I can do. We have to let Jeff and my father handle this." He paused and then added, "And they *will* handle it."

Maggie wished she felt as convinced as he sounded.

"One other thing, sweetheart—"

Maggie's mind was racing, her thoughts so scrambled she didn't answer him.

"Maggie?"

She looked at him.

"I don't think we should tell your parents about this. Your mother's not strong as it is, and Matthew—well, you know how he'll be."

At first Maggie agreed with him. But then a new thought set off another wave of panic. "How can we *not* tell them? Gracie is alone with Mum through the day while we're at school. Oh, Jonathan, what are we going to do? We don't dare leave them by themselves with no one else at the house!"

He turned toward her, and Maggie saw her own fear reflected in his eyes.

❧·❦

After he called Lexington and started home, Jonathan tried to think if there was anything more he could do. Had it not been for the obvious need to provide Maggie and the baby with some sort of around-the-clock protection, he might have felt a little less troubled after talking with his father. Jeff Prescott had unearthed some decidedly unsavory information about Barlow. Those findings, combined with the evidence of the beatings he'd inflicted on Eva Grace—documented by not only Maggie and her mother, but by Dr. Sally Gordon as well—should be enough to make any court refuse the man custody of Gracie.

His father had assured him that Jeff would seek a restraining order against Barlow right away to keep him away from Gracie, and they would proceed from there to build a case against his gaining custody.

But Jonathan wasn't totally ignorant of how fickle the law could be. With Eva Grace deceased, there were only three people who had witnessed the evidence of Barlow's mistreatment: three women, of whom two were family members and could only be expected to support Eva Grace's account of Barlow's beatings. Just how seriously a judge would consider the evidence against Gracie's natural father was anyone's guess.

For the first time since he'd settled in Skingle Creek years before, Jonathan felt the remoteness and isolation of their small community. In Lexington he would have been able to work closely with his father and Jeff Prescott in building a case against Richard Barlow. He could have also arranged some manner of protection for Gracie until this entire ugly business was settled. As it was, he could stay in contact only by the occasional telephone call or letter, and there was really no one he could count on to provide an extra measure of security for Gracie.

He found himself delaying his return home, wanting more than anything to have a solid plan in mind before facing Maggie. He understood her fear. Understood it and shared it. Even though he'd never met Barlow, Maggie's depiction of what had been done to her sister and her account of the day Barlow showed up and tried to take Eva Grace back to Lexington with him had been enough to convince him that they were dealing with a vicious, perhaps mentally disturbed or at least conscienceless man. Indeed the information that Jeff had uncovered made it clear that Barlow was not only abusive, but corrupt as well.

How in the world did such a man convince his business associates—including his pastor and local congregation—that he was an upstanding Christian and an exemplary husband? For that matter, how had he managed to win over a young woman as astute as Eva Grace and convince her he was worthy of her love?

It was growing dark, and the temperature had dropped considerably over the past couple of hours. But the chill that gripped Jonathan had nothing to do with the cold of the winter's night. He couldn't shake his memories of Maggie's tragic sister. From child to young woman, Eva Grace had been lovely, bright, and full of promise, yet she had ended up destroyed by the very one who had once vowed to honor and cherish her.

How can one human being do this to another, Lord? What kind of darkness twists the heart of a man like Richard Barlow to the extent that he would wreak such betrayal, such savagery, on his own wife?

Maggie was right. If Barlow was capable of doing what he'd done to Eva Grace, there was no telling what he might do to a defenseless infant…to Gracie.

Shaken and now possessed by an urgency to get home, Jonathan snapped the reins. He hated feeling helpless, being powerless to provide Maggie and his child—yes, his *child,* for Gracie had become just that—protection from the malevolence of the likes of Richard Barlow. For now, however, the reality was that all he could do was stay as close to his family as possible while leaving any real solution to their dilemma up to his father and Jeff.

Please, God, let them find that solution soon.

Chapter Fifteen

A Blast from the Mine Whistle

Wherever man oppresses man
Beneath the liberal sun,
O Lord, be there, Thine arm made bare,
Thy righteous will be done!

John Hay

⟶

Maggie's mother always said that troubles seldom travel alone but usually arrive in the company of others.

These days Maggie was finding Mum's wisdom bitterly true. Only three days after they received the letter from Richard Barlow's attorney, her brother, Ray, learned that soon he would be without the weekend job he prized so highly at the Taggart farm. Their cousin, Jeff, had decided to sell out and move to Indiana.

Ray's disappointment and discouragement were palpable. As bad as Maggie felt for her brother, though, what came next, on the following Monday, was a harder blow still.

As was always the case when the mine whistle sounded in the middle of the day, most of the town came to a halt. Maggie and Jonathan were in their respective classrooms when they heard the blast early that afternoon. Maggie froze for a moment and then went to the open door of her room and looked out. Jonathan was already crossing the hall on his way to her.

He took one quick look at her face and said, "I'll have Carolyn take your students. Go ahead."

Maggie ran the entire way. Her da was in that mine. Da and their friends and neighbors. Indeed, most of the men from town were below ground, at the mercy of the mountain from which they dug out a living. With the whistle piercing her heart like jagged glass, she ran as fast and as hard as she could until she reached the pithead, where a crowd made up almost entirely of women, except for a few retired miners and town businessmen, were already gathered, clamoring for news.

She looked around for her mother, half expecting to see her standing there with Gracie bundled in her arms, but as yet there was no sign of her.

❖·❖

At any other time Kate MacAuley would have been one of the first women at the pithead. But with Gracie down for her afternoon nap and the day so cold and raw, she steeled herself to wait at home for any news. Oh, how she hated the dread sound of that whistle when it went off without warning. In all their years in Skingle Creek, she had been through too many explosions, had seen her husband carried out under a blanket, or watched him stumble from a cage, his eyes burning and his body hunched with pain.

Outside, Figaro alternated between howling at the mine whistle and barking at the folks who pounded down the road, headed for the mine. Kate called the big dog inside, as much for his company as to quiet him. With wee Gracie asleep, the house was too still entirely. She needed some normal noise about her, something other than the sound of the whistle and the shouts of those running by the house.

With the dog bounding ahead of her, she went upstairs where she could stand at the window of their bedroom and look toward the mountain. She couldn't see the mine itself from there, but perhaps she could pray with a clearer head if she were looking in the direction of the trouble.

❧·❧

The February wind was raw with heavy, gun-metal clouds that hinted of evening rather than early afternoon. Maggie stood waiting, her heart banging against her chest, her mind frozen in this instant, in this place.

Nearly every face in the crowd was known to her, and the low voices murmuring, along with an occasional choked cry, were familiar as well. All at once she caught a whiff of smoke and went rigid. Nothing sparked terror in a miner's heart or that of a family member faster than the word coming down that there was "fire in the hole." What with the constant presence of "black damp"—the deadly, invisible gas that was only one of the dangers in a coal mine—and the kegs of dynamite stored behind wooden doors, a fire might trigger explosions and deadly infernos that could rage out of control in a matter of minutes.

The women's voices were growing louder now, some of them shrill. The questions circulating among the crowd were the same ones heard over and over again: "What happened? Does anyone know what happened?"

Maggie whirled in surprise when she saw Ray threading his way through the crowd. Nearly a head taller than most of the women, he came to stand beside her.

"Ray?"

"Mr. Stuart—Jonathan—said I could come." He gave her a long, steady look. "He's my da too, Mags."

Maggie nodded and squeezed his hand. "I'm glad you're here," she said.

"What about Mum? Have you seen her?"

"No, but she might not come, not with Gracie."

"Have you heard anything?" he asked.

"Nothing. But there's smoke."

A muscle beside his mouth jerked, and Maggie tried to reassure him. "Not much. It's scarcely noticeable."

He lifted his face. "I smell it too."

With an uncharacteristic protectiveness, he put a hand to Maggie's shoulder. "It'll be all right. It must not be too bad, or we'd have heard something by now."

This small act, so unexpected and yet so indicative of her brother's new maturity, warmed Maggie's heart. And how odd it was looking up at her "little brother," who by now was nearly as tall as their father, if not yet as thickly muscled. Studying him, in that moment she saw something else that hinted of Matthew MacAuley. Nearly obscured by the strong jawline and increasingly handsome features, a watchful calm spoke of the man waiting to be discovered by this youth poised on the precipice between his boyhood and the future.

Maggie couldn't shake the image that both intrigued her and saddened her. Ten years his senior, to this day she often thought of Ray as "Baby Ray." Her "little brother." Now it seemed that he was almost a man grown, and she had missed so many of those years along the way. Yet how connected they all were as a family. Her mother and father, Ray, Nell Frances, and herself...and Eva Grace, still a special part of the blood and the love that bound them together.

She couldn't think about Eva Grace, not now. She turned her attention back to the mine as she waited and prayed for the appearance of her father, the one who risked his life day after day, year after year, in the darkness under the mountain, sacrificing his safety and his health in an effort to protect his *family's* health and safety.

Maggie's blood flamed at the thought of the unsafe working conditions the miners faced...and had faced for as long as she could remember. Although he never said much in front of them when they were children, of late Da was more open about the uncaring mine owners—"the men in their mansions, sitting on their money"—who refused to even consider making the improvements and repairs necessary to keep the miners safe.

When her mother would point to the increasing drive toward a union and what it could mean to the men, Da was quick to warn that, as much as he was willing to work for a union in Skingle Creek, it would not come without a hard price to pay. "In a number of places, men have had to die before the union ever saw the light of day. There's no reason to think it will be any different here."

Her mother had never made any secret of the fact that she would give almost anything to see their father out of the mine. "Your da pokes fun at me for believing it could happen," she would say. "But it *can* happen. I know it can. I've prayed for years that the Lord would give him something better—something *safe*. And I'll not stop praying until it happens. It's so hard to see him leave the house every morning and know he's going to a place where he's never safe, where he's always at risk."

Sometimes they forgot why he did what he did, why he was willing to work in such treacherous conditions, constantly placing his life in jeopardy.

God forgive them, they sometimes took him for granted.

Please, Lord, bring him safely out of that mine again. Bring him back to Mum and all the rest of us. And if You will, please answer my mother's prayer. Give Da a better place, a safer place to work. For both their sakes, Lord—for those of us who love him more than he'll ever know—please answer Mum's prayer.

❖•❖

Kate stood at the window, the great hound at her side. She was aware of the way he watched her, glancing back and forth from where Gracie lay sleeping in the little bed Matthew had fashioned from some smoothly sanded sideboards and a mattress filled with soft scraps of flannel. Occasionally the big dog whimpered like a pup, as if he sensed the danger in the air.

Kate felt like whimpering too. Fear froze her in the moment, closing off her sense of hearing and sight, leaving her unable to function. How many times had she waited like this? Not here, not in the warmth of her own home, but at the opening jaws of the mine that at any hour of the day could steal her husband from her in a dozen different ways. How many prayers had she uttered for his safekeeping, for his *life*? How many more times would she go through this same soul-numbing vigil, this insane death watch that almost certainly could be avoided if only the right people cared enough to *fix* what was wrong with the mines.

She couldn't stand here any longer…she *couldn't*. Whipping around she went to the baby bed and gently scooped up Gracie. After bundling the baby in multiple layers of outerwear and blankets, she grabbed her own coat, and, telling Figaro to stay, hurried from the house.

❖·❖

"There's Mum," Maggie said to Ray, watching her mother make her way through the crowd on the other side of the pithead as she hurried toward them with Gracie against her shoulder.

Kate was obviously out of breath when she reached them. "What's happened? Have you heard?"

"Nothing yet," said Maggie, noting her mother's ashen skin and the tremble of her lower lip. "But we've been here only a few minutes."

"Ray?" Their mother frowned when she saw him. "Why aren't you in school?"

Ray's reply was to cross in front of Maggie, pull back the blanket to grin at Gracie, and touch a finger to her nose.

"I'll take her, Mum," Maggie said, reaching for Gracie.

But Ray had already lifted the baby from his mother's arms. Holding Gracie against his shoulder, he patted her gently on the back. "Jonathan said I could come," he finally replied.

Not for the first time, Maggie was struck by her teenaged brother's unusual tenderness with Gracie. None of the boys she remembered from her own teen years, with the possible exception of Kenny, would have given a baby a second glance, much less the unabashed affection Ray lavished on his tiny niece.

The sound of three bells, a signal to hoist the cage, brought silence to the waiting crowd. "Someone's coming up," Maggie's mother said quietly. "That's good."

Maggie held her breath. At the first sign of the miners emerging from the cage, she pushed forward as far as she could, only to see that her da wasn't among the other men. She turned to look at her mother, whose taut expression had tightened still more as she searched for her husband and didn't find him.

The men who did come up were immediately besieged by the crowd and plied with questions. "What happened? Is anyone hurt? How many? Is there a fire? An explosion? How bad is it?"

Maggie took the baby from Ray and gave him a meaningful look. "Why don't you go see what you can find out for Mum?" she said.

He nodded and wedged his way through the crowd toward the miners who had emerged from the cage.

A moment later he stepped back a little to make room for Judson Tallman, who pushed through the waiting family members and began to question the miners.

Gracie had been so quiet that Maggie was surprised when she parted her blankets and saw that she was wide awake. She dropped a kiss on her nose, and the baby wriggled and waved her tiny fists. "You're such a good girl," she murmured, kissing her again.

Her arms trembled as she held the baby against her heart. Her throat felt swollen with fear. There was no getting used to these mine alarms, though there was nothing new about them. She couldn't count the scares she'd had while growing up. More times than not, her da had walked out entirely unscathed.

But not always.

It wasn't only her father she feared for. She had neighbors, family friends, and former schoolmates in the bowels of that mountain.

The people of Skingle Creek were so connected to each other that what affected one family affected them all.

Tallman turned toward the crowd just then, raising his hands to get their attention. Not a tall man, he nevertheless emanated a sense of strength and authority with his powerful shoulders and heavy, low-set brows over dark eyes.

"All right, folks. Here's what we know. There was a bump, but not a bad one. So far as we can tell, nobody's badly hurt. A couple of men with some sprains and bruises maybe. There was a small fire, but it's already out. We'll be bringing all the men up, a few at a time, and we'll know more then. Now move back apiece and give them room."

"A bump" was what the miners called it when a pillar exploded. With tons of rock resting on them, if the energy wasn't concentrated exactly as it needed to be, the pillars could explode. One of the worst fires at the mine had happened from a bad bump that occurred when Maggie was still a baby. Her father still had a burn scar on his back from that explosion.

Another cage came up just then, but as they watched the men step out, there was still no sign of Matthew MacAuley. At the same time a murmur passed through the crowd as Dr. Sally Gordon pulled up in her buggy a few feet away and stepped out, her medical case in hand.

"What's Dr. Gordon doing here?" her mother asked. "Where's Dr. Woodbridge?"

Mary Sheehy, standing close by, turned and answered. "He and his wife went to Pittsburgh last week to visit their daughter and her family. My man said they won't be back until the end of the month."

The doctor nodded to Maggie and Kate as she passed by but hurried on to the pithead.

"Those men aren't going to let a woman doctor lay a hand on them."

Maggie put a hand on her arm. "Mum, if they're hurt—"

"Then they'll just be hurt. And you know good and well your

da is no exception." Maggie *did* know and prayed that Da wouldn't need a doctor's attention—that *none* of the men would, for that matter.

Poor Dr. Gordon. Maggie hated to see her feelings hurt, but these men were so stubborn they'd limp off like injured dogs before they'd let a woman doctor help them.

Ray had made his way back to them and now to his mother. "Mum, don't be scared now, it's not bad. But Terry Maguire said Da is hurt some."

Kate MacAuley closed her eyes in resignation. "Hurt *how?*"

"He wasn't sure. But he said Da wouldn't come up until all the other men were out."

Maggie watched her mother's mouth go hard, her eyes flare. "He can be *such* a fool! He thinks he's a daddy to them all."

"It's just his way, Mum," said Maggie, trying to soothe her. "You know how he is about his men."

"Oh, I know how he is all right! Never mind that he'll be the death of me yet for worrying about him, thanks to his devilish stubbornness. I should just go on home and leave him on his own."

As if she would. Maggie had heard this kind of tirade before when her mother was vexed. She knew it was simply her way of blowing off steam to keep from flying apart.

"If the man would ever…just once…think of himself first." Her mother's grumbling was barely audible. "Just once. But no, he's got to be the hero, always the one who stays."

Another cage came up just then, and this time Matthew MacAuley was in it.

Her anger clearly forgotten, Kate broke through the lines, ignoring the deputy and two of the mine bosses who had been stationed at the edge of the crowd to keep control.

Maggie had to crane her neck to see past the wide shoulders and considerable height of Sheila O'Brien directly in front of her, but she caught a clear enough glimpse of her father stepping out of the cage, his right arm hanging limply and crookedly at his side.

Chapter Sixteen

In Need of a Helping Hand

He cannot heal who has not suffered much,
For only Sorrow sorrow understands;
They will not come for healing at our touch
Who have not seen the scars upon our hands.

Edwin McNeill Poteat

The pain knifing up Matthew's arm was an agony, but not so great that he didn't see his wife making her way toward him, as well as two of his children watching him from the crowd. He felt as though he might pass out at any instant, but that would rattle Kate something fierce. And hadn't the woman already suffered enough misery on his behalf? So he ground his teeth and steeled himself to stay upright. He even tried to manage a smile for his wife's benefit. Then Ray and Maggie, wee Gracie in her arms, made a move as if to come to him and he sighed, preparing to be fussed over when what he needed more than anything was a pain powder and a long hot bath.

Another glance closer up and he saw the tall form of Dr. Gordon making her way through the crowd, her broad features set in resolve, her long, silver-streaked hair blowing in the wind. Clearly a woman on a mission.

Matthew had no quarrel with Dr. Sally Gordon. Hadn't she worn herself out spending nearly the entire day—Eva Grace's last day—doing all she could do to save the girl, and then, when her passing couldn't be avoided, seeing her through to the end?

No, he had no ax to grind with the woman doctor, other than the fact that she *was* a woman doctor. And in spite of the fact that not a miner on the grounds was about to let her touch him, here she came, clearly thinking to ply her trade with the lot of them. Where was their own doctor anyway? Woodbridge might be little more than a hack, but at least he was a *man*.

The darkness came at him with a rush then, the blood racing to his head like a river overflowing its banks. The ground swelled up to meet him, blackness engulfed him, and the last thing he saw was Kate running toward him, calling his name.

❧·❦

Maggie saw her father go down, her mother run toward him, followed by Dr. Gordon. She stopped, putting a hand to her brother's arm to restrain him. She wanted to go to her parents, but she had Gracie in her arms. The smell of smoke was stronger here. In spite of Tallman's assurances, there was no telling what might be going on inside the mine. Any member of a miner's family knew that even a small explosion could be dangerous. It would be foolhardy to expose the baby to that kind of risk.

Yet seeing Da on the ground, her mother on her knees beside him as the doctor threaded her way through the crowd, she had all she could do to stay put.

Ray stepped out again, and once more Maggie caught his arm.

"We'd best stay here," she said. "Dr. Gordon needs room to tend to him."

Her brother frowned, looking from her to their father. "Ma might need help."

Maggie shook her head. "Only the doctor can help, Ray. There's nothing we can do."

When he still looked doubtful, she pressed, "We'll only be in the way. Let's wait."

He looked from her to their parents, drew a long breath, and shoved his hands into his pockets and stood waiting.

❖·❖

Matthew MacAuley felt himself swimming up from the bottom of a dark, cold river. Something—driftwood? stones?—weighted his arms, especially his right arm, making it difficult to thrash his way through the water. Pain knifed through his shoulders and up the back of his neck. His head pounded as if someone were pummeling him with one blow after another. And he was cold, bone-freezing cold.

When he finally reached the surface, he gasped for air, choked, then filled his lungs again and opened his eyes. Kate was on her knees, watching him, while Dr. Gordon perched at his other side, holding a vial of some strong-smelling stuff to his nostrils.

"Ah, you're back," said the doctor. "Good. We'll get you in the buggy and take you to my office."

Dazed, Matthew watched the woman doctor. She seemed to be speaking from a tunnel or the far side of a cave.

"Home," Matthew said, struggling past a swollen throat and thick tongue. "Take me home."

"Your arm is broken, Mr. MacAuley. I'll need to set it, and I'm not going to do it here on this cold ground in the wind."

"Not...broken."

"Oh, but it is."

"Where's...Doc Woodbridge?"

"My understanding is that he's in Pittsburgh visiting family."

Gradually Matthew became aware of the other miners gathered around them. "See to the other men," he said. "If they'll let you."

"The other men don't need seeing to," she said shortly. "The foreman said no one was badly hurt but you. Why is that, I wonder. What happened, Mr. MacAuley?"

Matthew meant to shrug, but the slight movement made him catch his breath with pain. "Just a bump," he muttered. "Nothing much."

"Then how did you break your arm?"

"It's not broken, I tell you. Just sprained."

The doctor sighed. "I have a medical degree, Mr. MacAuley, and in spite of your poor opinion of me, I know a broken arm when I see one." She stopped. "I need two of you men to get him into my buggy so I can take him back to my office. Now, please!"

Matthew's eyes wouldn't focus quite yet, but he saw well enough the look that passed between Zeb Yorkey and Pat Callahan. Neither man made a move.

Matthew turned to look at his wife. "Get someone to take me home, Kate."

The doctor interrupted before Kate could reply. "I can set your arm at your house if that's what you want, Mr. MacAuley. But you'd be better off at my office. I have everything I need there, including something to dull the pain."

"I don't drink spirits," Matthew growled. "Curse of my people."

Dr. Gordon's lip curled. "I was referring to laudanum."

"Kate—"

But for one of the few times in their married life, Kate paid him no heed. Getting to her feet, she faced Yorkey and Callahan. "Would you men please help my husband into the doctor's buggy? I'd appreciate it," she said.

The two men quickly replaced their caps, and with a furtive glance at Matthew, moved in on him, supporting him on each side to help him up.

So shot with pain and so weak that even anger wouldn't rise

in him, Matthew couldn't quite manage a glare in Kate's direction. When she continued to ignore him, he drew an exaggerated sigh and, with the help of Yorkey and Callahan, limped away from the crowd toward the doctor's buggy.

Chapter Seventeen

The Proud and the Proud

I was too ambitious in my deed,
And thought to distance all men in success,
Till God came on me, marked the place, and said,
"Ill-doer, henceforth keep within this line,
Attempting less than others"—and I stand
And work among Christ's little ones, content.

Elizabeth Barrett Browning

Kate resented Matthew's insistence that she stay in the waiting room while Dr. Gordon set his arm. Any other time he'd want her with him, but heaven forbid she might see a sign of weakness in him. Ah, no, of course not. He could be so insufferably proud at times. Proud and stubborn. He knew very well she wanted to stay with him in the examining room, but rather than allow her to see his pain up close, he banished her to the other side of the wall.

Well, she'd tell him soon enough what she thought of his foolishness. Once he was feeling better, she'd give him an earful all right.

And Dr. Gordon was no better. Telling her to make herself comfortable, that she'd take good care of her husband. Dr. Woodbridge had never shut her out when *he* tended to Matthew's injuries.

Make myself comfortable indeed!

Finally she paced, tracking from one side of the dimly lit examining room to the other, casting an approving eye on the obvious cleanliness and order of the place. The white curtains were crisply starched, the bench and chairs neatly painted, the floor swept. Even as miffed as she was, she had to admit that she would have been surprised if the doctor's office hadn't spoken of order and cleanliness. Dr. Gordon was that kind of a woman, Kate was sure of it.

From the examining room she could hear the low sounds of voices, mostly Matthew's, and she wondered how he was behaving. Surely he wouldn't insult the doctor, and her having been so kind to them throughout Eva Grace's confinement…and at the end.

Dr. Gordon had arrived early on the morning of their daughter's last day, had stayed and supported and comforted throughout the hours to help bring Gracie safely into the world, all the while fighting furiously to save Eva Grace's life. Clearly the doctor had been near the point of exhaustion herself by the end.

Kate would never forget how tears had tracked the physician's face when Eva Grace finally passed over. She had looked as sorrowful as if she'd lost a member of her own family. That day had given Kate—and hopefully Matthew as well—full and certain proof that Dr. Sally Gordon was not just a medical doctor with a strong professional conscience, but also was a good woman of great compassion.

This memory alone was enough to banish her pique with the doctor—if not with her husband.

Remember what she did for us, Matthew. What she did for our daughter…and mind your tongue. Mind it well.

❖·❖

"If you'll take the pain medication, Mr. MacAuley, this won't hurt as much."

Matthew shook his head. "I've had broken bones before. Just set it and be done with it."

The doctor shot him a look of uncertainty but proceeded. "How did it happen?"

Matthew shrugged and was again reminded that he had a broken arm. "A piece of slab fell when the pillar exploded. I pushed one of the men out of the way before it hit him, but my back went out at the same time, and I came down on my arm. I heard the bone break. I know the sound."

She nodded. "If you'll just remove your shirt, please."

Matthew felt blood rush to his face. He wanted nothing so much as to bolt from the room and out the door. All this fuss by a woman who wasn't even his wife. He reckoned he'd have been better off to let Kate come in with him.

She was watching him. "Your shirt, Mr. MacAuley. Here, let me help you."

Matthew fumbled at the buttons. "I'll do it." *Ach, this is mortifying.*

Yet when the shirt was off and she began to work on his arm, something about her quick, precise touch wasn't nearly as awkward as he'd expected. It was a lot like having Doc Woodbridge work on him. Except that Dr. Gordon didn't pinch or press as hard as the company doctor. Matthew always had thought Lebreen Woodbridge enjoyed his work a bit too much.

"We're in luck, Mr. MacAuley. It's only your upper arm that's affected."

What is this "we" business? There is nothing wrong with her arm, after all. And didn't he already know it was his upper arm where the bone had broke? He knew more about broken bones than he'd like to, and that was the truth.

"You won't need a cast. I'll just splint it, and you can use a sling."

"No cast?"

Did the woman really know what she was doing? Doc Woodbridge always used a cast with broken bones.

He didn't know whether to be worried or relieved. "Then I can work."

She lifted an eyebrow. "Well, *no*. Not for a few weeks. You'll have to give the bone time to heal."

"A few *weeks*? I can't lay off for weeks!"

She flipped a strand of spiraling silver hair out of her face. Matthew had never known a woman—especially one her age—to wear her hair hanging in such a way. How could she see what she was doing? Besides, it wasn't seemly. Not at all.

Of course, the doctor didn't have a husband. Or did she? He wondered if there was or had ever been a *Mister* Gordon. Probably not. What self-respecting man would marry himself to a woman who spent her days gallivanting around the countryside delivering babies and working on half-dressed men? He couldn't think of a man in Skingle Creek who would put up with that kind of brass.

"I have to work," he said flatly. "There's no way I can lay off for any length of time. I have a family to feed."

She was doing something across the room at a counter, her back turned toward him. "You won't do your family any favors by making yourself worse. I expect you're right-handed? I can tell you that if you want the full use of your arm back, you have to let it heal before you go back to work."

Before Matthew could manage a sharp retort, she said, "You've had your back broken too, haven't you? And your shoulder? Kate mentioned it to me."

She calls my wife Kate, not Mrs. MacAuley. When did the two of them get so chummy?

He swallowed. He knew when. Still, he didn't like it. Not that her impudence was likely to rub off on Kate. Kate was a lady. She knew how to behave.

"Aye, I've had some breaks," he said sullenly.

"And your knee as well?"

"That too. Doc Woodbridge said it was crushed pretty bad."

"I expect you live with a fair share of pain, given all that."

Oh, I have some pain, all right. That I do. Matthew said nothing.

She came back to him, continuing to talk as she worked. To Matthew's surprise, it was over within minutes—and with an unexpected minimum of pain.

"I'll send some pain medicine home with you. You'll probably need it, at least for the next couple of days. And have Kate help you put ice on the break every few hours," she said. "Keep the sling in place the rest of the time."

"I'll need you to sign me off," Matthew said, bearing more humiliation as she helped him on with his shirt. "But not for weeks, mind. A couple of days only."

She straightened, her expression stern. "Mr. MacAuley, a couple of days won't do. Besides, just how do you plan to work with a broken arm?"

Matthew started to lift his shoulder, but winced with the movement.

The doctor's expression softened a little, which for some unaccountable reason irritated Matthew.

"I *know* you have to work, Mr. MacAuley. I understand. But—"

"No offense, ma'am, but I doubt that."

She frowned.

"I doubt that you understand."

She studied him for a long moment. "I might understand more than you think I do."

Still perched on the end of the examining table, Matthew thought about that. "Why do you do it?"

His question seemed to puzzle her.

"Are jobs that scarce for lady doctors?"

To Matthew's surprise, she laughed. "Well, I'll be honest, Mr. MacAuley, we can't go pulling them off trees."

"That's the reason you came here then, to Skingle Creek? Because it was all you could find?"

She still looked amused. With a shake of her head, she replied, "No. I came here to get out of the city. And I wanted a private practice I could actually call my own. In Philadelphia I was subject to the whims of a few good old boys who allowed me only conditional hospital privileges."

She paused and then went on. "I was very proud when I was younger. Too proud. I thought I was such a fine physician I could overcome the best the male doctors had to offer. But I had to eat too, and for a long time the only patients who came my way were indigents. I helped as many as I could, but eventually I ran out of money."

"Well, I don't mean to be rude, ma'am, but you've picked a poor place to eke out a living. This is a dirt-poor town as it is. And miners are never going to take kindly to a woman tending to them. They're proud men."

"Yes, I've caught on to that," she said, her tone dry. "Let me be blunt, Mr. MacAuley. You might say I'm an independent sort. I wanted the freedom to practice medicine my way. When my husband died, I had no ties to the city, so I opted for a new start. It was time."

So she *had* been married. Matthew felt a bit sheepish at his earlier supposition that a woman like herself couldn't get a man. Yet some perverse streak turned his sheepishness to petulance. Her reasons seemed sound enough, but shouldn't she limit her doctoring to *women?*

"I have no illusions that the men will line up to fill my patient list. But not everyone in the county is male. I believe, in time, at least some of their wives and daughters will find their way to my door."

"I wouldn't count on it, ma'am," he said, his voice sounding more gruff than he'd intended. "The Company deducts from our wages to take care of our doctor bills, and everyone's used to Doc Woodbridge—though in truth, I don't hold him in such high regard."

She took her time answering. "Think about this. You know how awkward you feel, being a man and having to subject yourself to a woman doctor? Just having me set a broken bone was difficult for you. Well, what do you think it's like for a woman who has to depend on a man for all of her medical care—even her most *intimate* care? Do you know what often happens? Women simply don't see a doctor at all unless it's a matter of life or death, and sometimes not even then."

Matthew had no comeback for that. She had a valid point, and he knew it. More than once Kate had waited out a problem rather than subject herself to Lebreen Woodbridge. And Eva Grace had also been dead-set against going to Woodbridge.

"I'm a good doctor, Mr. MacAuley. If the people around here will give me a chance, I can help them. And I can help *you* if you'll let me."

Matthew shot her a look.

Saying nothing, she turned and went to the counter, opened a long, wide drawer beneath and pulled out an odd-looking contraption. She brought it back to him. "I believe this will help your back if you'll wear it."

Matthew didn't know what to make of the thing she was holding up in front of him. It looked...well, it looked just a little like a corset.

"It's a back brace," she told him. "I've seen the way you walk, and if I'm not mistaken, you're in constant pain. This will support your back, which will ease the pain. I wish you'd try it. Just wear it through the day, not at night. Oh, and one more thing."

Again she crossed the room, this time opening a door to the cabinet above the counter. When she came back to him, she had something in her hand that looked like a long, stiff sock, but with clamps on it. "Slip this over your knee when you're working or when you're going to be walking any distance. Use the clamps to secure it and keep it tight. It will help brace your knee and keep it straight."

"I don't have time to bother with such contraptions. Besides, I'm not in that bad of shape. Doc Woodbridge gives me medicine for the pain when I need it."

Something flared in her eyes. "What kind of medicine?"

"Well, I don't know what it is," Matthew grumbled. "Just pain powders."

"Does it help?"

Matthew didn't answer right away, but the bullish expression on the woman's face plainly said she was waiting for a reply.

"I only take it at night."

"And why is that?"

"Because it makes me too tired and sluggish to work, that's why! A miner can't be crawling around underground without all his wits."

Faith, and wasn't she a harridan!

"It's laudanum, isn't it?"

"I don't know exactly what it is. It might be that, aye. Are you done with me?"

"Take the braces, Mr. MacAuley," she said quietly. "At least try them. If you won't do it for yourself, then do it for your wife. She worries about you."

Now that was too much. She was overstepping her place. Matthew didn't know what to say, so he remained silent.

The doctor regarded him with a look that made him think she had something more to say. And so she did. "I wish you'd take the pain medicine I'm going to give you instead of the laudanum. You're not as likely to become dependent on it. And Mr. MacAuley? If you're concerned about paying me, you needn't be. You don't owe me anything for today."

It struck Matthew then that part of his resentment toward the woman might not be due entirely to her boldness. It might also have to do with the fact that they still owed her for taking care of Eva Grace. He was paying her, a bit at a time, but they were still in debt to her for more. But Evie had wanted her, so they'd gone along with her wishes. And now he'd be owing this woman for who knew how long a time.

"You'll be paid," he muttered. "It might take me a spell though."

"I said it's not necessary—"

"I pay my own way."

Again she studied him. "Yes, I know you do." She paused. "Well, you're set to go then," she said, her tone brisk. "I'll just write a note for you."

When she returned with a slip of paper, she handed it to him with a smile. "I expect Dr. Woodbridge will be back before you need to be seen again. But in case he's not, I hope you—or your family—will feel free to get in touch if necessary. And you do need to let me—or Dr. Woodbridge—check your arm in about ten days."

He stood and she continued to face him. "I'll make you a deal, Mr. MacAuley."

Matthew eyed her, suspicion adding to his aggravation. "What kind of a deal?"

"You wear the back brace and the knee support for six weeks. If they don't help, give them back and I'll not say a word. And I'll wipe the bill you're so intent on paying off my books. But if they *do* help, you'll put in a good word for me with some of the men and their families. Let them know they can trust me. Especially," she added with a faint smile, "the *women.*"

Matthew gave her a long, hard look. Without a word he reached behind him to retrieve the contraptions she'd left on the examining table.

"I'll think on it, ma'am," he said, crossing to the door.

"Mr. MacAuley?"

Matthew stopped and turned. "Aye?"

"Please don't call me 'ma'am.'"

Again Matthew turned, making a supreme effort not to drag his bad leg as he started for the door.

Chapter Eighteen

Changes of the Heart

The innocent and the beautiful
Have no enemy but time.

W.B. Yeats

～

It was hard to watch a man like her husband suffer idleness. Matthew had never known the meaning of the word except for those times when he'd been injured. Even then he'd always done his best to keep busy.

Kate had always counted herself blessed to be the wife of a man who hadn't a slothful bone in his body. All she had to do was look about her home, which at one time had been a typical coal company camp house, and she was reminded to give thanks for her man.

While other less fortunate families shivered and grew ill through the raw winters, Matthew saw to it that their hastily, inexpensively built house was insulated with weather boarding. The only drafts in the MacAuley house rose from the thin floors, which even Matthew hadn't been able to do much about. The windows were few and poorly fitted, but he filled the cracks with putty each year. In the worst of winters he tacked cardboard or oilcloth over them to keep in as much heat as possible. Knotholes and cracks were filled nearly as soon as they appeared, and Kate prided herself on being married to one of the few men in Skingle Creek who allowed not a single leak in the roof to go unattended longer than necessary.

Thanks to Matthew, their home was warmer and dryer than most. Indeed, Kate was convinced that her husband's industriousness was one of the primary reasons their children stayed as healthy as they did, even in the harshest of weather. Her husband was the kind of man who brooked no laziness, not from himself or from his family. So finding himself in a position where he was useless at the mine and could do only minor chores about the house gnawed at him like a starving wolf.

The only thing that helped take some of the bite out of this particular turn of idleness was the fact that he still had the use of one good arm—and the presence of wee Gracie. As the only one of their grandchildren they'd ever had close by, and because of the loss of Eva Grace, the baby was doubly dear to them.

Finally they experienced first-hand the joy of being grandparents. Although he liked to tease Kate that she would spoil their infant granddaughter, to Kate's way of thinking Matthew was doing a far more thorough job of it than she ever could.

Early Friday afternoon, a few days after the explosion at the mine, she stood at the doorway of the front room, watching her husband with Gracie. Matthew was entirely unaware of her scrutiny as he cradled the babe in the crook of his good arm, bracing her bottle with his broken one as he fed her. Every now and again Gracie would stop tugging at the nipple and simply go still, studying him as if she found him the most intriguing sight ever. As for Matthew, he wore a smile that could crack his face in half.

Next week things would go back to a more normal routine again. Judson Tallman, the mine superintendent, had assigned Matthew to the temporary job of cleaning and counting tools and equipment, as well as other tasks he could perform with one good arm. At least it would keep some pay coming in, if not as much as he made working the coal.

Savoring the sweetness of this moment, Kate watched them for a long time. It was a bittersweet scene, one that reminded her of the days of Eva Grace's infancy. Her eyes stung with the memory. Gracie's golden hair, Matthew's tenderness as he studied her—it didn't seem that long ago that he had held their firstborn daughter just like this. Now it was the daughter of their firstborn who captured his attention.

Matthew had never been a man to shirk his role in caring for their babes, as was the case with some of the other husbands in town. He had seemed to enjoy tending to the children when they were tiny, even changing their diapers when necessary.

Kate had watched him with Eva Grace often enough to realize that he treasured those intimate hours with his tiny daughter. Indeed, the children's infant years were the only time he allowed himself to be softhearted and playful with them. As they grew older, he gradually turned most of their care over to Kate. Once they were of school age, he found it difficult to be easy with them, to be...*soft* with them. Consequently, she used to worry that the girls and Ray might grow up without knowing how much their father really loved them.

Somehow, though, they knew. Even Ray, despite his tendency to test his father's patience in the worst way, seemed to know he was loved—and loved deeply. Kate had seen it every now and then in the expression that would cross the boy's face when Matthew paid him an unexpected bit of praise for a job well done or slung an arm around his shoulder as they headed off to the woods on a hunting expedition.

Perhaps she shouldn't enjoy it so much, but she loved having Matthew at home. Not only was he company for her, but she felt... safer. What with Richard Barlow's threat to claim Gracie constantly hanging over them and the fear that he might show up at any time, she scarcely drew a deep breath these days. But with Matthew in the house, she didn't worry quite as much. Even with a broken arm and a lame leg, he was a stronger, brawnier man than most. Eva Grace's awful husband would find himself faced with a formidable opponent should he try to take wee Gracie away from them.

As if sensing her scrutiny, Matthew turned to look. "Does she always take it all?" he asked, indicating the empty bottle.

"She does," Kate said, walking over to the rocking chair to stand beside them. "Indeed, there are times when I believe she'd actually take another if I'd give it to her."

Matthew turned back to the baby. "No wonder you're such a pudding of a girl."

"And didn't you always say there would be no skinny babes at the MacAuley house?"

He chuckled. "I did, didn't I? Well, there's no worry about that with this one." He studied the babe in his arms, who regarded him right back just as intently. "She's a pretty wee thing, isn't she?"

"Like her mother," Kate said, thinking back to a different time.

"Aye, like her mother," Matthew said softly, and Kate knew that he too was remembering.

❖•❖

Jonathan loved his work. He was altogether convinced that the teaching profession brought him more fulfillment, a greater sense of accomplishment, and a more contented life than world renown or great riches ever could have. Nevertheless, he was glad it was Friday.

That hadn't always been the case. Before he and Maggie were married, he'd often dreaded the final school day of the week. In fact, some weekends he'd actually suffered a mild case of depression. Coming home to an empty house at the end of the week had been a source of discontent and restlessness. Those Fridays when he was without plans for dinner with friends or a social event at the church, he'd had to fight against an encroaching loneliness.

He hadn't remained a bachelor so long by choice. He simply

hadn't fallen in love. Well, once, when he'd still been little more than a boy. But she'd gone away to Europe and met someone else, ending their engagement. For years there had been no one else. Yet the never-quite-relinquished longing for a home and family created in him a reluctance to face the weekends when families normally did things together.

How long had he yearned for someone to be *together* with?

And then Maggie had come back to Skingle Creek. Maggie, his former student, later his friend, and at last the love of his life. Now he welcomed each Friday as the time of dismissal approached for the promise of time to be with his family.

And Maggie's parents, of course. They almost always got together with Matthew and Kate on weekends, at least for a few hours. Both he and Maggie were keenly aware that her folks faced their own kind of loneliness these days. With Ray almost grown and choosing to spend time with his friends when he wasn't working, and with Eva Grace no longer with them, surely the weekends must be difficult for them as well.

Jonathan hadn't missed the shadow that fell across Kate's face when he and Maggie bundled up Gracie and left for home on Friday evenings. Except for Matthew needing his wages from the mine, it was most likely good for Kate to have him home these days.

Although he hadn't mentioned it to Maggie, Jonathan had also felt relief the past few days, knowing that Matthew was there with Kate and Gracie. It bothered him that *he* couldn't be with Gracie all the time, given the fact that Barlow had threatened to come for her at some point. He consoled himself with the fact that, even with a broken arm, his father-in-law could be an intimidating man. Barlow would find more than he'd bargained for if he came looking for Gracie and found Matthew standing in the gap.

Jonathan looked up from his desk to see Maggie marching two of the six Conibear children—"the Conibear rascals" as she called them in private—into his office. The duo she had in tow were the twins, Willy and Billy. These all too frequent visitors to his office were the youngest of the tribe. Jonathan had the next three in age in his class. The oldest of the six, Jerome, was no longer a student, having left school for the mine at age fifteen.

There had never been a Conibear who didn't cause trouble in or out of class, and seldom did any one of them act alone. What with five of them still in school, Jonathan's—and now Maggie's—patience was tested on an almost daily basis.

Part of his mind registered the fact that Maggie looked particularly fetching today with her starched white shirtwaist and green silk ribbon tied in a neat bow around her neck. The bun at the nape of her neck, as was more often than not the case, had failed to securely anchor her heavy hair. A few curls slipped free in places, giving her the look of a slightly carefree schoolgirl.

He stood as they entered, his eyes meeting his wife's just long enough to note the blend of exasperation and grudging amusement in her expression.

"Billy and Willy have something to tell you, Mr. Stuart," she said, her tone impressively stern.

Jonathan clasped his hands behind his back and waited. *What this time?*

"What's going on, boys?" he asked.

They sneaked a look at each other. Willy grinned and Billy bit his lower lip as if to restrain himself. They somehow managed to lift a hand in unison and swipe a dark shock of hair off their foreheads, which promptly fell forward over their eyes.

"Billy?"

The six-year-old's face flamed. He opened his mouth as if to speak and then thought better of it.

In the meantime, Willy peered at Jonathan from under the hair falling over his eyes. Jonathan lifted an eyebrow, and the boy stopped grinning.

"It seems that neither wants to speak first, Mrs. Stuart," Jonathan said. "Why don't you fill me in on the situation?"

Maggie sighed. "They put a toad in Livvie Ferguson's desk and made her cry."

The two boys shot a self-satisfied look at each other and then at Jonathan, who had all he could do to swallow down a wave of hilarity.

The last thing he needed, however, was to have them thinking he was amused by their behavior. He straightened to his full height and donned his most severe frown.

"Why would you boys do such a thing? Surely you knew you'd frighten Livvie."

They looked down at the floor. In unison, of course.

"Well?" Jonathan said. "I'm waiting for an answer, boys."

He saw Willy poke his brother in the back, and as if a button had been pushed, Billy poured out a stream of words that added up to a pathetically lame excuse. "We was just funnin' her. We din't mean no harm. We wanted to see her jump, that's all."

Beside him, Willy snickered. "And she *did* jump too."

Jonathan darkened his expression still more and deepened his voice to a rumble. He *must* not look at Maggie. "You find it amusing to frighten a schoolmate?"

The two boys again stole a glance at each other, their expressions sobering.

"No, sir," said Willy.

"No, sir," said Billy.

"I should hope not," Jonathan said, settling what he meant to be an intimidating look on first one and then the other. "Well, boys, you've had your fun. Now you're going to have to face the consequences."

Willy turned red, while his brother went pale.

"Mrs. Stuart," said Jonathan, not quite meeting Maggie's gaze, "you'd best go back to your class. The boys can stay here with me for the next several minutes while we consider a proper punishment for their behavior."

In what Jonathan knew to be a deliberate ploy to make him meet her eyes, Maggie made no move to leave.

Finally Jonathan donned the face that his wife referred to as his "stuffed-shirt schoolmaster expression" and looked at her full on. Her eyes danced and her mouth quirked, but he thought he withstood her mischief fairly well.

She went back to her class then, leaving Jonathan to deal with the twins.

He watched her go, more eager than ever for the sound of the dismissal bell.

A mutual throat clearing reminded him of his mischievous young charges, and he turned his attention to the two scamps eyeing him across the desk.

❧•❧

Back at her desk in her classroom, Maggie admitted to herself that she loved Fridays. In fact, she looked forward to them so much that she wondered if she ought to feel guilty. She enjoyed being a teacher. She loved her students and loved everything about the school: the smell of chalk and schoolbooks, the sight of little girls in pigtails and pinafores, even ornery little boys like the Conibear twins, who couldn't behave more than half an hour at a time, if that.

Lately though she welcomed the end of the school week more and more. Too often she found herself thinking about the weekend when it *wasn't* Friday. It unsettled her, this preoccupation with the weekend, and she wondered if her earlier love and passion for teaching might be on the wane.

The truth was, she was beginning to not mind so much the fact that after March she would no longer be teaching. She hadn't admitted this to Jonathan because she hated the thought that he might be disappointed in her. He made no secret of the fact that he was loath to even think of the time when she'd no longer be with him at the school every day. How would he feel if he learned she was beginning to look forward to the very thing he dreaded?

Her emotions were at war with one another. Although she wasn't all that comfortable—at least not yet—with the idea of giving up teaching entirely, the reality was that she wanted to be at home with Gracie. On the other hand, she had to question how content she would be staying at home all day after so many years of being

away, first at college and then in the classroom. She thought she'd
still like to teach in some capacity—but not full-time.

She didn't want to cause any inconvenience for Jonathan, but
if he and the board set their heads to it, surely they could find
another teacher willing to settle in Skingle Creek. And he did have
Carolyn Ross, the highly efficient school secretary, to help out in
the meantime.

In truth, there was something else prompting her increasing restlessness besides the desire to spend more time at home. She never
doubted that Gracie was in good hands with her parents. They had
raised four children of their own, after all, and they loved Gracie as
much as if she *were* their own. But next week Da would return to
work, and her mother would again be alone most of the day with
the baby. What if Richard Barlow were to show up when there was
no one with Gracie but Mum?

Even if her father *were* at home, would he make a difference?
She knew Jonathan and her mother believed Da could halt any
attempt on the part of Richard or his attorney to take Gracie away.
And not so long ago, Maggie wouldn't have doubted their confidence. But now? Da had a broken arm, a crushed leg, and a back
that failed him when he least expected it. Would he really be able
to stop Richard or anyone else?

Maggie had seen the heat and strength of her former brother-in-
law's rage for herself. She had seen the wildness in his eyes and the
evidence of the brutality he'd wreaked upon her sister. And because
she *had* seen, she couldn't allow herself to be lulled into believing her father, in his present condition, would present any kind of
defense against Barlow.

While she wasn't so foolish as to imagine she could match
Richard Barlow strength for strength, she couldn't help but believe
that, at least for now, she might be the only one who could offer
any real protection to Gracie during the day.

She would die before she let anyone take away Eva Grace's
baby.

Her baby.

She could only pray that Richard wouldn't come before the end of March. After that she would be at home with Gracie.

Please, Lord, don't let him come before then.

Maggie thought about her prayer for a long moment and then revised it.

Better yet, Lord, don't let him come at all.

Chapter Nineteen

Sunday Surprises

Love is the one constant of a heart…
God's love is the one constant of a life.

Anonymous

When Jonathan walked into the Sunday afternoon rehearsal with his "Singing Miners," as he'd dubbed the new choral group, the question foremost in his mind was whether or not he'd misjudged his own idea—and his father-in-law's influence. At the first rehearsal the week before, no more than half-a-dozen men had shown up, including himself and Matthew. He had already steeled himself for an even poorer turnout today.

He hadn't been in the church meeting room much more than ten minutes when he got his first surprise as Matthew walked in with four other men. Each wore a dubious, almost sheepish expression. They stopped, leaning against the back wall as if ready to bolt from the room. A few minutes later Tommy Byrne and Luc Penryn, a Welshman who hadn't been in Skingle Creek more than a few months, came in and joined the others.

By the time Bernard Kelly and Nevan Flynn sauntered in, the men had begun to talk among themselves and appeared to be losing some of their uncertainty. The brightest moment for Jonathan was the appearance of James Egan, followed by Benny Pippino—"Pip"—a former student who had lost a hand in a machinery accident while still a child and working as a breaker boy. Jonathan had befriended the lad, convincing the school board to let Pip attend classes in exchange for doing odd jobs about the schoolhouse for a nominal wage. He'd gone on to graduate as one of the top students in his class, eventually working himself into a good job keeping books for Charles Ferguson at the company store.

Something that might not be known to everyone else but was well-known to Jonathan was that Pip possessed an achingly lovely tenor voice.

He walked up to Jonathan upon entering and grinned widely. "I know I'm not a miner, Mr. Stuart. But I was hoping maybe you'd let me sing anyway. You remember, I always did love to sing when I was still in school."

Jonathan couldn't reply fast enough. "I can't tell you how glad I am to see you here, Pip! Of course you can sing with us."

Before Jonathan commenced rehearsal, five more men arrived, making a total of sixteen besides himself. He was feeling downright jubilant when he walked to the front of the room and coaxed them to come forward.

He spoke only a few minutes, welcoming them all, and reviewing for the newcomers the type of music they'd be singing, as well as the main objective behind the group's formation. "I'm simply hoping to provide something that, even in a small way, might help lift the spirits of our neighbors every now and then, and music has been proven to do that in a number of ways. So that's what we're about, fellows."

There was no missing their skeptical looks. These men lived hard lives, lives in which the very act of survival was a struggle for them and their families. The monotony of their work, the grind of their everyday trials, could at times be enough to crush their spirits and dampen their hopes. Jonathan had no illusions about how difficult it would be for such men to trust the word of a schoolteacher who seldom got his hands dirty except to plant a garden, a man who knew next to nothing about never having sufficient wages to pay his bills. Yet that was exactly what he was asking them to do: trust that he was right in his conviction that they could make a difference for the town.

Watching them, taking in the way they were studying *him*, he decided it was time to dispense with words and turn to the music. "Enough talk," he said. "Let's just sing a song or two."

A few heads nodded. This was definitely not the kind of group in which one "tried out" for placement, so he lined them up according to the kind of voices they told him they had: "low," "not too low," and a "little higher than some."

❧•❦

Jonathan expected to have his work cut out for him in training the men to sing parts, perhaps even in singing unison. He couldn't have been more wrong. What he had forgotten was that these men sang together nearly every day on the way to work, on the way home, and in church on Sunday. After a couple of verses of "Barbara Allen" and "Froggie Went a Courtin'" he was fairly bursting with delight. These men could *sing!* They harmonized almost as well as a professional group. They knew how to cue each other and sang with heart. And it came naturally to them. Even the words he'd so carefully written on the chalkboard of the meeting room proved, for the most part, to be unnecessary.

What pleased him even more than the musical ability evident within the group was the awareness that they were enjoying themselves. Gone were the diffident mumbles, the skeptical expressions, the slumped shoulders. Once they started singing, they stood tall, watching Jonathan intently for direction and smiling when he expressed his pleasure. Before long they were even calling out requests.

Jonathan discovered that Civil War songs were still popular among them, as were the tunes of Thomas Moore. Irish pride surged with Moore's "The Minstrel Boy," and after the Italian Pip Pippino's tenor soared above the other voices on the final verse, the men declared him an "honorary Irishman."

Then someone got the bright idea of naming Jonathan the same. "Aye," cracked Matthew MacAuley, "seeing as how he married my daughter, let's give the man a title to wear with pride."

It wasn't long before Jonathan could detect individual voices. Matthew's rumbling bass could probably shake the timbers in the mine, and the Welshman, Luc Penryn, possessed a strong lead voice that would pull some of the others along and give them confidence. As for Pip's tenor—well, as Matthew might say, it was a voice that could charm the birds from the bushes.

He couldn't wait to get home and tell Maggie about his "Singing Miners."

⟫⟪

As it turned out, however, Jonathan had only enough time to begin his account of the evening before Ben Wallace paid an unexpected visit.

"I'm sorry to drop by like this," the pastor said after hanging up his coat in the hallway and following Jonathan into the living room.

"You don't ever have to apologize for dropping in on us, Pastor Ben," Maggie told him from her place on the sofa, bringing Gracie up to her shoulder and rubbing her back.

He declined her offer of coffee as he took a chair by the fire. "So, Jonathan, how did rehearsal go this afternoon?"

"Much better than last week." Jonathan sat down beside Maggie and Gracie on the sofa. Still brimming with excitement, he recounted his experience with the newly formed choral group. Suddenly he realized he'd been completely dominating the conversation. "I'm sorry," he said "I didn't mean to go on like that."

"But you've every right to be pleased," Ben said. "I'm excited *for* you. I think this is going to be a good thing for those men. And for the town as well."

"I hope so. But that's enough about the miners for now. You said you had something to tell us, Ben."

"Yes. Well—" The pastor's expression sobered. "That's why I came. I couldn't put this off any longer."

"Is something wrong?"

"I'll just take Gracie to the kitchen," Maggie said, starting to rise from the sofa.

But Ben stopped her. "No, Maggie. This is for you to hear too."

Something about his friend's pinched features stirred uneasiness in Jonathan. "Ben?"

The pastor leaned forward with a hand on each knee. "I'll just come right out with it. I wanted you both to hear this from me first. I've accepted a call to another church just outside Louisville."

Jonathan couldn't have been more surprised if the older man had said he was leaving the ministry altogether. "Another church? But why?"

A faint smile relieved his friend's earlier seriousness. "Because I believe it's God's will, of course. Otherwise I'd never consider such a move."

"But I thought—I mean, you've never mentioned even the thought of leaving Skingle Creek."

The other nodded. "That's because I *hadn't* thought about it before now. I love the town, you know that, and the church. I love these people. But I'm convinced God has another plan for us. And I think part of that plan has to do with Selma and Huey."

"You've changed your mind about the adoption?"

"Oh, goodness, no! Your father's lawyer has already started the paperwork for us. He's filed the petition, and when I talked to him by phone last week he said he believed the adoption would go through quickly now that Lazlo's prison sentence is in effect. He's trying to work through the red tape as quickly as possible."

Jonathan felt as if he'd been punched in the stomach. He was only vaguely aware of Maggie's hand covering his. "I don't quite know what to say, Ben. This is the last thing I expected."

"I know. And I'm truly sorry to dump it on you like this, without warning. But I didn't want to say anything until I knew for certain I had a definite call. And I also had to make sure I can legally move the children with us."

When Jonathan made no reply, he went on. "I genuinely believe this may also be God's way of helping Selma and Huey. I've been concerned just what it would be like for them to stay here, where they've been so unhappy and where there are constant reminders of their parents and everything that happened. I'm convinced that getting away from the bad memories will be best for both of them."

Jonathan hadn't thought of that, and as much as he hated to admit it, he supposed Ben was right. But life without this friend whom he'd come to love as a brother? He couldn't even imagine such a thing.

"I simply don't know what to say, Ben."

"We'll miss you and Regina terribly," Maggie put in.

"Yes," Jonathan murmured. "Terribly."

Ben leaned forward even more. "Jonathan—Maggie—I hope you'll be happy for us. We're excited, Regina and I, about the future. We hate to leave our friends, of course, especially the two of you. But we're finally going to be parents! We love those children, you know that. And if God wants me with a new congregation, He has a reason. In all honesty, I'm looking forward to this."

Jonathan looked up and studied his old friend. And then he saw it: the conviction and genuine eagerness. And something else. A look of expectancy, as though he were waiting for a word of affirmation or at least some acknowledgment that Jonathan was happy for him.

He struggled to find the words Ben seemed to be waiting to hear.

How could he *not* wish his friend well when he was so clearly convinced that God had placed a call upon his heart and when he was so intent on heeding that call? He had stood by Jonathan for years, as a counselor and spiritual confidant as well as a friend. Whatever it took, Jonathan could not bring himself to disappoint the man seated across from him.

Even so, with that awareness came a great sorrow. Still, he knew what he needed to do. He stood and approached his friend, who also got to his feet.

"You know I want only what's best for you," Jonathan said, his voice not as steady as he would have liked. "And if this is God's will—well, then we both know it *will* be the best."

He extended his hand, and Ben took it between both of his. "Thank you, my friend. That means a great deal to me."

"When will you tell the congregation?" Jonathan asked after the moment's emotion subsided.

"Tomorrow. That's why I came here this evening."

"That's going to be difficult. For you as much as the people, I expect."

Ben nodded. "I can scarcely bear to think about it. I was hoping you and Maggie would pray for me tonight and during the service tomorrow."

Maggie got up with the sleeping Gracie in her arms and came closer. "You can be sure we'll do just that, Pastor Ben. When will you be leaving? Or do you know yet?"

"I hope to stay until a new pastor is in place," he said. "I don't want this to be any more inconvenient for the people than absolutely necessary. If possible, I'll help my replacement settle in before I leave."

"No one can *ever* replace you," Jonathan said firmly, still feeling somewhat ill about the evening's unexpected turn of events.

"Now, Jonathan," the other said, "I'm going to speak to you as your pastor instead of as your friend. Don't you be thinking that way. I'm trusting you to pray with the rest of the congregation that

God will send exactly the right man here who will not only replace me, but be a better pastor to the people than I've ever been."

"Impossible!"

"I mean it now. I'll not have you thinking that way. No man is irreplaceable." He paused, a faint smile touching his features. "Although I'll have to admit that as friends go, I'm not likely to find another like yourself. But when it comes to preachers, I fully expect you and the congregation to be blessed with someone very special in no time at all."

His words puzzled Jonathan a little. He almost sounded as though he knew something he wasn't telling them. Still, Ben could be unintentionally cryptic, usually because his mind was continually working, always racing ahead.

In any event, this was scarcely the time to speculate, not with his own thoughts and emotions in such turmoil.

❖•❖

Later that night, after they'd tucked Gracie in and prayed together, Maggie sat down beside her husband on the edge of the bed and took his hand. "I'm so sorry, Jonathan." She rested her head on his shoulder. "I know how hard this must be for you. And you were so happy when you came home, so enthusiastic about your time with the miners."

He ran a hand down the side of his face and shook his head. "It was just so unexpected."

"I know. But even if you'd had more warning—some sort of preparation—it wouldn't have made it any easier. The two of you have been such good friends for so long." She stopped and then added, "You'll stay good friends, of course. Louisville isn't so far that we can't take turns visiting now and then."

He looked at her. "That's true. And we'll want to stay in touch with the children as well."

Maggie nodded, hoping to encourage him. "And they'll want to stay in touch with *you*. You mean a lot to Selma and Huey."

"No more than you do. And you're right, we won't lose touch, but—"

"But it won't be the same," she said softly, squeezing his hand.

"No. No, it won't. But then nothing really stays the same, does it?"

The sadness in his tone made Maggie want to weep. But that was the last thing he needed from her. Instead, she framed his face between her hands and held his gaze. "We'll stay the same, Jonathan. We *will*."

She saw the effort it took for him to return her smile. "We've already seen quite a lot of change in our lives, don't you think?"

"*Life* changes. But what we have together *won't* change. Not ever. No matter what."

He studied her for a moment, then covered her hands with his and brought them to his lips. "No matter what," he promised.

He kissed her, and Maggie's heart opened to him like a window to the warmth of the morning sun.

Chapter Twenty

A New Teacher in Town

The temple the Teacher builded
Will last while the ages roll,
For that beautiful unseen temple
Was a child's immortal soul.

Author unknown

⌐‿‿⌐

Maggie remained vigilant, even when there was no word from Richard Barlow for another two weeks, but her days were too busy to dwell on her fear that he would eventually show up in Skingle Creek.

She had all she could do to keep up. The school board hadn't located a teacher to replace her, so she spent every spare minute she could manage between classes and after school preparing lessons and projects ahead, hoping to make things as easy and as convenient as possible for Jonathan or the teacher who would ultimately take

over her classes. Her time at home was taken up with Gracie and
Jonathan, in addition to drafting out some early chapters for a new
children's book she had in mind.

For months now her publisher had been urging her to provide
them with a new manuscript. Although she loved the process of
developing a story and creating the people for that story, she found
it difficult—some days impossible—to spend any quality time on
the work. Perhaps when she was no longer teaching she'd be able
to make more progress on the manuscript, but for now she had
other priorities.

Jonathan also was busier than ever. To his surprise there had
been three applicants for Maggie's position. In conjunction with the
school board, he'd begun to hold interviews, only to come home
thoroughly disgruntled after each. Apparently most of the board
would have agreed to any of the three, none of which, according to
Jonathan, was qualified. He worried that the board members simply
weren't looking past the need to hire a teacher—*any* teacher.

"They would have hired this last fellow—a martinet if I ever saw
one. Why, he gave every indication that he doesn't even *like* children. I ended up just shy of an all-out quarrel with Ernest Gibbon,"
he told Maggie.

The bank president was known to be contentious when least
expected. More than once Jonathan complained that if Gibbon
couldn't find a point to argue, he'd create one. "The man is enam-
ored of his own voice."

After hearing about the "martinet" and the other applicants so far,
Maggie could only agree with Jonathan. Not one of them sounded
as if he belonged in a classroom. Hopes for hiring a teacher in the
near future were looking dimmer all the time.

At least his work with his singing miners was going well. *More*
than well. The rehearsals were a high point in his week, and Maggie
was relieved he enjoyed them so much. To her way of thinking, if
the men to whom he was devoting his time received even half the
blessing Jonathan insisted he did, then the benefits of the choral
group definitely ran in both directions.

Maggie hoped his work with the miners would also help ease the approaching loss of his friend, Ben Wallace. She could only imagine how difficult it was going to be for the two men to say goodbye. For her part, she considered herself doubly blessed in that Jonathan was not only her husband, but her best friend as well. She wouldn't want to face the onerous task of saying goodbye to a special friend.

As she bundled Gracie up for their outing, she smiled at the thought that she also had a *new* friend these days: Anna Tallman. At least she hoped they would become good friends. Certainly they never ran out of things to talk about. Indeed, any time they were together they seemed to find something else they shared in comon. Maggie fervently hoped Anna and Kenny would stay in Skingle Creek; already she didn't like to think about the possibility of saying goodbye.

Anna was far enough along in her time that she no longer went out, so today Maggie would visit her instead. Jonathan was dropping her and Gracie off on his way to the school, where he and the board would be conducting yet another interview before his afternoon rehearsal with the miners. He hadn't much liked the idea of interviewing on a Sunday, but there was always difficulty getting all the board members together on weekdays.

Maggie suspected Kenny was a bit uneasy about leaving Anna alone in case the baby put in an early appearance. He had stopped one evening the past week to see if Maggie would keep Anna company this afternoon while he and his father drove out to the Runyan farm to pick up some eggs and other produce.

Maggie tied Gracie's cap and tugged her blankets snugly around her. She tweaked the babe's nose, eliciting a squeal and a bubble from the rosebud mouth.

"This," she told her daughter as she lifted her into her arms, "is going to be fun. But we'd best get downstairs before your papa loses his patience with us."

Jonathan stood at the table near the back of his classroom studying the application for today's interview before the others arrived.
He hadn't told Maggie the applicant's identity yet; he'd been surprised himself when he learned who was interviewing today, so he
decided he would wait to see how the meeting went before saying
anything.

Henry Piper was a member of the school board. The man had
always been a private person. Some in town speculated that he was
somewhat of a hermit and perhaps even eccentric. To save him,
Jonathan couldn't imagine Henry in a classroom surrounded by
children. Yet rumor had it that Piper was well-educated, that he had
even studied law before returning to the area to help care for his
mother and sister after his father's death. Not long after his return,
Henry's mother also died, his sister married and moved away, and
Henry was left alone on the farm. For years he rarely came into town
except for school board meetings and weekly church services.

Henry walked into the room just then, and Jonathan took a second look. Seldom seen in anything other than overalls and a flannel shirt—usually with a pipe in his mouth and the pungent smell
of tobacco circling his head—today the middle-aged farmer was
decked out in a well-tailored dark blue suit, his silver hair brushed
and shining. No pipe, no tobacco.

Jonathan again glanced at the application in his hand, surprised
to find that Henry was only in his early fifties. Up until now he
would have taken him to be older. The suit and tie whittled a few
years off his age. It wasn't that Jonathan hadn't seen the man in his
Sunday best before, just never up close. Henry attended the Baptist
church a few miles out, so they seldom ran into each other.

They shook hands and made small talk for a few minutes until
the other board members filed in and exchanged greetings.

Matthew shot a quizzical look in Henry's direction, and then
arched an eyebrow at Jonathan.

Ben Wallace was there too, of course. As president of the school
board, he introduced today's applicant. The skepticism of the other
board members couldn't have been more obvious. For the most

part, they remained silent, obviously expecting Jonathan to conduct the interview.

As soon as everyone was seated, Ben led them in prayer. Jonathan then made an attempt to put Henry at ease. "Well, Henry, I think I speak for us all when I say we're surprised to see you here—but pleased, of course. We had no idea you'd be interested in a teaching position."

From the other side of the table, Henry Piper leaned slightly forward and straightened his eyeglasses on the bridge of his nose. "To tell you the truth, Mr. Stuart, neither did I. As it happens, I believe the Lord placed this on my heart. That's why I'm here."

Jonathan paused for a moment at the man's frankness, then cleared his throat and started in on the questions he asked every applicant. "Do you have any teaching experience, Henry?"

The man nodded. "I do, yes, sir. I taught at an elementary school in Frankfort for three years and before that I studied law."

Jonathan glanced up from the application. "I had no idea, Henry. Did you finish law school?"

"No, but I have my college degree. I only went to law school in the first place because of my uncle Eber. He talked me into it. I never wanted to be a lawyer. I left law school and took some more classes to finish my degree. Then I started teaching."

Jonathan studied the man across from him. "Did you like teaching?"

Henry Piper nodded eagerly. "I liked it a lot. Had it not been for my family needing me back here, I expect I'd have gone on teaching in Frankfort."

Jonathan took note of the deeply seated intelligence that brimmed in Henry's eyes and the air of composure the man emanated. He'd always suspected that Henry Piper was, by nature, a gentleman. A gentleman *farmer* perhaps, but a gentleman all the same.

"So you have some kind of a teaching certificate, do you, Henry?" Ben Wallace asked.

"I brought it with me," Henry said, handing the paper to Jonathan

"It's been a long time since I've used it, but I've kept it up to date just in case."

Jonathan scanned the certificate and found everything in order. "I'm curious as to why you'd want to take up teaching after so many years out of the classroom," he said, watching the other man closely.

"I know it might seem a bit strange," Henry replied. "But I've missed teaching. Even after all these years, I still miss it. I liked being with children. And just being in a schoolhouse with books and chalkboards and lessons—" He stopped, a faint pink stain rising up his neck and face. "Maybe that doesn't make sense—"

"On the contrary, Henry," Jonathan said, "it makes a great deal of sense. I expect I'd never stop missing the classroom if I had to leave teaching for some reason. Being a teacher is what you *are,* not necessarily what you *do.*"

Henry brightened. "Yes!" he exclaimed, grateful for Jonathan's understanding. "That's it exactly!"

"Well, one thing concerns me—" Ernest Gibbon put in.

The others turned to look at him, and once he had their attention, he went on. "Don't take offense, Henry, but the idea of an unmarried man like yourself as a schoolteacher might not set very well with some of the parents."

His words fell with a thud and brought total silence to the room. A few of the men looked at each other. Matthew looked at Jonathan, who felt compelled to offer an observation.

"Ernest, did you forget that I taught here for many years before I was married?"

Gibbon didn't seem inclined to meet Jonathan's eyes. "We all know that."

That was all he said. But what was he *really* saying?

"Your point, Ernest?" asked Ben Wallace. "I don't know that anyone here has a problem with hiring a teacher who's also a bachelor. It certainly didn't have a negative effect on Jonathan's work. If anything, he had more time to devote to the children than a married teacher might have had."

As if he realized his words could be taken the wrong way, Ben turned to Jonathan. "I don't mean that you don't give the children enough of yourself now that you *are* married, Jonathan."

Jonathan waved away his friend's attempt to explain. "I know what you mean, Ben." But he did wonder what Ernest Gibbon wasn't saying.

When Ben moved to bring the subject to a halt, casually pointing out that he didn't believe they needed to consider Henry's single-ness an issue, Gibbon resisted. "I don't mean to offend, Henry, you understand. But you've kept to yourself over the years. Folks don't really know you very well. There could be a problem of trust—"

At that point Jonathan would have objected, but Henry lifted a hand to indicate that he wanted to address Gibbon's concern.

"I understand what you're saying, Mr. Gibbon. And you're right, I haven't been all that sociable. There was always the farm and the house to take care of and the animals to tend. And I've never been one who's all that comfortable with folks I don't know. And I expect I'm pretty quiet by nature." He stopped, folded his hands together on top of the table, and went on. "But I *am* comfortable with chil-dren. And I was a good teacher. I think I'd still be a good teacher, given the chance. I'd like to work with children again, and that's why I'm here."

He held Jonathan's gaze for a moment and then looked down at his hands. Jonathan glanced around at the others and saw what he needed to see. He waited for Ernest Gibbon to offer another objec-tion. When none came, he told Henry he would hear from them soon.

Ben Wallace waited until Henry left the room, then asked Jonathan if he had anything to add before they voted.

"Only that I'm in favor of hiring Henry Piper," he said, "assum-ing his background and credentials are verified. He's an excellent candidate for the job. He's intelligent, experienced, and a member of the community. And he's eager for the job."

Everyone nodded their accord—except Ernest Gibbon, who, as they all knew, was inclined to always have the final word.

"Well, now, we don't want to rush things, do we?" Gibbon said. "There's been talk, you know, that Henry might be kind of...eccentric. By his own admission he's not a bit sociable. And I can't help but wonder why a man his age has never married—"

Jonathan sighed. "Did you wonder the same thing about me, Ernest?"

"Now, Jonathan, you're a much younger man than Henry Piper," Gibbon replied, fingering his shirt collar. "And you *did* take women out, after all, before you were married. You weren't some kind of hermit. You didn't shut yourself off from everybody else in town."

Ever the peacemaker, Ben Wallace broke into the conversation. "I don't think we can assume that Henry is odd, Ernest, just because he stays home most of the time or because he's not married." He paused and smiled. "There's no abundance of unmarried women his age in Skingle Creek, you know. Could be he's just never met the right woman. I don't believe we ought to count that against him. Why don't we go ahead and take a contingent vote so we'll know where we stand? Jonathan seems to think Henry is well-qualified for the job, and his opinion counts with me."

Matthew, the only miner on the board, spoke up before Ernest could. "Agreed."

Gibbon muttered something Jonathan couldn't catch. With no further objection, they voted. By the end of the meeting Henry Piper had been approved as the new schoolteacher for Skingle Creek, subject to his background information and credentials being in order.

❖·❖

This was the first time Maggie had ever been inside the Tallman house. Although she and Kenny had been friends as children, their friendship didn't include visits to Kenny's house.

Judson Tallman had always kept the rest of the town at arm's length, and even as a child Maggie sensed Kenny wasn't allowed to bring friends home. The Tallmans simply didn't do that. And even though it was said that Judson Tallman had softened some toward his son and his employees at the mine, he had never been a man to warm up to. People instinctively kept their distance.

The Tallman house was large and neatly kept. Maggie wasn't surprised to find that it was furnished sparsely, and with little attention given to the niceties that made a house a home. Mr. Tallman had lived alone for years now, ever since Kenny had graduated and gone off to college. His lack of interest in his home couldn't have been more obvious. The draperies were dusty and frayed in places, and the upholstered pieces looked as though they might shed a cloud of dust if anyone sat down on them too hard. This was a place where someone slept and sometimes ate. No pets curled up for naps or came running to the door when someone arrived. It was a place that might just as well have stood empty had it not been for a few crocheted layette pieces here and there and the aroma of fresh coffee drifting down the hall.

As if sensing Maggie's thoughts, Anna glanced around at the front room with a wry smile. "Awful, isn't it?"

Maggie felt as if she'd been caught stealing the silver. "What? Oh no! It's very nice, Anna. Really."

"No, it's not. It's horrible. It breaks my heart to think of Ken growing up in such a cold, *vacant* place." A plaintive expression crossed her features, as though she were actually looking into the past and seeing Kenny here as a lonely young boy.

"I *hate* it that Ken had such an unhappy childhood!" she said in a heated outburst unlike the quiet, reserved woman Maggie had come to know. "I can scarcely wait until we have a place of our own and the baby is born so I can make a real home for him."

Unexpectedly Maggie's eyes filled. This woman would change Kenny's life—had *already* changed his life, and all for the best. "He's so fortunate to have you," she said, propping Gracie against her shoulder. "I'm so glad the two of you found each other."

"May I hold her?" Anna asked, reaching for Gracie from her end of the sofa.

Gracie went willingly when Maggie passed her over to the other woman, and once settled in the crook of Anna's arm, lay studying her.

"What a darling she is! I'd love to have a little girl too, but between you and me, I'm hoping our first is a son. I think it will be so good for Ken to have a son."

"He'll be a wonderful father," Maggie said, convinced of it.

"Yes, he will." Anna smiled at her. "Just as your Jonathan is. I love watching him with Gracie. He *adores* her."

As they talked, Gracie fell asleep in Anna's arms.

"She gets heavy after a bit, Anna. Let me take her."

"Absolutely not. I love this!"

Anna seemed keenly interested in Maggie's plans once her position at the school came to an end.

"I really haven't had time to think much about it," Maggie admitted. "I know it's going to be difficult at first, until I get used to not working. But taking care of Gracie and looking after the house will keep me plenty busy. I'm sure I'll adjust." She stopped. "You know, lately I've almost been looking forward to it. If it weren't for Jonathan fretting about not having me at the school, I think I might come to like the idea. Sometimes I feel so harried, rushing out every morning, dropping Gracie off at my mother's, hurrying through the evenings to get ready for the next day."

Anna nodded but Maggie didn't think she looked all that convinced.

"What?" Maggie prompted. "You don't think I'll be satisfied if I'm not teaching?"

Anna glanced down at Gracie and tucked the blanket more closely about her before shifting the baby a bit higher against her arm.

"Oh, I can't possibly know that, Maggie. It's just that I have an idea that I'm hoping you'll be interested in."

"What kind of an idea?"

"First, have you heard what Ken has been up to lately?"

Maggie hadn't. She listened with increasing interest as Anna told her of Kenny's efforts to establish a mission for the wives and families of deceased or disabled miners. "Ken found out about the need from Pastor Wallace. Many of the mine widows have to move out of their homes once their husbands are gone because they can't meet the rent. And there's the lack of food and clothing. Ken says some of the families don't even have enough bedding to keep warm."

"I know it can be disastrous for the family of a miner who's been killed or permanently disabled," Maggie agreed. "Ben Wallace has done what he can, but he's so busy as a full-time pastor, I'm sure it's impossible for him to keep up with everything. And once he leaves—"

"Well, Ken's quite the organizer. He's had to be, living on the mission field as it were. And he's a great one for raising funds as well. He has a good head for making things work."

"But he'll need to be paid," Maggie pointed out. "He can't just volunteer his time for free with a baby coming—" She stopped. "Oh, Anna! I'm so sorry. I can't believe I said that. It's absolutely none of my business!"

Anna laughed at her embarrassment. "Don't be silly. You merely stated what I've already told my husband. Once we have our own place, we'll need to pay *our* rent too. Not to mention put food on the table." She shifted Gracie a little. "I'm really not worried about us, Maggie. Not at all. Something will come along for Ken soon, I'm sure. He was so convinced about coming back here. He believes this is where God wants him, at least for now. I've learned to trust his insights and his instincts. If God has truly called Ken back to Skingle Creek, He'll take care of us."

Maggie nodded. "Meanwhile, Kenny—I'm sorry, I'm so used to calling him that—*Ken* is going to help take care of the town. The people in Skingle Creek may not know it yet, but they *need* you and Kenny. *I* need you."

"I think we need each other, Maggie. And in that regard, let me tell you my idea."

Maggie rested her hands in her lap and waited.

Anna captured her attention in an instant. "I'm thinking of starting a school," she said. "A school for younger children who can't attend regular school yet. Not until after the baby is born, of course, and Ken locates a permanent position."

She paused. "And I'm hoping you'll consider becoming my partner."

Chapter Twenty-one

Sharing News

A little love, a little trust,
A soft impulse, a sudden dream,
And life as dry as desert dust
Is fresher than a mountain stream.

Stopford A. Brooke

~~~

Maggie saw Jonathan's excitement as soon as he helped her and Gracie into the buggy. She decided to keep her own news for later.

They'd no more driven away from the Tallmans than he handed her a sheaf of paper.

"What's this?" she asked.

"A list of songs the men are ready to sing," he said with a smile as he turned his attention back to the road. "Consider it your own private invitation to come to the next rehearsal and hear them for yourself. I received their permission to invite you."

"Oh, that's grand! I'd love to come and listen. Can Gracie come too?"

"Naturally the invitation includes Gracie."

"There's more," Maggie said, watching him closely. "I can tell."

"You read me so easily, don't you?" he said, glancing at her. "Well, I hope you're pleased with the rest of my news, although I'm still not quite sure how *I* feel about it." He paused. "We're about to hire someone for your position, Maggie. On a trial basis, just until the end of the school year."

Because *this* piece of news was so completely unexpected, Maggie struggled to take it in. When she didn't reply right way, Jonathan reached for her hand. "Maggie?" he questioned, again turning to look at her.

"Oh, I'm glad for you, Jonathan. Really I am! I'm just...surprised, that's all. So tell me, who is it?"

"You'll never believe it. Henry Piper."

Maggie stared at him. "Not the same Henry Piper who owns the dairy farm?"

"That's the one."

"But is he qualified?"

"It seems so. He has a teacher's certificate and three years teaching experience at an elementary school in Frankfort. And he's eager for the job. The board approved him subject to checking out his background. As I said, we won't be offering him a permanent position, just to the end of the school year. After that we'll see what happens. But my instincts tell me he's going to work out just fine."

"Henry Piper," she said softly. "Who would have thought it?"

She'd have to mull it over, but after the initial sting of realizing what this meant, that it had just become possible for her to leave the school as planned, she thought she was glad.

"Well," she said cheerfully, "I can finally stop worrying about how you're going to get along without me."

He gave her a long, studying look. "Are you really all right with this, sweetheart?"

Maggie decided she was. "Yes, I believe I am. In fact, now that I know you've found a teacher, I might just as well tell you that in a way I'm relieved. I've been praying someone—the *right* someone—would come along so you wouldn't be left overburdened by my leaving. It's been difficult for me at times, trying to manage everything, what with the job and the house and Gracie. I was feeling as though I wasn't doing anything as well as I wanted to."

"That's not true at all. You've been wonderful. But I know it hasn't been easy. So you don't mind then?"

"No, I really don't. I want the best for you and the students, and it sounds as though everything is going to work out just grand. No, I don't mind. I think this will be best for everyone."

He squeezed her hand. "I'm glad. And now, tell me *your* news."

Maggie couldn't stop a smile. "How do you know *I* have news to tell?"

"Those green eyes of yours have been shooting fireworks since I came to pick you up. So tell me, what do you know that I don't?"

By now they were pulling up in front of the house.

"Let's wait until we get inside," Maggie said.

❦

By the time they got inside, however, Gracie was fretful. Before anything else, Jonathan gave her a bottle and put her down for a brief nap while Maggie started supper.

Later, when he came into the kitchen, Jonathan came up behind her and put his hands around her waist. He turned her around to kiss her soundly. The spoon in Maggie's hand went clanging against the stove, sending a splash over the side and onto Figaro's nose, which the big hound promptly licked and then looked up, obviously hoping for more.

"I missed you," Jonathan said, loosening his tie and watching as she retrieved the gravy spoon.

Maggie feigned a frown. "It's only been three hours."

He shrugged. "Too long."

"You'd best get used to it, dear. It won't be long now until we'll be apart all day."

Brightness left his face. "I'm not ready to think about that."

"Oh, Jonathan, I'm sorry. I was only teasing. You know it has to be this way. Besides," she said, ignoring a twinge of hurt on her own part, "don't they say that absence makes the heart grow fonder?"

Again he circled her waist. "If my heart grows any fonder of you, my love, it will explode. Now let's get supper on the table. While we eat you can tell me what has you so excited."

❖

He lost track of time as they talked. When he first heard Anna Tallman's plan, he wasn't at all sure it was a workable idea. Moreover, he wasn't convinced that he even *liked* the idea. He was already begrudging Henry Piper the position he still thought of as Maggie's. While he recognized the need to hire *someone,* and certainly Henry, by all appearances, would seem to be well-qualified for the position, he couldn't help but resist the idea of another teacher *replacing* Maggie. He knew he was being intractable, but there it was. He didn't even want to think of someone else in her place.

Even so, come the end of March—which by now wasn't all that far off—she would have to leave. The law required it. It struck him that as practical as Maggie had tried to be about leaving the school, more than once over the past few weeks he'd seen a shadow pass over her face when the subject was mentioned. She hadn't admitted it to him. She was even pretending to be relieved, but he knew her final parting from the school was going to be difficult to say the least.

Perhaps, then, this idea of Anna's might turn out to be a good thing after all. Unconventional, yes. But based on his own experiences as a teacher, he thought it just might work. As far as he knew, there was nothing to restrict two women, both talented, exceptional teachers, from conducting a private school on private property.

It was not without its obstacles, a major one being a way to fund it. But when he pointed this out, Maggie had another surprise.

"You're not going to believe this," she said, getting up to take their plates to the sink. "Kenny's father has offered to fund us for the first year."

Jonathan stared at her. "Judson Tallman? Are you serious?"

"Entirely. Isn't that unbelievable?

"Why in the world would he make such an offer? I mean, yes, Anna is his daughter-in-law, but Tallman's never been known as a generous man."

She came back and sat down. "I was surprised too. But do you know what I think? I think this might be his way of keeping Kenny in Skingle Creek. And don't forget there'll soon be a grandchild in the picture."

Jonathan considered her words. "You might be right. From what Anna's told you, it sounds as though Tallman genuinely likes her. Could be he really wants to help."

She looked dubious.

"Tallman has changed over the years," Jonathan reminded her. "He's not as hard a man as he was when Kenny was growing up. I'd like to think he's genuinely interested in helping out. A private school in Skingle Creek: that will be an event."

"Oh, don't call it that, Jonathan! A 'private school' sounds so pretentious."

"Nevertheless that's what it will be. We can probably help out a little with finances too. I don't know that I want Judson Tallman doing it all. You haven't said what ages you're thinking of."

"Anna mentioned four and five year olds."

He nodded. "A private kindergarten."

"You know about kindergarten?"

He lifted an eyebrow. "I'm not entirely ignorant of the education system, Maggie. I do read and go to seminars on occasion."

"I didn't mean…oh, you're teasing. Stop it! Has there ever been any thought of having a kindergarten at the school?"

Jonathan shook his head. "I've raised the subject a few times to make the board aware that a kindergarten is definitely part of the future, but as I'm sure you've noticed, we already have a space problem. We're not set up to take children younger than six or seven years old yet. That would mean adding on to the building again and getting at least one more teacher. There's simply no money for it. And more to the point," he added with a sigh, "not a man on the board believes it's necessary."

"I want to know what you think, Jonathan. Tell me the truth. Will this be good for the children? And if so, do you believe we can make it work?"

He took a sip of coffee. "Where would you locate?"

"Probably in one of our homes to begin with. I doubt that we'll have more than two or three children to begin with, and with both of us having our own babies to take care of—"

"Yes, how do you plan on managing that?" he interrupted. "Anna will have a new baby, and you'll have Gracie."

"We've already got that figured out. We're thinking of only half-day sessions. At least to begin with, the babies will still be taking naps once or twice a day. While one of us is busy with the children, the other can look after our own little ones. And I'd be awfully surprised if Mum isn't willing to help out as needed. You've seen how she is with Gracie. I think she'd love to help."

Jonathan sat back and studied her. "You two seem to have this all worked out. Is Anna that certain she and Kenny are going to stay here?"

"She says Kenny is convinced this is where God wants him."

Not wanting to discourage her, he said nothing for a moment.

"So?" she prompted. "Do you think the idea is too far-fetched?"

Did he? It was a lot to take in, with some fairly obvious complications that could crop up. "You'll need more than just space, you know. You'll need sanitary facilities, a play area outside *and* in. And supplies. In truth, you'll need quite a lot just to get started."

"You don't think we can do it, do you?"

He couldn't bear the discouragement in her eyes where only a few moments ago there had been nothing but enthusiasm. The last thing he wanted to do was hurt her feelings or spoil her excitement, but he wanted to be very careful not to give her false encouragement.

Besides, when had Maggie ever failed in something she set her mind to? Perhaps *that* was the key to making a venture of this magnitude work.

"You really want to do this? You're quite sure?" he asked.

"I am, Jonathan. I honestly believe we *can* do it. But I don't even want to try if you're against the idea."

He took in the firm set of her mouth, the light in her eyes, the conviction that molded her features. "I'm not against it, Maggie. Not at all. And, you know, it would be a tremendous help to me...and to the children, of course."

She brightened still more. "Do you really mean that?"

"Of course I mean it," he said firmly. "Why, Maggie, surely you've seen for yourself that we have children starting school who simply aren't *ready* for school. We get children coming into first grade who can scarcely speak English. Some of the immigrant parents are so overwhelmed and beaten down by the time they settle in that it's all they can do to function, much less prepare their children for school. Not to mention the families where the fathers are working the mine while the mothers spend every spare minute taking in laundry or sewing to make ends meet."

"And don't forget the farm children," she put in. "Their mothers spend almost as much time working outside as the men do. Some of those little ones still can't hold their eating utensils properly or speak more than a few comprehensible words."

"All right then," Jonathan said, draining the last of his coffee from the cup. "It seems that all that's left is for you and Anna to draw up your plans. When are you planning on starting up? In the fall?"

"Probably not until after winter break. That should give Anna time to get situated with the new baby. It's going to take some doing to work out all the details and get set up."

Abruptly she stopped. "You don't think this is too ambitious for two women? We're not taking too much on ourselves?"

He reached across the table and took her hand. "What I think is that you can do anything you make up your mind to do. As I recall, the word 'can't' has never been part of your vocabulary."

"You sound like Eva Grace," she said with a smile.

"How's that?"

"Oh, she was always telling me I could do anything I wanted to. Like when she found out I was in love with you—she told me to fight for you."

"Eva Grace told you that?" he said, unable to suppress a smile.

"Remember when I was changing my hair styles every other day?"

"Indeed I do. What was all that about?"

"Evie was trying to make me look more mature." She paused. "That was her way of helping me...gain your interest."

"Are you serious? That was for *me?*"

"In a manner of speaking. And you needn't look so pleased with yourself."

"So...Eva Grace knew you were in love with me?"

"Don't be smug, Jonathan. Yes, she asked me, and I told her the truth. She also knew that *you* were in love with *me*. It so happens that Evie saw it before *I* did."

"*Really?*"

"Yes, *really.* Now, can we talk about the school?"

"Of course. Just one more thing—"

Maggie sighed.

"Did Eva Grace happen to say *how* she knew I was in love with you?"

Now it was Maggie who looked smug. "She said she could tell by the way you choked on your own tongue every time you looked at me."

Well, he *had* asked.

"Let's do the dishes," he said.

Chapter Twenty-two

On Behalf of Good Men

When thy heart, with joy o'erflowing
Sings a thankful prayer,
In thy joy, O let thy brother
With thee share.

Theodore C. Williams

Was it Jonathan's imagination or was Matthew MacAuley walking a little straighter these days? And with a less noticeable limp? Curious, he watched his father-in-law enter the church sanctuary and walk down the aisle. This wasn't the first time he'd detected what he thought might be a difference in Matthew's gait. Especially noticeable was the improvement in his lame leg. What accounted for it? If Maggie had noticed, she hadn't mentioned it.

He would have pointed it out to her if she were here. She'd planned to sit in on rehearsal today, but at the last moment Gracie had shown symptoms of a light cold, so they stayed in.

Perhaps he would just ask Matthew. Surely a son-in-law had a right to inquire about such things.

He had moved the men's rehearsal into the sanctuary today because the acoustics were clearer. Now that they were more firmly established as a group and had reached the point where they harmonized surprisingly well, he wanted to get an idea of their communal voice and the depth of their projection. He had an idea he'd like to try with them, though admittedly even *he* questioned whether it was too ambitious for such a new group. Still, he saw no harm in stretching them a little and giving them a goal.

The larger part of his idea was to give the town a *gift*. He sensed the time was approaching when the men would be ready to do just that.

❧❦

Jonathan and Matthew usually stood talking a few minutes after rehearsal, so when they finished today Jonathan took advantage of the opportunity to satisfy his curiosity.

"I can't help but notice something, Matthew. Would I be out of line in asking what accounts for the difference in the way you're walking these days?"

The older man regarded him with a measuring look. "You just might be, you know," he said in a tone that hinted more of amusement than impatience. "Not that it would be the first time."

The thing about Matthew, it wasn't all that easy to tell when he was serious. "I'm sorry. I couldn't help but notice—"

"I'm funnin' you, lad. Be easy." He glanced around as if to make sure no one else was nearby. "In truth, I'm glad it's that noticeable."

He dropped his voice even lower. "That woman gave me some braces to wear. I've been feeling better. If you've noticed a difference that's good. It means I'm not imagining it."

"The woman—that would be Dr. Gordon?"

Matthew nodded. "She gave me a contraption to wear for my back and another for my knee."

"They've helped with the pain?" It was all Jonathan could do to contain himself and not let the other see how pleased he was. He'd tried more than once to talk his father-in-law into seeking out Dr. Gordon's help, but each time Matthew had been adamant in his refusal.

"Aye, that seems to be the case. I don't much take to the idea of wearing the things for any length of time, but so long as they help, I'll give them a try."

"Well, I'm so glad Dr. Gordon was able to help. I tell you, Matthew, from everything I'm hearing about her, she's a fine doctor."

"The woman is a bully is what she is," Matthew said, his lip curling. "She doesn't let up."

Jonathan bit his tongue to keep from laughing. "Could be she recognizes a difficult man when she sees one."

Matthew shot him a squint-eyed look. "Some men need to show more respect for their in-laws, I'm thinking."

It struck Jonathan that if the other knew just how much respect he *did* have for him it would likely embarrass him to pieces. He ventured a suggestion. "You know, there are other men who could undoubtedly benefit from Dr. Gordon's attention—if they only knew she could help them."

"Now listen, Jonathan—" Again Matthew cast a furtive look around to make certain no one was within listening distance. "I don't want any of the men knowing about these braces. Bad enough I had to have my arm set by a woman doctor. If they find out she's got me wearing a corset and a knee band, I'll never hear the end of it."

Jonathan considered that for a moment. "You wouldn't have to tell them anything specific. But it does seem only fair to put in a good word for her. It couldn't hurt to at least let them know you consider her a good doctor and that she's been of some real help to you."

Clearly unmoved, the other waved off his suggestion. "I'd best be getting away now. I need to get in some wood and see what else Kate might need done before bedtime."

"Is Ray home?"

"No, he won't be in from the farm until a bit later. This is his last weekend out there." He stopped. "The boy's down in the mouth about losing that job. I wish Jeff and Martha hadn't decided to sell out. It's a good farm with great land."

"Yes, he's going to miss it, I'm sure. Listen, I'll stop by on the way home and help you with the wood."

"No need for that."

"You've no business chopping wood with a broken arm, Matthew."

"Who said anything about *chopping* it? I'm just going to carry some in. I chopped it last evening."

Jonathan shook his head in exasperation. "You chopped wood with one arm?"

"Nothing wrong with the good arm. But thanks for offering."

Jonathan sighed as he watched his father-in-law walk away. Matthew always managed to have the last word.

❖•❖

Matthew grinned to himself as he left the church. He was actually feeling *good* today. And he felt even better now that he knew the improvement was obvious, at least to Jonathan. The woman doctor might be a bit of a harridan, but these contraptions she'd put him in were making a difference, he had to give her that. Whatever accounted for the way they worked, neither his knee nor his back pained him quite as much as they had.

Consequently, he'd cut down on the laudanum. Truth was, he'd cut it out altogether. He was taking the pain powders the woman had given him in its place. And they didn't make him feel nearly as groggy and as worthless as that other stuff. That in itself made the woman worth whatever he'd have to pay her eventually.

He picked up his pace a bit more as he started for home, almost enjoying the sting of the evening wind on his face. For the first time in what seemed an age, he felt like a man *ought* to feel.

He caught up to Lem Odle and Thom Moloney along the road.

When Lem started complaining about the cramps he got in his legs if he stood in one position for any length of time, Matthew thought about it, cleared his throat, and said, "You ought to see that Dr. Gordon, Lem. I'll wager she'd know what to do. She's a woman, and all, but she's helped me a good bit, and that's the truth."

❧·❧

Jonathan stood outside the church building, watching his father-in-law as he headed toward home with two of the other miners. He didn't even try to suppress the wide smile that broke over his face at the sight of Matthew advancing along the road at a good pace. Why, the man very nearly had a spring to his step.

It did his heart good to see something going well for his father-in-law. Life had been hard for him, painfully hard. He was a good man—as good as they came—and he deserved something to break well for him for a change.

With God's help—and Maggie's agreement—he had a plan that just might bring some more good fortune Matthew's way.

Chapter Twenty-three

Jonathan's Plan

To be honest, to be kind;
To earn a little and to spend a little less;
To make upon the whole a family happier for his presence...

Robert Louis Stevenson

All week Jonathan mulled over the idea that had been working at the back of his mind for more than a month now. It had also been near the top of his prayer list for just as long. By Friday he knew it was time to raise the subject with Maggie. She would be the one to say yes or no.

If he followed through with this, it would involve both responsibility and change for both of them. Seeing as how they'd already experienced a fair share of both, he had no intention of going any further without a clear show of approval and enthusiasm from his wife.

When they stopped at the MacAuleys after school that afternoon, instead of taking Gracie home, he surprised Maggie by asking her mother if she'd be good enough to mind the baby that evening so he and Maggie could have a quiet evening alone.

The discussion he had in mind was serious business, and he was resolved that they would have all the uninterrupted time they needed to talk it through.

❖❖

That evening they drove out to Holly Hill House, a country inn and the only refined dining place in the area. Jonathan thought the combination of the inn's cheerful decor and a leisurely ride into the country might be good for both of them.

Maggie's excitement convinced him he'd made a wise choice.

"I've never been here, you know," she told him after they were seated in the private corner he'd requested. "Candles, tablecloths, paintings on the walls!" Maggie couldn't stop staring at her surroundings. "The only time I've ever been to a place this nice was when some friends took me out to a birthday supper in Chicago. This is lovely, Jonathan. Thank you!"

He smiled at her enthusiasm. "I thought you might like it."

But in an instant her lively expression gave way to a look of suspicion. "Wait. Is something wrong?"

He laughed at her. "Because I want to take my wife out to dinner? No, dear heart, nothing is wrong."

"You're quite sure?"

"*Maggie—*"

"All right then. I'll relax and enjoy myself."

"That's what I was hoping for."

"I suppose you're used to nice places like this," she commented, "growing up in the city and all."

"Lexington has its share of good restaurants, yes. When we go back one day, I'll take you to some of them."

Her eyes clouded, most likely from the memory of their interrupted honeymoon trip to Lexington, when they were called back to Skingle Creek because of Eva Grace's death. Unwilling to let anything cast a shadow on the evening, Jonathan quickly changed the subject. "I saw you had the Conibear twins cornered again this afternoon. What happened this time?"

She brightened. "Actually, I took them aside to tell them how proud I was of the way they behaved today. I can't think what struck them, but I didn't have to call them out once."

"You're sure they're well?" Jonathan asked dryly.

"Isn't that the way with them though? They behave for an entire day, and we think they're ill!"

The waitress appeared with menus, and they went on exchanging school stories until their dinners were served. About halfway through the meal, Jonathan realized he'd been quiet for too long when Maggie put her fork down and asked, "There *is* something wrong, isn't there?"

He hurried to reassure her. "No, I promise you there isn't. There is something I'd like us to talk about, but it's a good thing—at least I hope you'll think so."

She studied him for a moment. "It's really something good?"

"I believe it is, yes. But I want your opinion."

She tilted her head a little. "So...I can have a piece of that fancy chocolate cake on the dessert cart while we talk?"

"Absolutely."

Jonathan beckoned the waitress.

"All right then. Tell me," Maggie said when the cake arrived.

And so he did.

❧•❦

A good twenty minutes later—or was it longer—she was still staring at him as if he'd just announced he was running for governor.

"Of course," he said, "if you're interested we'll have to drive out and talk with your cousin as soon as possible." He paused. "Well, what do you think?"

Maggie seemed to finally remember the glazed piece of chocolate cake on her plate and lifted a bite to her mouth.

"What do I think?" she finally said. "I think you are absolutely the most wonderful, generous, sweetest man in the world." She took another bite of cake. "And quite possibly just a little mad."

"Just a little?"

She laid her fork on the side of her plate. "Jonathan, you can't do this. As much as I love you for even thinking of it, it's out of the question."

"I assure you it's not."

"But the *expense*. You can't possibly—"

"Maggie, I thought we'd already settled that. I explained to you—"

"About your mother's inheritance and your savings because bachelors don't spend much money and interest accumulated from the bank. Yes, I heard all that. But you can't possibly have *that* kind of money. And even if you did—"

"I do." Jonathan reached into his coat pocket.

"What? What are you doing? What's that?"

He slid the paper in front of her. "My—*our*—bank statement."

"Your bank—"

She picked it up, looked at it, stared at it, and gasped.

She gaped at him in disbelief. "I married a rich man!"

Jonathan laughed out loud, drawing raised eyebrows from people across the room. "Hardly. I merely wanted you to see that I'm not going to bankrupt us with this idea. We'll still have a savings account afterward. If that weren't the case, I wouldn't even consider such an idea."

"But, Jonathan, this is *your* money, your savings. Why would you want to spend it in such a way? Why would you do this?"

He folded the statement and put it back into his pocket. "My reasons have much to do with my love for you and your family, Maggie. But even more, I want to do God's will for all of us. While I don't pretend to have an inside track to His wishes, I do believe that this much, at least, is from His hand. And for all I know, it's the very reason I've been blessed with a bank account to begin with."

He leaned forward, taking both her hands in his. Maggie glanced around, but for once she didn't seem concerned about who might be watching.

"Is this real, Jonathan? I can't believe it's real."

"It's as real as what you and I are and what we have together."

"Are you sure, Jonathan? Are you sure it's the right thing? The thing you're meant to do? That it's what you *want* to do?"

"I think this will benefit us all, Maggie. And, yes, it's something I genuinely believe I'm to do. But I *won't* do it unless you want it too. We're married, Maggie. This is *our* money, *our* future. I can't undertake something like this without your blessing."

"My *blessing?*" Her eyes gleamed as if sprinkled with sunlight. "Oh, Jonathan! If we weren't in a public place, I'd be on your lap hugging you until you cried for mercy!"

His eyes went over her face. "Let me get the check."

Chapter Twenty-four

Maggie's Goodbye

Live day by day.
Why art thou bending toward the backward way?
One summit and another thou shalt mount.
Why stop at every round the space to count
The past mistakes if thou must still remember?
Watch not the ashes of the dying ember.
Kindle thy hope. Put all thy fears away—
Live day by day.

Julia Harris May

The last day of March, and thus Maggie's last day at school, fell on a Friday.

She spent most of the day trying not to weep. She was going to miss the school, miss the children, and miss being a teacher—at least for now. Moreover, at different times of the day the thoughtfulness and kindness of her students very nearly unglued her already fragile composure.

Each child brought her a gift, almost all homemade, and every one of them precious and to be kept with her other mementos. Even the Conibear twins showed up, grinning and obviously pleased with themselves, with a somewhat bent twig, explaining that it was a "baby maple tree" she could plant in her front yard to "'member them by."

"I assure you, Willy and Billy, I could never, ever forget the two of you."

She was packing up her treasures in advance of the dismissal bell when Huey Lazlo edged up beside her at her desk and tugged at her hand.

"Miss Maggie?"

Maggie looked down at the small face with the pointed chin. "Yes, Huey?"

"Selma and me drew you a picture."

He handed her a drawing of a dark-haired little boy and a taller girl. The picture had been matted and framed on hardboard. Obviously, Regina Wallace had had a hand in the project.

Maggie had all she could do not to break into tears. Months ago Selma, Huey's big sister, had drawn a picture for Jonathan: a picture of herself and her little brother. In that earlier drawing, the girl wore an utterly solemn face, and the boy's cheeks were tracked with tears—clearly a reflection of their troubled hearts and their unhappy life at home with their parents. This time the children in the picture were smiling and holding flowers. And at the bottom were printed the words: "Thank you for helping us."

And thank you, Ben and Regina. Thank you for taking these children into your home and into your hearts, she thought.

Tears burned Maggie's eyes, but she managed a smile. "This is the finest picture I've ever seen, Huey. You can be sure I'll keep it forever. Please thank Selma for me too."

His answering smile was shy but bright. "Will you and Mr. Stuart come to visit us sometimes after we move to Louisville?"

"Of course we will, Huey! And no doubt the Wallaces will bring you and Selma back to visit *us* too." She bent over and hugged the boy.

The dismissal bell rang then, and the children—every last one of them—filed up to Maggie's desk and gave her a hug and said goodbye. Huey hung back until the last student had left the room. He came forward to collect one more hug before starting for the door. At the last moment, he turned back and waved. "I'll miss you, Miss Maggie!"

Maggie put a fist to her mouth to keep from crying.

I'll miss you too, Huey. I'll miss every one of you...all my children...

She waved to him and turned away so he wouldn't see her weeping.

※·※

Jonathan found her facing the chalkboard, her slender shoulders heaving, sobs tearing from her throat.

"Oh, my dear..." He crossed the room and took her by the shoulders, turning her around and pressing her face against his chest. "I'm so sorry, Maggie. I *hate* this for you. I'd give anything if I could have kept it from happening."

She choked on a sob, pulled in a steadying breath, and wiped a hand over her eyes. "No, I'm all right, Jonathan," she said, looking up at him. "Really, I am." She still held Huey's picture in her hand, and she showed it to him.

He studied the picture and felt his own eyes sting. "This has to be so hard for you."

"I don't think I'm crying because I can't teach here anymore. Can you understand that? I honestly believe it's *right* that I leave...and leave now. I'm crying because it's...such a bittersweet goodbye. Yes, I'll miss the school—being here with the children and with you. But I can come and visit, and you and I will still have our time together at home. I think I'm simply realizing just how much of my life has been lived here in this building. So many years. Growing up here, then leaving, and coming back. Finding you again—there's so much of *me* inside this school, Jonathan. It's almost like leaving a part of me behind."

He held her close, saying nothing.

Finally she eased back enough to look at him. She smiled. A brave smile, made all the more poignant by the tears that still glistened in her eyes. "That's the sadness. But there's a sweetness, also, there really is. I'm leaving for the right reasons, and I have a nice home and precious baby girl waiting for me. Not to mention a wonderful husband. I have parents and a brother who love me, and now I can spend more time with them. And eventually, God willing, I'll be a teacher again, thanks to Anna. I'll even have a school that's partly my own."

She stopped, straightened her shoulders, and pressed his fingers with her own. "It's time to go. I'm ready now. Let's pick up our daughter and go home."

At the exit, Jonathan waited as she turned for one last look behind her. Then they stepped outside together.

Chapter Twenty-five

A Grateful Heart

O my Love and Life,
O my Life and Love,
Thank God for you!

James Thomson

⟋⟍

April. Even in a coal town the promise of spring made itself known, drifting down from the mountains, weaving its gently scented fragrance among the dust-covered houses and streets, bringing a hint of brighter skies and warmer days.

On Saturday Maggie and Jonathan took advantage of the nicest weather they'd had in months to take Gracie for a buggy ride out of town. It wasn't merely a pleasure ride, although Maggie was enjoying every minute of it. The excitement simmering just beneath her appreciation of the sunshine and light breezes had to do with the objective of their excursion.

Their destination was the Taggart farm, where they planned to speak with Maggie's cousins, Jeff and Martha, about a plan that would change the lives and future of two families: the MacAuleys and the Stuarts.

They stopped only once before reaching their destination, pulling over to the side of the road to admire a patchwork field of early wildflowers. While there, they added yet another prayer to the myriad others they'd been sending up for weeks.

❧⊰⊱

Saturday was a long day, and a lonely one at that, for Kate. No sign of Maggie or the baby. Matthew was at the mine, and Ray off with his friends, now that his job at the farm had ended. When she was alone like this, her mind betrayed her with memories and with fear. The memories were filled with thoughts of Eva Grace—what her oldest child had gone through at the hands of a man who'd said he loved her, Kate not knowing until it was too late to help—and the suffering Eva had endured at the end.

The fear. The fear centered around that man who had deceived her daughter, who beat her and humiliated her, threatened her, and threatened to take her child. Surely he would come one day. No matter how they all avoided speaking of it, Richard Barlow would come for Gracie. Of this Kate had no doubt.

Matthew kept reminding her that the law had placed a restraining order on Richard. But knowing what she knew about him, having seen for herself the rage in the man that day he'd come and tried to force Eva Grace to go home with him, Kate was convinced the question wasn't *if* he would come, but *when*.

She was eager for Matthew to come home. But when he finally came in, one look told her he was hurting and exhausted. After he cleaned up, they ate a quiet supper, their conversation limited to her few, careful questions and his mostly one-syllable responses.

He did ask after Ray, as well as Maggie and her family. When she refused his offer to help with the dishes, telling him to rest, he wandered off to the front room where he promptly fell asleep in his chair.

Kate woke him after finishing her mending, and as soon as he checked the locks and changed his clothes, they went to bed.

Late into the night Kate lay staring at his back, wondering how many lonely days like this she could endure without going completely mad.

❧•❧

Too excited to sleep, Maggie sat at the vanity, brushing her hair.

"You're going to pull it out by the roots the way you're attacking it," Jonathan observed. He relieved her of the brush and began to wield it in even, gentle strokes.

This had become a nightly routine, and Maggie was hard-pressed to say who enjoyed it most. Jonathan claimed he did, but she didn't see how that could be possible.

"When will we tell them?" she asked. "I don't want to wait too long. Mum has seemed so…so heavy hearted lately. This is going to make such a difference for her."

"How about tomorrow? Kate's already asked if we'd come for a late supper after rehearsal. I could drive you over before then, and you could spend some time with your mother while Matthew and I are at the church."

"That would be perfect."

"Just don't let anything slip to Kate until Matthew and I get back."

"I won't. But I doubt that I'll close my eyes tonight. Oh, Jonathan! I still can't believe we're going to do this. That *you're* going to do this!"

"First things first, Maggie. We can't do anything unless your folks are agreeable. And it's hard to tell what Matthew will say."

"How could he *not* agree to it? Surely he will."

"Your father is a very proud man," Jonathan pointed out. "And if you don't mind my saying so, at times he can be a very *stubborn* man. We'd best not count on anything until we see his reaction."

Jonathan was right, of course. Her mother wasn't exaggerating when she fussed about Da's hardheadedness.

"Ray will be positively wild for the idea," she said. "And Mum is going to kiss your feet." She reached behind her, stilled his hand with the brush, and then patted the vanity bench for him to sit down beside her.

He looked dubious. "Are you sure this spindly thing will hold both of us?"

"We'll find out, won't we?"

He sat and she took his hand. "I need to know something."

"What's that?"

"Why are you doing this? For that matter, why do you do *any* of the things you do? You're always giving, Jonathan. You put everyone before yourself. You always have."

"What are you talking about?"

"Don't be evasive. You know what I mean. You think I don't know about some of the things you do? I *do* know. For instance, I know you're helping Kenny fund the mission. Anna let it slip. And you're forever buying things for the school out of your own pocket. I expect you've done that for years." She stopped and then added, "And look what you're doing with your singing miners. The time and effort you give them just because you think it will be good for them and the town. And now *this*—what you're doing for my family."

The more she said, the more he fidgeted. But Maggie wasn't finished. "You've been pouring yourself and your wallet out for as long as I've known you, Jonathan Stuart. I've wanted to ask you for years what motivates you. I figure now that I'm your wife, I have the right to ask. Why do you do it?"

He still didn't meet her gaze. "I don't believe I've ever thought about it. But gratitude perhaps?"

It was no surprise to Maggie that he hadn't thought about it. But his answer confused her.

"I don't understand. All the people you've helped over the years, why would *you* be grateful to them?"

"I'm not grateful to *them.* I'm grateful to *God.*"

Finally he met her eyes. "I've had an incredible life, Maggie. I've never wanted for anything. I've had…so much: a happy childhood, wonderful parents, a good education, good friends." He stopped, running a hand down the side of his face before going on. "Let me explain something. When I came to Skingle Creek, it was with the somewhat patronizing notion that the people here needed me. I was young and idealistic and convinced that God called me here to give these poor people a blessing."

"Well, what's wrong with that? You *have* been a blessing to the town."

He put a hand to her arm. "No, Maggie. I had it all wrong. *I'm* the one who received the blessing. These people have given me more than I could have ever hoped for in a lifetime. The children, their parents—the people of Skingle Creek—gave me a reason for existence, a purpose I would never have found on my own.

"Moreover, it was here that God showed me what He wanted *from* me and *for* me. It was here that He healed me, physically and spiritually. And it was here," he lifted her hand and brushed a light kiss over it, "it was here that He gave me the most precious gift of my life—He gave me *you.*"

His voice caught and he hesitated before going on. "You and your family. Gracie. Don't you see? He's given me everything I've ever prayed for and so much more. The little I do for anyone else, and it *is* little in comparison to what He's done for *me,* I suppose I do it because I live with an overflowing heart. I am so deeply *grateful.*"

The room was completely quiet. Jonathan's eyes caught the glow from the kerosene lamp, and Maggie felt herself drawn to the light in his gaze. She touched his cheek with the back of her hand and left it there until he covered it with his own.

She'd thought she was finally coming to know him well, this man she had loved almost all her life. But she realized that tonight, more than at any other time, she had seen his heart and felt the very pulse of his being.

In that moment, her own heart rose up in response and matched his gratitude with her own.

Chapter Twenty-six

Shadows over Sunday

Our deeds pass by as shadows
In pursuit of what we are.

Anonymous

These songs you've got us working on now, Jonathan. They're not so easy to sing as some of the others, are they?"

Jonathan shook his head, waiting for Matthew to step inside the church before closing the door. "No, they're not. Even so, I think the men are coming along nicely with them, don't you?"

His father-in-law made a low sound in his throat as they started into the sanctuary. "If you say so. I think you might have chosen a few pieces easier to learn."

"Now, Matthew, don't you go letting on as though the music is troublesome to you. The men take a lot of their signals from you. If they see that you're fine with the songs, they'll try to match you."

Matthew made the same guttural sound as before. "You and your ideas. You do come up with some dandies. You really think we're up to this?"

"I *know* you are. It's going to be wonderful." Jonathan slid him a sideways look. "You don't trust my ideas?"

"Some more than others perhaps."

"Your daughter tends to like them...for the most part," he said with a grin.

"And would she be telling you so if she didn't, do you think?"

"We're talking about Maggie, Matthew."

"Aye. I expect that one would tell you quick enough."

"Indeed."

A few of the other men were already down front waiting.

"I'll give you a ride home after we finish," Jonathan said, hard put to suppress a smile as he considered the evening ahead. "I'm having supper at your house."

"Again?" Matthew said, clearly making no effort to suppress *his* smile.

❧·❦

Richard Barlow had ridden into Skingle Creek in the afternoon after spending the night in a fleabag inn just outside of town. Acting on information he'd pried from his milksop attorney, he first made his way to the Stuart house. It seemed that his sister-in-law, little Miss Maggie, had married the local schoolteacher and the two of them were raising the baby.

His baby.

He had planned to confront them at their own front door and take the infant, thinking that late Sunday afternoon would be the optimal time to catch them at home. Were they really so ignorant as to think a stupid restraining order would keep him away from his own flesh and blood?

He wasn't worried about them putting up a fight. If the husband was a schoolteacher, he wouldn't be worth much. And while Maggie might think she was a spitfire, she was still just a woman. Neither of them would be a match for him. Or for the gun in his pocket.

When he found no one at home, he knew where to go next. Ordinarily he wouldn't be all that eager to come up against Eva Grace's old man. Big as a tree and just as rugged, Matthew MacAuley had never made any secret of the fact that he wasn't impressed with his daughter's choice of a husband.

Too bad. What MacAuley didn't know was that his son-in-law wasn't overly impressed with his darling daughter either.

He still fumed when he thought about the cold, unfeeling way they'd advised him of his own baby's birth and the death of his wife. Sending a cut-and-dried note through Randal, his attorney. And then almost immediately slapping a restraining order on him.

He knew they would underestimate him, and that was in his favor. By now they probably assumed he'd given up on claiming the baby. That he would heed the restraining order and not venture near. Ha! That's exactly what he wanted them to believe.

That's why he'd waited so long, why he hadn't made a move until today. But now the time was right. That baby was his, and he was taking her home. What he would do with her later was of no concern to him just yet. He'd find someone to help take care of her. He would see that she was raised to be obedient and behave herself, unlike her foolish mother.

There was no way she was going to grow up in Skingle Creek among these no-account people he detested.

❧⚜❧

Maggie was setting the table, trying to keep as busy as possible so her excitement wouldn't bubble over. "How many places, Mum? Will Ray be here?" she asked, fervently hoping he would be.

"He said he'd probably be back by four. But I wouldn't count on it. He's out on The Hill with Tim Duggan and his father, looking for that black bear that's got everybody so spooked."

Maggie looked at her mother. "A bear? I thought they'd disappeared from around here."

It was an unusually warm day for early April, and the kitchen had quickly grown steamy. Kate went to open some of the other windows, and then came back and opened the kitchen window over the sink as well. "Your Da says there is no bear, but the Duggans have got it in their heads that they saw bear scat a few days ago. They told everyone who'd listen. Nothing would do for your brother but to go along with the others today."

"Well, I hope Da's right. I don't like the idea of a bear anywhere near town."

"Oh, you know the Duggans," Kate said. "Always looking for something that isn't there." She wiped her hands down her apron and turned toward the pantry.

Just then Gracie cried out from the back bedroom. "She's waking up. I'll get her," Kate said. "Keep an eye on the potatoes."

Maggie went to the stove and lifted the lid on the pot, stepping back a little to avoid the steam. When someone knocked at the front door, she quickly replaced the lid on the pot and started for the front room.

"I'll get it, Mum," she called.

One moment she was hurrying out of the kitchen, still humming with happiness and anticipation, and the next the world roared and shifted like a giant earthquake, splitting the ground beneath her, almost knocking her senseless.

Richard Barlow stood just inside the front door, one hand in his pocket, the other holding a gun trained directly on her.

Chapter Twenty-seven

An Intrusion of Darkness

And the dark lava fires of madness
Once more sweep through my brain.

James Clarence Mangan

Had he been wrong? Had he misjudged the miners' ability or overestimated his own?

Jonathan stood thinking a moment with his back to the men, pretending to listen to the chorus. Today's rehearsal was only a short straw away from disaster. It was as if the men had never sung together. Even Luc Penryn, his lead singer, fell off pitch several times and took the others along with him. Moreover, Luc was clearly having trouble with some of the words, not a usual problem for the Welshman. The one number that Jonathan had been accompanying with his flute at each rehearsal—and which had gone extremely well until today—would have been ludicrous had it not been such a frustrating experience for him and, no doubt, for the men as well.

Finally, he turned back to them and called the singing to a halt, still making a concerted effort to keep his unsettled thoughts to himself. "Well," he finally said, "we're not doing all that well today, are we?"

A few chuckles sounded from the back row, but for the most part his words were met with glum expressions and a few bewildered stares.

They didn't understand what was happening either.

One thing was certain: They were on the border of discouragement. If Jonathan wasn't careful with what he said, it was altogether possible he might tip them over the edge.

"You know, I thought we did surprisingly well on these numbers last week. I expect we're just having an off day. That sort of thing happens. I'm not worried about it, and you don't need to worry either. Let's stop for now and spend the rest of the day with our families. We'll do better next week."

That broke the tension. There were some audible deep breaths and murmurs of relief. Within a few minutes everyone was out of the building and on the way home.

Only Matthew remained, waiting for Jonathan to collect his things.

"You're free to say 'I told you so,'" Jonathan admitted as they walked out of the church.

"What do you suppose went wrong?"

"I have no idea."

"Well, don't let it get you down. Like you said, next week will be better, I expect."

Jonathan hadn't realized how dejected he must have sounded until it struck him that Matthew was making an effort to cheer him up. Not exactly typical, that. "Let's hope so," he said, forcing a brighter note into his tone, although his head throbbed like thunder. "We have only three more weeks until Easter."

Matthew delayed his reply. "Three weeks is it?" His words were laced with uncertainty.

"I'm afraid so. I'd thought Easter Sunday would be the perfect day for the men's first performance, but now I'm beginning to wonder."

"That's not a lot of time."

Jonathan rubbed the back of his neck. "No, it really isn't." He could sense Matthew watching him. "If you have any suggestions, I'd welcome them."

A long breath. "I might have one."

Jonathan hadn't expected this. "Feel free, Matthew," he said, going around to the other side of the buggy and stepping in. "I'd be pleased to hear anything you have to offer."

"These past few weeks—perhaps you've made things too much like work, lad."

Lowering himself into the seat, Jonathan turned to look at his father-in-law. "Work?"

"Aye. When we first started with the singing some weeks back, it was mostly a good time. The men were enjoying themselves. Lately, though, especially since you've started with the new music, you've been working us like you're the drill master of a Royal regiment. Some of the good times have gone out of it, don't you see? We want to do our best for you just as much as you want it from us, but not like this."

Taken completely unaware by the other's observation, Jonathan stared at him for a moment before turning his gaze straight ahead. "I've done that? Taken the 'good times' from it?"

As if he'd gone too far and might have hurt Jonathan's feelings, the older man waved a hand. "Oh, it's not all *that* bad. The men still like to come and sing. I enjoy it myself. But it seems to me that if you handled things more as you did when we first started up, it might raise their confidence in themselves again. You see, lad, these men—if they don't believe in their ability to do something the right way, they're likely to lose faith in themselves and refuse to do it at all."

He paused. "All we know is mining, son. We don't know a thing about anything else. So when this singing idea of yours seemed to catch on, we felt pretty good about ourselves. We began to believe you were right, that we could make something of this and do the town some good."

"And you *can*, Matthew! I know you can. You men have every right to feel good about what you've achieved. Most of the time you sound as if you've been doing this for years."

"Ah, but don't you see? It doesn't take a great lot to shake loose that sense of achievement and take the starch out of our sails. I know these men. Being good at what they do is important to them."

Jonathan frowned. "So what do I do now?"

Matthew rubbed his bearded chin for a moment. "Let them lead the way. Let them have fun with it again and do it their way, even if it's a bit of a departure from what you had in mind. Give them some slack. You just might be surprised at the outcome. If they get too far off direction, you can always rein them back in. But in the meantime, they'll enjoy themselves."

Jonathan stared at him for a long moment and slowly nodded his head. "You're a wise man, Matthew MacAuley. The longer I know you, the smarter you get."

Matthew tapped his head and grinned at him. "I have a thought every now and then, that's true. Now let's get home. Supper's waiting."

Jonathan thought about what else was waiting—the news he and Maggie were planning to break tonight. He had high hopes that the reaction of his in-laws would more than make up for the disappointment of the afternoon.

He snapped the reins and the buggy lurched forward.

❖

Reason deserted Maggie. Her darkest nightmare had come true, her cruelest fear realized. The only thing she could think of was Gracie. Her mother would come walking through the door with her at any moment, and there was no way to stop her.

"Where is she?"

Richard's voice was as hard as his eyes. He was different somehow, different from the way he'd been before when he'd come after

Eva Grace. The same florid face, the same arrogant jaw, the same insolent sneer in his tone of voice. But *something* was different.

His eyes. There was a wildness…a rage.

"Where *is* she?" he demanded again, this time pushing the gun out a little further toward Maggie.

And then Gracie squealed.

Mum would have her on the changing dresser by now, making faces at her to get her to laugh.

Don't, Mum! Don't! Oh, Gracie, hush, baby…hush.

Richard's eyes cut to the right, to the side of the house where the bedroom was. He smiled. "Finally I get to see my daughter."

"Richard," Maggie said carefully, fighting down the cold river of panic surging inside. "For goodness' sake put that gun away. What are you thinking? Coming in here like this…with a gun. Do you realize the trouble you're bringing on yourself? You shouldn't be here. You're under a restraining order as it is."

"Restraining order? Ha! I'm under *nothing*. And as far as orders go, I'm the one giving them today. Go get her. Go get my daughter."

Maggie's legs threatened to buckle. Blood roared in her head like a waterfall. She couldn't let him see that he could bully her.

"If you think I'm bringing the baby into this room while you have a gun in your hand, think again!"

For an instant he actually wavered. Then his eyes cleared, and he took a step toward her. "You get her or I will."

"You'll not touch her!"

Maggie jumped at the sound of her mother's voice behind her. Richard snapped a look over her shoulder. And Gracie…Gracie started making her little nonsense sounds, her baby noises that Maggie loved so much.

"Bring her to me, Kate."

His tone was calm, almost curious. Like that of any father asking to see his child.

How could a madman sound so normal? And he *must* be mad. What else but madness would prompt a man to demand that his child be turned over to him while he held a gun?

With her gaze riveted on him, Maggie stepped in front of Gracie and her mother. "Take Gracie back to the bedroom, Mum," she said, managing to keep her voice steady. "Take her now."

Richard took a step toward them, the gun trained directly at Maggie's heart. "You do that, Kate, you take even a single step and Maggie is dead. I mean it."

Maggie saw it in his eyes. *Hatred.* Hatred for her and for her mother. But wait...something worse than that, more vicious. *There!* The madness she'd suspected. Not the humanity Eva Grace must have once seen there, but the ugliness that had replaced it. There would be no reasoning with him. How could you reason with madness?

If she risked her life—and he took it—there would be no chance of saving Gracie and most likely no chance of saving Mum. They would both die, she and her mother, perhaps Gracie too. That couldn't happen...she couldn't let it happen.

What do I do? What can I do?

Gracie was close enough to reach her tiny hand to the back of Maggie's head and tug at her hair while squealing.

"I said *bring* her to me!" Richard pointed the gun at the ceiling and fired.

Maggie and her mother screamed. Gracie shrieked in terror and started to wail.

"Did you really think I'd give up my child? That I'd just turn her over to you?" He was shouting now, shouting over Gracie's cries, which only made her cry harder.

"Stop that crying!" he ordered Maggie, waving the gun in her direction. "Make her *stop!*"

"She's a *baby,* Richard!" Maggie shouted back at him. "She's terrified! Of *you!* You're frightening her!"

That stopped him, but only for an instant. "You're as much of a witch as your sister was, you know that?"

An almost blinding fury exploded in Maggie's head, but somehow she groped and found within herself a measure of control. She could smell her own rage now, coupled with fear, but she kept her voice from trembling. "Richard, *think* what you're doing. You can't possibly get away with this. Do you really want to go to jail for kidnapping? That's what will happen, you know. You're violating the law by being in this house."

He merely sneered at her. "Not only are you a witch, you're a fool. Get out of the way!" he ordered, motioning with the gun for Maggie to step to the side.

When she made no move, he started toward her, leveling the gun at her head.

Chapter Twenty-eight

Shattered Silence

Oh, thou! who comest, like a midnight thief,
Uncounted, seeking whom thou may'st destroy;
Rupturing anew the half-closed wounds of grief,
And sealing up each new-born spring of joy.

John Keegan

Ray came tramping out of the woods and across the railroad tracks with his rifle slung over his shoulder, most of his earlier excitement about the black bear left behind with the Duggans.

He was more than a little impatient with both Tim and his father, what with all their talk about seeing evidence of the bear with their own eyes. Da had probably been right about there being no bear to begin with. He said the "scat" the Duggans had seen was more likely the droppings of their over-excitable imaginations.

They'd been out for hours with no sign of anything bigger than a white-tail buck, who skedaddled to the other side of the mountain the minute it spotted the three men with their guns. The rest of their expedition had been boring, to say the least.

As he reached the turn to the house, he stopped dead at the sight of a strange horse and buggy pulled up a few yards short of the house. No one he knew drove such a vehicle. Jonathan's rig was smaller and shinier. He had a chestnut mare. Pastor Wallace had a big brown buggy and an ugly black horse.

He stood looking at the carriage a minute, wondering if there was company coming to supper, though Mum hadn't mentioned it. Who could it be? He smelled meat cooking and something sweet. Apples. Maybe a pie, he hoped.

Hitching his rifle a notch higher, he started across the road.

A gunshot broke the stillness. Someone screamed and a baby began to cry hard.

Gracie!

❖ ❖

Maggie's ears hammered with the furious drum of her heart. Something inside her pulled back like a bowstring drawn taut. She felt breathless, lightheaded, yet at the same time she sensed a calm welling up and spreading over her. With her baby's shrieks filling her ears, she thought of nothing but protecting her mother and Gracie.

At that moment, her life had no value, no meaning to her except as a shield to protect her loved ones.

She snapped.

❖ ❖

Something exploded inside Ray. He tore across the road, heading for the front porch. The sound of a man shouting and Gracie's continued shrieks made him pivot and haul himself over to the house. Head down, he went at a crouch, stopping at the narrow front room window, which was open.

He inched his head up just far enough to see his mother and a wailing Gracie standing behind Maggie. Facing them, with a gun in his hand, was Richard Barlow.

Hatred ripped through Ray. Loathing for his former brother-in-law quickly turned to fear. Barlow was shouting for Gracie to stop crying, waving the gun at Maggie like a madman. Maggie looked as if she was about to hurl herself at him. Barlow appeared to be flying apart, the gun in his hand shaking and jerking every which way.

"Get out of the way!" Barlow ordered again, waving the gun.

Gracie wailed louder, her crunched little face scarlet.

Ray's eyes cut to his mother, clinging to wee Gracie.

His stomach in knots, his hands trembling, Ray shook his head to clear it. In one quiet move, he slipped his rifle from his shoulder and stood just as Maggie took a step toward Barlow, her face pale and drawn.

Ray saw what she intended. Barlow trained the gun directly at her head, and Ray knew what was going to happen.

Barlow sidestepped, half turning toward the window with the move, his gun still leveled on Maggie.

Ray brought his rifle up and took aim just as his sister stepped forward.

❖❖

When the explosion shattered the room, Maggie screamed and bent double, waiting for the pain, waiting to fall. She looked up and saw Richard, a look of astonishment whipping across his face, grab his chest. The gun clattered to the floor as he went down.

Maggie stared in stunned disbelief at the man at her feet, blood seeping from his chest, his eyes locked open in amazement. Finally, she found her wits and stumbled toward her mother to lift the screaming Gracie from her arms. Cuddling the baby against her heart, she stood shaking, staring at the lifeless body on the floor as she hushed and soothed her hysterical child.

Ray charged into the room, rifle in hand, stopping only long enough to nudge the body on the floor with one foot before going to Maggie and his mother.

"Are you all right?"

Maggie nodded, choking on a sob. "Richard—"

"Richard's dead."

At the sound of Ray's voice, Gracie squirmed in search of him, and after placing the rifle on the floor, Ray gave her his fingers to clutch. She watched him, her choked sobs finally easing as she held onto his thumb.

Maggie noticed her brother's hand was shaking. "Ray? Are you all right?"

He looked at her, his gaze starting to clear now. Finally he nodded. "I had to shoot him, Mags. I had to."

"I know…I know you did. You had no choice. You saved our lives, Ray…mine and Mum's. And Gracie's as well. You did what you had to do."

The three of them were still standing there, huddled together, when a white-faced Jonathan lunged through the door, Da right behind him.

Chapter Twenty-nine

A Child Is Born

The hope lives on, age after age.

George William Russell

Nearly a week later, the investigation wrapped up and Ray was exonerated by the authorities, the entire family enjoying a hard-won peace.

Jonathan and Maggie again made plans to break the news they'd been holding back for days. Without giving anything away, Jonathan let the MacAuleys know that Sunday was to be a special day, one not to be compromised by extraneous events except in an emergency situation.

That "emergency situation" arrived late Saturday night when Judson Tallman showed up at the Stuart's house. Jonathan and Maggie were sound asleep when they heard pounding on the front door well past midnight. By the time Jonathan found his robe and eyeglasses and stumbled down the steps, the pounding came again, louder this time.

Disoriented and struggling to focus his eyes, Jonathan opened the door to find Kenny's father in a state. Somewhat disheveled, he appeared highly agitated and harried. In fact, Tallman didn't look like himself at all.

"Mr. Stuart. I apologize. But it's Anna! She's—the baby is coming! She's asking for your wife." His words spilled out in a breathless volley as he wrung his hands.

Maggie was already on her way down the steps. She came up behind Jonathan. "Mr. Tallman! What is it? Is it Anna? Is it her time?"

Tallman wilted with relief at the sight of Maggie. "Yes! Yes, it's the baby. Maggie—Mrs. Stuart—will you come? Anna said she'd asked you to be with her for the birthing."

"Yes, of course I'll come. Just give me a few minutes."

"Thank you. Anna will be most grateful. Kenneth has gone for Dr. Gordon, so Anna sent me to collect you."

At Jonathan's insistence, Tallman came inside to wait while Maggie dressed. In the living room the mine superintendent recovered his usual air of stiff formality. "I apologize for disturbing you and your wife, but Anna was set on my fetching Maggie—Mrs. Stuart."

"It's no trouble at all, Judson." Jonathan purposely used Tallman's given name, hoping to break through a layer or two of the other's defenses and put him more at ease.

He motioned for him to sit down, but when Tallman remained standing, Jonathan did likewise.

"This is an exciting time," Jonathan said, hoping to help the man relax. "Is Anna doing all right?"

At last Tallman managed a deep breath. "I think so. Anna never complains. She insists she's quite all right."

"And Kenny?"

"He's...ah...very nervous. *Very* nervous."

Jonathan couldn't stop a smile. "Well, I imagine that's to be expected. I'm sure everything will be fine. And this will be your first grandchild, isn't that so?"

Tallman looked startled, as if this fact hadn't yet occurred to him. "Why…yes. Yes, that's right."

Jonathan continued his attempts to make conversation, noting that Tallman was obviously trying to control—even conceal—his nervousness. He kept glancing toward the stairway. Seeing no sign of Maggie, he would then turn his attention back to Jonathan, as if preparing himself for the next question.

"Maggie thinks highly of Anna, you know. She truly values their friendship."

Tallman nodded. "Anna is a good woman. Kenneth is very fortunate."

"And so is Anna," Jonathan couldn't resist saying.

"Oh yes. Yes, indeed."

Jonathan expelled his own breath of relief when Maggie came hurrying into the room, dressed and ready to leave.

At the door, he squeezed her hand and told her goodbye. He then turned to Judson Tallman and said, "I'll be praying for all of you."

Tallman shot him an awkward but not ungrateful look before following Maggie out the door.

Jonathan watched until Tallman's buggy disappeared into the night. He remained sleepless after going back to bed, so he spent the time in prayer. He lifted up Anna, Kenny, and the baby, and also Judson Tallman, a man who always seemed excessively keen on protecting himself from any display of feeling—or any sense of faith in God.

He smiled a little at the thought of the stoic, stone-faced Welshman at the mercy of the charming Anna and the coming new baby. Judson Tallman couldn't possibly know how much his life was about to change.

❖•❖

Maggie worked hard to hide her nervousness on the drive to the

Tallman house. The mine superintendent seemed wound tightly enough on his own. He certainly didn't need a show of anxiety on her part.

In truth, though, she was frightened nearly to the point of being sick. She hadn't wanted to do this. It had taken an act of sheer will to agree when Anna asked her to attend the baby's birthing. If she weren't so fond of Anna....

Well, I am fond of her, I did promise, and so here I am.

She swallowed hard, trying to ignore the stomach spasms. Never in her life had she seen a baby born. She knew only the narrowest facts about the entire process, little more than what she'd overheard from snippets of conversation from her mother and other women. Even in Chicago most of her friends were as ignorant about giving birth as she was.

And then there was what happened to Eva Grace. Her sister's entire waiting time had been difficult, even painful, finally resulting in her death. Consequently, when she thought of watching Anna give birth, fear gripped her. She had all she could do not to concede to raw terror.

She suspected her mother sensed her misgivings. When Maggie told her about Anna's request, Mum had fixed one of her long, searching looks on her and said bluntly, "And you're all right with that, then? You mustn't give your word for something so important unless you're quite certain you can keep it."

Maggie had assured her that this was something she felt compelled to do for Anna and that she would be just fine. Her mother had seemed satisfied, yet Maggie had noticed her watching her now and then that same afternoon with a thoughtful expression.

At the moment Maggie wanted to tell Mr. Tallman to turn the buggy around and take her home. But she couldn't do that. Moreover, Kenny would probably need someone to talk with and wait with tonight. And from everything she'd seen of his somber-faced father, *he* would be of little comfort.

Maggie stole a glance at Judson Tallman, whose features seemed set in stone as he stared straight ahead. She couldn't stop a small sigh at the thought of Kenny growing up with this hard, seemingly cold, undemonstrative man to parent him. And now there was Anna. Anna and a baby on the way. Judson Tallman was in for a shock.

A smile slowly broke across her face. At least for the moment her heart lightened. Who knew better than she what a difference a baby could make in someone's life, even in the life of a man like Judson Tallman?

⋙⋘

Upon entering, Maggie went directly upstairs to Anna. Her friend was well into labor. To Maggie's dismay, Dr. Gordon and Kenny hadn't arrived yet. Anxiety returned in full force, but she managed what she hoped was a brave face and a reassuring smile as she took Anna's hand.

"Oh, Maggie, you came! I'm so grateful."

Maggie bent to brush a strand of hair away from her friend's face. "Of course, I came. I promised, didn't I?"

"Has Ken come with the doctor yet?" Anna asked, gripping Maggie's hand with surprising strength.

"Not just yet, but I'm sure they'll be here any minute now. Can I do anything for you?"

Anna smiled and shook her head. "Just...keep an eye on Ken once they get here. He's *terribly* nervous. You'll have to be a rock for him—for both of us, I'm afraid."

Maggie suppressed a groan. She didn't feel like anyone's "rock." She felt like mush. Even so, she managed to keep a smile in place. "Kenny will do just fine. And so will you."

"Oh, I believe *I* shall," Anna asserted. "I'm not so sure about Ken."

Maggie sat down beside her on the bed. "Is there anything you want, dear? Anything at all I can do?"

Again Anna shook her head. "Just stay with me. And Maggie?"

Maggie leaned toward her.

"I don't want Ken in the room while I'm in labor. He's agreed, although I don't think he understands. But you do, don't you?"

Maggie didn't understand anything about this entire ordeal, but at the moment it seemed best to agree with anything her friend said. "Whatever you want, Anna."

"He'd only get himself into a state, and that won't help me at all. Only another woman can understand the act of giving birth. My mother said my father was the bravest man she'd ever known until he entered the birthing room, and then he turned into a coward. Poor man—and there were five of us."

Maggie laughed in spite of herself. Her humor was short-lived when a sharp labor pain seized Anna and she cried out. Maggie shot to her feet, still holding the other's hand.

After the pain had passed, Anna gave her a weak smile. "You have a very strong grip, did you know that?"

Just then Mr. Tallman cleared his throat from where he'd apparently been waiting in the hallway. "Anna, are you all right? Can I do anything? Get you anything?"

Maggie and Anna exchanged a look. "Anna's fine, Mr. Tallman," Maggie called out. "She's doing just fine."

"Yes...well—" Again he cleared his throat. "I'll wait downstairs then. Kenneth will be coming with the doctor soon."

"I think my pains are coming closer together now," Anna said after a moment. "I wish the doctor would make an appearance soon."

It struck Maggie that she wished the exact same thing even more.

❧·❧

Kenny's father didn't stay downstairs long. In a few minutes he was back, asking if there was anything he could do. Maggie sent him to boil water.

"Lots of water, Mr. Tallman, please," she ordered. That was one thing she *did* know. Women having babies always needed boiled water, though she had no idea why.

Minutes later the pains were coming much more frequently and with more intensity. Maggie stood in awe before Anna's calm and her continuing cheerfulness despite the pain so obviously gripping her.

"Does it hurt terribly, Anna?" she asked, and then could have kicked herself. "Oh, what a stupid thing to say! I'm so sorry."

Between pains, Anna reassured her. "It's not stupid at all. And, yes, it hurts. But then most things of value don't come to us easily, do they? This child is going to be worth every single...ah..." She gasped as another pain seized her. Maggie bent to lay a cool cloth on her forehead, and Anna squeezed her hand in gratitude. "You're doing wonderfully, Maggie," she said with a smile.

"*I'm* doing wonderfully?" Maggie almost laughed at the absurdity of Anna's assurance. "*You're* the one having the baby, Anna. And you're incredible!" In that instant she heard the downstairs door open and close. The sound of voices came up the stairs. Kenny and Dr. Gordon!

Thank You, Lord! Maggie prayed.

She heard Kenny come at a run, taking the steps at least three at a time, followed by Dr. Gordon, warning him to slow down lest he break a leg.

Anna gave him only a moment after he charged into the room before ordering him out. "Now, Ken. I mean it!"

Maggie stepped aside so he could lean to kiss Anna before she threatened him again.

He left the room like a recalcitrant schoolboy headed for the principal's office, casting a wide-eyed look of anxiety at Maggie as he went.

"Good girl, Anna," the doctor said, making ready to examine her. "The birthing room is no place for a man. They haven't the stomach for it."

When Maggie offered to leave while the doctor examined her, Anna gripped her hand with such force she winced. "No. Stay, Maggie. Please."

Maggie stayed.

"Ah! We're doing nicely, Anna," Dr. Gordon stated. "Sorry it took me so long to get here. I was at the Finnegans delivering Mary's baby.

I've never quite understood why babies seem to delight in making a grand entrance late at night and all at the same time. Anyway, your husband was waiting for me at my house when I got back."

She glanced at Maggie. "Bring me my case, would you, Maggie? Over there on the chair by the door. Anna, your husband is in quite a fix. I thought I might have to treat *him* before we got here." She laughed quietly.

In the throes of another labor pain, Anna nevertheless managed to say, "Oh, he's been just awful tonight. I hope this doesn't take much longer."

Setting the medical case at the foot of the bed, Maggie went back to Anna and took her hand.

"Actually, my dear," said Dr. Gordon, rising from her chair at the foot of the bed, "it's not going to take much longer at all. Give me one more good push, now. And another. Yes! Here we go!" She shot a look at Maggie. "Don't you faint on me now, Maggie Stuart. You've done well so far."

Just before she turned her attention back to her work, she added, "I expect we'll be doing this for *you* one day."

Her words set off an alarm in Maggie's head. Something at the back of her mind struggled for attention. So much had happened and in such a brief time. So much.

But something else hadn't happened…not for some time now. She drew in a startled breath, choked, and made a small sound of recognition.

The doctor looked up. "What? What's wrong?"

Maggie looked at her, pulled in yet another sharp breath, and again choked. "I…nothing…nothing is wrong. I don't think…I just might need to talk with you…later."

Dr. Gordon gave her a measuring look through narrowed eyes, but only for a second or two. "That's fine," she said, clearly distracted by the more important event taking place.

❯❯·❮❮

Maggie quietly exited the room more than an hour later to give Kenny and Anna their privacy. Anna looked wan and exhausted, but she was smiling at her new son held securely in the crook of her arm. Kenny stood watching, a slightly dazed smile about to crack his face in half.

She waited in the kitchen with Judson Tallman. He actually talked to her most of the time. They talked about the baby, about Kenny's experiences on the mission field, and about Anna, of whom he was unabashedly fond.

Maggie suspected she was witnessing a side of the mine superintendent seldom seen before. His face was alive with an enthusiasm she would have previously thought impossible for the man. Not only did he seem on fire with excitement, but the usually dark house blazed with light. Candles, kerosene lamps, and hallway sconces glowed. It was like being in a different house entirely.

They were deep in conversation about the prospects of the school—the new school that she and Anna would manage—when Kenny walked into the kitchen holding the baby.

His father nearly knocked over the chair as he jumped to his feet, but he said nothing.

Maggie also stood, enjoying the look of pride and happiness shining in Kenny's eyes.

It struck her in that moment that in spite of the fear that preyed on her, she wanted to see that look on Jonathan's face someday. The pride, the elation of holding his own newborn.

"Dr. Gordon said it was all right to bring him down and show him off," Kenny said. Giving no warning, he handed the small bundle over to his father, who looked for all the world as if he would pass out on the spot.

"Let me introduce you to your first grandson, Dad," Ken said. "Jonathan Judson Tallman, meet your grandfather. We decided," he said with a look at Maggie, "to name him after two very special men in our lives."

Maggie fought against the tears burning at the back of her

eyes. "Thank you, Kenny," she said quietly. "Jonathan will be so pleased."

Judson stared down at the wee boy in his arms with wonder. Finally he looked up. "He looks just like you, son. A fine boy!" Now it was Kenny's father who glowed with pride.

With that Maggie lost the battle. She let the tears flow as they would and her fear no longer held sway.

Chapter Thirty

Family Gathering

He'll meet the soul which comes in love
And deal it joy on joy—
As once He dealt out star and star
To garrison the sky,
To stand there over rains and snows
And deck the dark of night—
So, God will deal the soul, like stars,
Delight upon delight.

Robert Farren

Jonathan and Maggie were out for an early evening walk when he raised the subject of the farm. Figaro ran well ahead of them, trotting into the woods behind the house while they slowly followed the road. "We've waited long enough. Let your mother know we'll be over Thursday evening."

"But Jonathan, that's a workday. You know how tired Da is when he's been in the mine all day. And he'll have to be up early the next morning as well. That won't be a good time to tell them *anything*."

"Maggie, I'm not waiting. Something is sure to happen if we do. Besides, we have to give your cousin a definite answer."

She looked at him, drew a long breath, and said, "All right. But don't say I didn't warn you."

"Matthew will be fine once he hears what we have to tell him," her husband said, taking her hand as they turned onto the path that led to a small pine grove near the pond.

"If we can keep him awake long enough to hear it."

"The word 'news' almost always grabs your father's attention, I've noticed. He's the only man I know who reads his newspaper twice through."

"Da's always been one for knowing what's going on."

"He is indeed. Sometimes to a fault."

She looked at him. "You two are always nettling each other."

"You mean he's always nettling *me*. I simply respond in kind."

She shook her head, smiling. "You're both incorrigible, not letting on what good friends you really are. I hope that friendship will be a help when Pastor Ben moves away."

"I'm not looking to Matthew to take Ben's place, if that's what you mean. Your father is my friend in his own right. But, yes, I'm sure it will help."

"Do you know when the Wallaces are leaving?"

"Well, Ben hasn't wanted to move on until the church board calls a new pastor."

"And they still haven't found anyone?" Maggie stopped to button her sweater all the way up. The sun was going down and the air was turning cool.

They started walking again. Not too far ahead, Figaro stopped, as if to make sure they were following, and then he charged ahead and disappeared.

"I thought perhaps you knew," Jonathan said, not looking at her.

"Knew what?" Again Maggie stopped, forcing him to stop with her.

When he made no reply, she tugged at his sleeve. "Knew *what*, I said."

"Anna hasn't said anything?"

"I haven't seen Anna since last weekend. Why? What does Anna have to do with Pastor Ben?"

He turned to face her. "They've called Kenny. The church board has called him as our new pastor." He paused, still smiling. "And he accepted!"

"Oh! Oh, Jonathan! How wonderful. They'll be staying. And Kenny will have a job."

He laughed at her, but Maggie couldn't restrain herself. "I'm so happy for them. And for the church. Kenny will be a wonderful pastor. And Anna the perfect pastor's wife."

"Yes. They're well-suited for the work, there's no doubt about that."

She narrowed her eyes. "How long have you known about this?"

"Well, the church board asked me for a reference a couple of weeks ago, but—"

"A couple of *weeks* ago? And you didn't tell me?"

"I *couldn't* tell you. The board asked that I say nothing until they made their final decision and Kenny his."

She feigned a pout, but she was too happy to carry it through.

They took up walking again, stopping only when they reached the grove. It was an absolutely beautiful day, and the grove was fragrant with pine and wildflowers. It was one of their favorite places to go and talk.

Maggie leaned against one of the older pine trees, digging her toe at the soft earth packed around the base of the trunk. Figaro bounded up, circled them as if to make certain they were safe in their surroundings and took off again.

"This is simply the best news," Maggie said, still a bit overwhelmed. "And Kenny and Anna must be overjoyed." She plucked a pine needle off her sweater. "And whether he shows it or not, I happen to believe Kenny's father must be just as delighted."

Then, as if noticing a shift in Maggie's thoughts—and a wry new smile on her face, Jonathan said, "Tell me."

"What do you mean?"

"There's something on your mind."

"Why would you think that?"

He moved closer and lifted her chin with one finger, forcing her to meet his gaze. "*Tell* me," he demanded gently.

Maggie smiled a little but fixed her eyes just over his shoulder. "Well, I *might* have some news of my own if you're interested."

"Stop that. You know very well I'm interested."

"Truly?"

"*Maggie!*"

Finally she looked at him. "Do you remember when you told me you'd like a large family someday?"

He nodded.

"Do you still feel that way?"

Without touching her, he moved in closer, dipping his head to meet her gaze. "Very much so." His eyes burned into hers as he put his arms around her.

"Well," she said, melding into his embrace. "It would seem that we're on our way."

For an instant his entire face went slack as he tried to take in her words. The last of the sun fell upon them, streaming down through the canopy of trees overhead. His eyes caught the light, and he tightened his embrace.

"*Maggie?*"

She nodded.

"You're...quite certain?"

"Oh, yes," she said softly. "There's no doubt. Dr. Gordon says that Gracie is indeed going to have a new little brother or sister before another winter."

"Maggie!" he said again, sounding as if he might strangle.

He pulled her as close as possible, burying his face in her hair. "What a gift you are to me. You've given me an entire *world* with your love—and made me feel like a giant in that world."

Maggie smiled a little to herself. Jonathan could be so unexpectedly, so endearingly romantic at times. "I'm glad, dear," she said. "But then you've always been a giant in *my* world."

❖–❖

By six-thirty on Thursday evening, supper was finished, the

table cleared, and the family settled in the front room while Gracie napped in the bedroom. Matthew had no more than sat down when he made it clear he would be patient no longer.

"So then, Jonathan," he said, leaning back in his chair, "you mentioned wanting to talk. What's on your mind?"

Maggie, sitting beside her husband on the sofa, shot a nervous glance in his direction.

"Actually," Jonathan said, "we'd hoped to bring this up before now, but things kept happening."

"Well, now seems a good time," Matthew prompted. "First, though, Kate and I have an idea we want to pose to *you.*"

Maggie's attention snapped from Jonathan to her parents, only to find them smiling rather suspiciously at each other.

Too curious to wait, she asked, "What kind of an idea, Da?"

Her father ignored her, directing his question to Jonathan. "Didn't you tell me you were going to Lexington when school's out for Easter vacation?"

"That's right. We need to sign the papers to initiate Gracie's adoption."

"Maggie and Gracie are going with you, are they?"

"Well, yes. Maggie has to sign too."

"How long will you be gone?"

Maggie and Jonathan exchanged looks. What was Da getting at?

"How long? A couple of days, I suppose. I'd like to spend at least a day with my father and sister while we're there."

Matthew gave a nod. "Of course you would. Well, here's what Kate and I were thinking. We thought perhaps you might want to take most of the week for your trip to Lexington—and leave Gracie here with us."

Maggie looked at Jonathan. He was as bewildered as she.

Matthew leaned slightly forward, his gaze going from one to the other. "We've been talking, you see. You've had no time for a real wedding trip—"

"A honeymoon," Kate interrupted.

"Aye, that," Matthew continued. "No honeymoon—" He pursed his mouth over the word as if it had a peculiar taste. "And the next thing you knew you'd taken on the responsibility of a babe. Kate and I, we think it only right that you have some time together, just the two of you, for a real honeymoon. And now that you don't have to be afraid to let wee Gracie out of your sight, you could take some time for yourselves while we look after her."

Maggie turned to her mother. "You're serious?"

"Of course we are. We love having Gracie with us. She'd be fine without you for a few days, don't you think?"

Ray, who had been quiet up until now, finally spoke up. "I won't be in school, so I'd be around to help."

They were all smiling, clearly waiting for a reply. More than *waiting*, Maggie sensed. They were offering a gift and genuinely hoping it would be accepted. Yes, that was it. They wanted to make her and Jonathan happy.

She looked at Jonathan. He smiled, eyebrows raised as if leaving it to her.

Could she do it? Could she really leave Gracie for a week? Without seeing her, without holding her—and do so with any peace of mind?

She saw the answer in Jonathan's eyes and knew what he wanted her to say.

"I can't believe you're offering to do this," she said, turning back to her family. "I'm going to say yes before you change your mind!"

Looking around the room and seeing their expressions— including Jonathan's—she knew it was the right thing to say, the right thing to do, despite her reservations.

❖·❖

It took another half hour or more before Jonathan and Maggie finally managed to put *their* idea to the test. Maggie could scarcely control her anticipation as Jonathan, seated on the sofa, knit his hands together and said without preamble, "I'm most likely going to be buying the Taggart farm. Your cousin has agreed to sell it to me, but there are a few details to iron out first."

From her place beside him, Maggie looked from her da—who was staring blankly at Jonathan—to Mum who was looking at *her*. She smiled at her mother, who then snapped her attention back to Jonathan.

"*Jeff* Taggart's farm?" Da asked.

Jonathan nodded. "That's right. But Maggie and I wanted to talk to you and Kate first."

"You're going to buy my cousin Jeff's farm?" Da repeated, still watching Jonathan, trying to comprehend.

Maggie's mother again turned to look at her. In that instant Maggie saw something pass across her features then quickly disappear. Mum could have no idea what was coming next, but she clearly knew *something* was coming.

"Wow!" Ray said.

"What do you know about farming, lad?" Matthew said. "A city boy like yourself."

Jonathan smiled at Maggie before replying. "I know absolutely nothing about farming, Matthew. But I've always thought I'd love living in the country. And that's part of the reason we're here."

Matthew quirked an eyebrow, still studying his son-in-law as if he might be a little daft.

"Matthew, I believe you *do* know something about farming from some of the things we've talked about now and then. So I—we— were hoping you might be interested in a partnership."

"A partnership?"

"That's right," Jonathan confirmed. "It would mean a move. You'd have to live at the farm, to be on the premises. I thought perhaps you and Kate—and Ray—could live in the farmhouse that's already there. It's a big house so there's plenty of room. I plan to build a home for us on the property as well. We've been looking at the hill on the south end. Maggie and I would like to get out of town a ways. We don't want to raise a family in this coal dust. It can't be good for anyone."

Matthew was leaning so far forward in his chair he looked about to fall out. But it was her mother Maggie was watching. Kate had brought her hand—trembling as it was—to her mouth. She stared wide-eyed at her husband.

Matthew shook his head. "Why, I can't do what you're asking, son. I don't have enough money to go partners on anything, much less a farm. Not that I wouldn't be interested if I *had* the means."

"Ah, that's what I wanted to know," Jonathan said, getting to his feet. "So you *would* be interested if it were financially feasible?"

Da swallowed so hard Maggie could see his throat working. "Oh, I'd be interested all right."

"Well, good," Jonathan said. "Because you don't need to *buy* a partnership, Matthew. What I have in mind is for you and Ray to *work* your part."

Da shot him a sharp look. "I don't take your meaning, lad."

Jonathan moved to the front window, hesitating for a moment before turning to face them all. "The thing is, Matthew, I don't want to farm. I like to garden, and I've been wanting some land so I could have a much *larger* garden. And we'd like some animals. I'm actually quite fond of animals. I'd help out with the work on weekends and evenings as I could, of course, but I'm a teacher at heart. I plan to go right on teaching. I want the farm for the land and the clean air. I want to get my family away from the coal dust."

He stopped, fixing his gaze directly on Maggie's father. "You're my family too, Matthew. You and Kate and Ray. Jeff Taggart told me that Ray is a natural at farming, and I suspect after you get settled the same will be true for you. I need someone to look after the place full-time and manage it. Someone who can be there all the time. Someone I can trust. I would very much like that someone to be you."

Matthew's frown seemed locked in place. "But how would we live? I don't have the stamina to work the mine and farm at the same time. And if I were to leave the mine, I'd have no wages." He glanced down at his hands with a look of defeat.

Excitement glinted in Jonathan's eyes. "Yes, you would."

Matthew's head came up with a snap.

"Jeff Taggart showed me his books for the farm. The dairy income and the money he makes from his corn and soybeans won't make you a rich man, but it will provide you with a decent living. You, Kate, and Ray will take half of the income the farm brings in. And," he added, "until things level out a bit, I can manage a small salary for you and a part-time wage for Ray. At least enough to supplement your farm income for a time…until we expand."

"Expand?"

Jonathan nodded. "Horses," he said. "I've always thought I'd like to raise horses. Good ones. I don't know anything about farming, but over the years I've done some reading about horses." He stopped. "Is it true what I've heard? That an Irishman has an instinct for the horse?"

"Wow!" Ray said again.

Matthew wiped a hand over his eyes as if his vision were failing. Maggie's mother was also wiping *her* eyes, but Maggie suspected it was for an entirely different reason. Ray simply sat staring at Jonathan.

Unable to sit still any longer, Maggie went to stand beside her husband. "Please, Da, don't say no. Jonathan has planned this for a long time, and it's something we really want to do. We want it for all of us."

"You can do this?" Matthew asked, his voice a pitch higher. "You can afford such a venture?"

"Oh, he *can*, Da!" Maggie burst out before Jonathan could answer.

Beside her Jonathan cleared his throat and looked at her as if he would like to speak for himself.

"I'm sorry," she murmured. But she knew her father, and she knew that his decision hung on his understanding exactly what Jonathan was offering and why.

"If your daughter will let me get a word in—" Jonathan said dryly. "Let me assure you, Matthew, that I'm not offering to *give* you anything. I'm offering you part of a business, a position that should prove a great deal more beneficial to you and your family than your job at the mine. This isn't a *gift*, if that's what you're thinking. It's a business proposition. I have my heart set on buying that farm. As much as I love Skingle Creek, we don't want to raise our babies in the coal dust. I'd really like you, Kate, and Ray with me in this."

"Babies?" The soft utterance came from Kate, whose sharp-eyed gaze locked on her daughter.

Maggie looked at Jonathan, who cracked a ridiculously proud smile. "*Babies,*" he asserted as Maggie nodded her confirmation.

Her mother began to cry in earnest.

"Matthew?" Jonathan said, waiting.

Maggie could almost plant herself in the middle of the struggle taking place inside her father, a fierce battle between pride and an old, once-believed-hopeless desire. She watched as he finally hauled himself to his feet and faced Jonathan square-on.

For a long moment he stood there, his eyes locked with Jonathan's. Then, as if he'd found what he was searching for, he nodded. "If you mean everything you've said, I'd be a fool to turn you down."

"If there's one thing you're not, Matthew, it's a fool," Jonathan said mildly. "So that's a yes?"

Jonathan extended his hand. After a slight hesitation, Matthew grasped it and said, "Yes."

"Done!" said Jonathan.

He turned to Ray, whose reply was an enormous grin and another "Wow!"

"God is good," Maggie's mother choked out.

And from the back bedroom came the sound of a baby's happy, high-piched squeal.

A Gift for Skingle Creek

Give my heart a voice to tell the world
About my Savior—
Give my soul a song
That will ring out across the years,
A song that sings Your boundless love
In sunshine or in shadow,
A psalm of praise for all my days,
Through happiness or tears.

B.J. Hoff

〜

It was a tradition in Skingle Creek to celebrate Easter at sunrise on Dredd's Mountain. No one but those new to town thought it peculiar to celebrate the Risen Savior at the top of a hill with such a name. The townsfolk had begun the custom as a way of defying the ash and dusty gloom hovering over the coal community by setting their annual celebration of the Lord above the mine itself.

By the time Pastor Ben wrapped up his Easter message, the sun, bright and warm and welcome, was on the rise. After a short prayer, the pastor announced a special tribute. As the sun struck its gold on top of the hill, Jonathan's singing miners stepped out from the back of the crowd and began to make their way to the front.

"O for a thousand tongues to sing…"

They came singing, fifty men strong, with voices deep and rich and powerful enough to echo across the mountain and into the valley.

Maggie, holding the sleeping Gracie in her arms, caught her breath at the sight and sound of them. She had heard them only once before, at a rehearsal that had been a bit rough-edged. Watching the procession now, her heart began to sing with them.

She was keenly aware of her parents on one side of her, her brother on the other, and her sister, the lively Nell Frances, her husband, and their little girls who had come to spend the week. Maggie glanced around at the other familiar faces in the crowd. It was probably no exaggeration to say the entire town had come to worship this Easter Sunday.

It was a blessing to look around and see these folks she'd known most of her life, the people with whom she'd grown up and gone to school. People whose weddings and baptisms she'd attended. Many were more than friends and neighbors; they were as dear as family.

Jonathan was speaking, and his voice snapped her attention back to him and the men standing directly behind him.

"…while not a one of us claims to be a musician, and that includes me, we thought we might have something to present as an offering to God and as a gift to you, His people. This town has seen more than its share of hard times and tragedy. On more than one occasion it seemed we might never rise above the worst of the oppressive winters, the devastating mine injuries and sickness and death. At times even the basic necessities have been hard-won. Too often we've watched a neighbor give up in utter desperation.

"Yet through it all I've seen the spirit of Skingle Creek—*your* spirit—triumph over the despair and help others do likewise by giving yourselves. In some cases, you gave everything you had to help a neighbor."

He paused for a moment, his gaze going to Maggie and the

rest of the family. "I love this town. I have loved it almost from the beginning. For years I've tried to think of a way to show you…all of you…how grateful I am to God and to you for taking me in, giving me a home here, and making me one of you.

"These men—" He turned and lifted an arm to include the miners. "These men are here today for the same reason I am: to express their gratitude to God and to offer you a gift—an enduring gift you can carry in your hearts long after today. We hope that even on the darkest days and in the most difficult times, you'll remember our gift and remember that there is *always* a reason to hope. The God who made us, the God who loves us and bids us love one another, is the reason for our hope."

Jonathan turned to the men and signaled them to begin again.

❧·❦

They took his breath away. From the mournful strains of "O Sacred Head" to the robust "Crown Him with Many Crowns" and on to the majestic power of "All Hail the Power of Jesus' Name" and the jubilant "Christ the Lord Is Risen Today," these men, this body of brothers, filled the mountain…and Jonathan's spirit. Finally, unable to remain silent any longer, he lifted up his voice and sang with them.

It was as if fifty voices became five hundred. The ground itself seemed to pulse until at last every person in attendance was singing.

At last they reached the final number, a personal favorite of Jonathan's. Though not an Easter hymn, it seemed the perfect choice for this day and for the town. A calm fell over the entire mountain as the achingly sweet tenor voice of Pip Pippino soared over and encompassed the men who now sang with him, ever so softly…

When peace, like a river attendeth my way,
When sorrows like sea billows roll,
Whatever my lot, Thou has taught me to say,
It is well, it is well with my soul…

Dear Readers:

The Song Weaver concludes the MOUNTAIN SONG LEGACY story. I hope you've enjoyed sharing the lives of Jonathan and Maggie and all the other Skingle Creek residents as much as I have.

Coming to the end of a series is always a bittersweet experience for me. I live with the people in my stories a long time, and they become so special to me that it's never easy to say goodbye.

Thank you for your interest in the trilogy and for the wonderful letters and e-mails you've sent me throughout its development and publication. You've been a huge encouragement to me. I can't begin to tell you how much I appreciate your kindness…and your prayers.

And now new projects await!

God's blessing and peace and hope be with you all.

About B.J. Hoff

B.J. Hoff's bestselling historical novels first appeared in the Christian market more than 20 years ago and include such popular series as An Emerald Ballad, The American Anthem, and The Mountain Song Legacy. B.J.'s critically acclaimed novels reflect her efforts to make stories set in the past relevant to the present. She continues to cross the boundaries of religion, language, and culture to capture a worldwide reading audience.

A former church music director and music teacher, B.J. and her husband make their home in Ohio, where they share a love of music, books, and time spent with family.

Be sure to visit B.J.'s website:

www.bjhoff.com

HARVEST HOUSE
PUBLISHERS

A Distant Music

In this first book of the Mountain Song Legacy series you'll step into a small Kentucky coal mining town in the late 1800s. Hope is found in the hearts of two young girls—the vibrant, red-headed Maggie MacAuley and her fragile friend, Summer Rankin.

When Jonathan Stuart, the latest in a succession of educators, wants to continue teaching in the one-room schoolhouse, Maggie and Summer know he is special. So when Jonathan's cherished flute is stolen, the girls try to find a way to restore music to his life.

Sorrow and joy follow in the days to come, and through it all Maggie, Jonathan, and a community rediscover the gifts of faith, friendship, and unwavering love.

The Wind Harp

B.J. Hoff's unforgettable characters from *A Distant Music* reunite in a gripping, dramatic story. When Maggie returns to the small coal town of her childhood, she has no intention of staying. Her life is in Chicago now. There's nothing to keep her in Skingle Creek...nothing but the discovery that a man who has lived most of his life for the children of Skingle Creek is no longer just the hero of Maggie's childhood. He now seems destined to become the love of her life.

In Maggie's quest for independence, she finds her greatest strength in sacrifice...and in her struggle to heal her family, she finds her heart renewed by love.

Harvest House Publishers
For the Best in Inspirational Fiction

Mindy Starns Clark
THE MILLION DOLLAR
MYSTERIES SERIES
A Penny for Your Thoughts
Don't Take Any Wooden Nickels
A Dime a Dozen
A Quarter for a Kiss
The Buck Stops Here

Smart Chick Mystery Series
The Trouble with Tulip
Blind Dates Can Be Murder
Elementary, My Dear Watkins

Roxanne Henke
COMING HOME TO
BREWSTER SERIES
After Anne
Finding Ruth
Becoming Olivia
Always Jan
With Love, Libby

Sally John
THE OTHER WAY HOME SERIES
A Journey by Chance
After All These Years
Just to See You Smile
The Winding Road Home

In a Heartbeat Series
In a Heartbeat
Flash Point
Moment of Truth

THE BEACH HOUSE SERIES
The Beach House
Castles in the Sand

Susan Meissner
A Window to the World
Remedy for Regret
In All Deep Places
A Seahorse in the Thames

Craig Parshall
Trial by Ordeal
Chambers of Justice Series
The Resurrection File
Custody of the State
The Accused
Missing Witness
The Last Judgement

Debra White Smith
THE AUSTEN SERIES
First Impressions
Reason and Romance
Central Park
Northpointe Chalet
Amanda
Possibilities

Lori Wick
THE TUCKER MILLS TRILOGY
Moonlight on the Millpond
Just Above a Whisper
Leave a Candle Burning

The English Garden Series
The Proposal
The Rescue
The Visitor
The Pursuit

The Yellow Rose Trilogy
Every Little Thing About You
A Texas Sky
City Girl

Contemporary Fiction
Bamboo & Lace
Every Storm
Pretense
The Princess
Sophie's Heart
White Chocolate Moments

Books by Lori Wick

A Place Called Home Series
A Place Called Home
A Song for Silas
The Long Road Home
A Gathering of Memories

The Californians
Whatever Tomorrow Brings
As Time Goes By
Sean Donovan
Donovan's Daughter

Kensington Chronicles
The Hawk and the Jewel
Wings of the Morning
Who Brings Forth the Wind
The Knight and the Dove

Rocky Mountain Memories
Where the Wild Rose Blooms
Whispers of Moonlight
To Know Her by Name
Promise Me Tomorrow

The Yellow Rose Trilogy
Every Little Thing About You
A Texas Sky
City Girl

English Garden Series
The Proposal
The Rescue
The Visitor
The Pursuit

The Tucker Mills Trilogy
Moonlight on the Millpond
Just Above a Whisper
Leave a Candle Burning

Contemporary Fiction
Sophie's Heart
Pretense
The Princess
Bamboo & Lace
Every Storm
White Chocolate Moments

To learn more about books by B.J. Hoff
and to read sample chapters, log on to our website:
www.harvesthousepublishers.com

HARVEST HOUSE PUBLISHERS
EUGENE, OREGON